THE DEMON OF MANSFELD MANOR

S.A. JACOBS

Published by Six-String Books

ISBN: 9781794447677

DEDICATION

For my wife Jennifer.

PROLOGUE

August 31, 1927 – Villa Ortenberg

The large clock in the main hall began to strike eleven. Ida gracefully stepped out of her parlor and walked down the grand staircase towards the immense double doors. Edgar, her butler, was waiting, a parasol in hand. As Ida got within ten steps of the doorway, Edgar opened the door and stepped out into the bright sunlight, waiting for her to pass. Without a word, Ida sauntered through the door. While the morning sun was bright, she was protected by the parasol in Edgar's hand.

The two walked in silence. Edgar moved rigidly as he followed her, anticipating each step. The brisk walk took them down a set of marble steps into an immense garden. The garden path led them to a large lily pond and finally to Ida's open-air tea house. As the two approached, a maid started pouring-steaming hot water into a cup. The beautiful gilded tea service sat alone on the marble table. As Ida and Edgar stepped into the tea house, the maid bowed, then immediately exited, retreating to the main house. Edgar set the parasol into a marble umbrella vase and pulled out Ida's chair. Once Ida was seated, he put the linen napkin on her lap. As she settled into her seat, he moved to her side where he stood silent and motionless. His hands were clasped together at his waist as he anticipated her next request.

This routine was precise and perfect. It was always that way. There were never instructions, never conversation. Only silence. The staff knew Ida, not personally, but through her patterns. Ida would never call out to Edgar and ask for tea. Nor would she ask for a walk. Yet, at eleven every morning, the same pattern was repeated. With no words or orders, Edgar would be at the door, ready to shield her from the weather. By the time they arrived at the tea house, her gilded tea service would be out and ready. It was simply the way it was, the way it always was.

While Edgar would not dare to look at his watch, he estimated he had another forty minutes of standing there motionless until he would again, like clockwork, escort her back to the main house. His mind began to wander. The heat of the morning was beastly. He felt droplets of sweat forming on his forehead. His mind became consumed with them. He was jolted back to reality when he heard her voice.

"Edgar," she said.

"Yes, Madam?" he replied.

"Please sit down."

"As you wish."

Edgar silently moved and took a seat across the table from Ida. He sat with impeccable posture as was expected in her presence. The two sat silently for a few moments. Ida eyed him carefully as she sipped her tea. When she set the cup down, she waved her hand in front of her face as if to dismiss Edgar's thoughts.

"Edgar, please be at ease. I wish to speak freely with you for a moment."

Edgar didn't move. He was filled with nothing short of confusion. He had been employed and lived at the Villa since even before it was completed. In all those times, there was never a moment to be at ease and certainly not one to speak freely without being behind closed doors.

"What is it?" he finally asked.

"I am concerned about the Villa."

"Whatever is concerning you, please let me know. I assure you that my staff and I will be able to make the needed modifications."

"I don't believe you can."

Edgar leaned back and crossed his arms in frustration.

"If I may," he said, "for the past seven years while you were abroad, this estate was kept precisely as you wished. Upon your return everything was just as you had left it. Without even a request from you, your meals were prepared exactly as you wished. Even the flowers in your parlor were replaced every day while you were absent in case you were to arrive back. Surely you cannot believe that we cannot make The Villa the residence you desire."

Edgar looked at her; her eyes flickered as they transitioned from wild with emotion to grief-stricken. He leaned back in his seat a bit. He immediately feared that he had said too much.

Ida abruptly smacked her hands on the table.

"I don't doubt your abilities or the abilities of the staff for an instant! My concerns are not with the grounds. I fear a much stronger darkness is overtaking the estate."

She paused, breathing deeply for a moment to regain her composure.

"You have been my most trusted confidant for many years," she continued. "You have seen a great number of the private dealings here at the Villa and never have you given me a reason to even suggest that you have not kept these matters private."

"But of course," he interjected in a much calmer tone. "That is part of my job,"

"It is, and you have done it impeccably. That is precisely the reason we are speaking now. I have some matters I need to entrust you with. Private matters of the utmost importance."

"What is it that you wish me to do?"

She stared at him quizzically as she leaned back and took another sip of her tea.

"As I was saying, The Villa is no longer the refuge it once was. This estate is being overtaken by the darkness of my past. It is as if the cloud in the sky will not allow a speck of sunlight to grace the doorstep. This darkness is growing and choking the life out of me and this estate. It is a spiritual darkness if you will. The estate has been cursed."

Not sure how to respond, Edgar leaned in closer to at least show that she received one-hundred percent of his attention.

"I have done everything in my power stop this from happening. I truly have. But I've failed. The power over this place is stronger than I am."

She stopped speaking and bent down to retrieve her handbag. She withdrew two envelopes and set them on the table. Both envelopes were fine stationery with a yellow hue. The top one was sealed with wax. Edgar recognized the seal. It was the same 'M' monogram inlaid on the floor of the foyer. It was the family seal.

"I am leaving the Villa, Edgar. I am not well, and this darkness is too much for me. I will live out the remainder of my life in the city."

A quick realization of where the conversation led filled

Edgar with a sadness. Not sadness for the darkness over the estate, but a sadness in feeling as though his life's passion was now gone.

"I understand," he said softly, looking at the envelopes. "I trust this is my severance and reference?"

"Not at all!" she waved her hand at him. "While I will not be returning here, you are the only one who knows that. You and the rest of the staff shall continue to care for the estate no differently than you have all these years. In fact, I have arranged for the estate to be maintained in this manner even after my death. For as long as the funds are available. There is but one notable exception to the care of the estate moving forward. This is one of the tasks I am entrusting you with."

She paused to drink some tea carefully, watching Edgar's expression. True to form, he did not waver.

"Do not be concerned, dear Edgar. I have also arranged for generous compensation for you."

"That is exceedingly kind, Ida, although I must admit I am a bit confused as to what services you wish me to perform."

"My apologies. I seem to have gotten sidetracked. First and foremost, after I leave this afternoon, my upstairs parlor is to remain locked. Absolutely no one, aside from you, is ever allowed to enter those doors. You are expected to continue cleaning the room. I only ask that you do so alone and only once a week. All other times, the door is to remain locked with you being the only one to have the key. Additionally, the inner chamber of the parlor is never to be entered again. Nor should its very existence be acknowledged."

"But of course," he replied.

"Edgar, you are the only one here aside from me that

knows the chamber exists. That secret dies with us. Do I make myself clear?"

"Absolutely!" he said.

"Finally, there are the matters described here." She handed him the bottom envelope.

"Here you will find my final instructions for the estate. As I mentioned, I trust that you will be here keeping up the property long after I am gone. I have made the proper arrangements for the estate to be bequeathed to its proper heir in time. This second envelope belongs to him. However, I am afraid that it will not be for a very long time. I am entrusting it to you to make the final arrangements to ensure it is delivered to him and no one else. When he takes possession of this estate, he will be the only one able to lift this veil of darkness covering the estate."

Edgar stared at the envelope a long moment before speaking again. "While I appreciate you entrusting me with this, I must confess I am a bit concerned. Would not these matters be better relegated to Thomas? After all, he is your lawyer."

"Absolutely not!" She rose from the table and began to pace. "You're right. Thomas is a great associate of mine. I entrusted him with all my legal affairs. However, he knows not the truth about the Villa, and I doubt he could even understand it. He is too grounded to see such things. Not to mention his association with Samuel. No doubt Samuel will make every attempt to attain this property despite having no legal grounds based on our divorce agreements. I digress; Thomas is not to have anything to do with these more sensitive arrangements."

Edgar hung his head solemnly for a moment and looked at the envelopes she had given him. He looked up at her, his brown eyes glassed over.

"With this, I have a request of my own," he said.

"What is it?"

"That your absence not be permanent. My loyalties are to this estate but also to you. I need to believe that one day this veil of darkness will be lifted, and I will again be able to escort you through these hallowed doors once more."

Ida rose to stand behind him. She gently set her hand upon his shoulder and took a deep breath.

"I have seen the cards fate has dealt to this estate. The darkness will be lifted but not by me. It is no longer my battle to fight. I can only leave the estate in the hands of the one person who can."

PART I

RELIQUE

1

—————

"THIS IS JUST PERFECT," I muttered, rolling my eyes.

I was sitting in my tiny cubicle when I overheard a man walk into our office and ask for Mr. James Bauer, my formal name.

Typically, when someone entered the office not wearing a delivery service uniform, it was obvious they had no business being there and were looking to sell something. I was working for a start-up marketing platform. As a start-up, the company was lean. We had no reason to purchase office supplies or shipping services from any of the suit-wearing salesmen who found their way to our door. The fact that he used my full name only exacerbated the situation as he clearly had no relationship with me. My name was Jim. The last time anyone called me James was on the first day of a class when the professor read the attendance list.

My job wasn't good. It wasn't bad. It was just a job. This day was among the many I'd spent hoping for more. It was the Monday following my twenty-fifth birthday. I had no need for a celebration. Still, it would have been nice to be in a real office where I could enjoy my required simple cake instead of replying to the overflowing inbox of emails. I minimized my email screen and stood up from my desk hearing Christine, my co-worker who had the unlucky seat near the door, asking the salesman if he meant Jim.

"I'm James," I said walking toward the stranger. "Listen, I don't want to waste your time. I am sure whatever service you're offering is great, but we are simply not interested. Even though you happened to find my name listed some-where, I would ask you to honor the 'No Solicitors' sign on the door."

"I'm sorry, Mr. Bauer. I have some documents to deliver to you. Is there a place where we can speak?"

"Uh yeah, there is a conference room over here, but I only have a minute. I'm scheduled to jump on a call in a few." It was a lie, but a harmless one. I showed him to the nearest conference room.

The man wasted no time and sat in the conference room unbuttoning his suit jacket. For a moment, I felt self-conscious about my casual jeans and t-shirt. He pulled out a sealed manila envelope from his expensive-looking leather bag and set it on the table.

"Mr. Bauer, I represent the law offices of Lutz and Hart-mann. I was asked to deliver this letter to you. First, I will need to see some identification to ensure you are the intended recipient."

In the back of my mind, I considered whether this was some sort of scam. However, his professional manner made me less skeptical. I didn't hesitate before pulling my wallet from my jeans and handing him my driver's license. He looked at it, then again at me as if I was buying beer with a fake ID. Then, he handed me the envelope and asked me to sign stating that I received it.

"Wait, what is this all about?" I asked.

"I believe all the information you need will be in here." He patted the manila envelope with his hand.

"Right, but what is it?" I asked again, becoming agitated at his evasiveness.

"I'm afraid I cannot answer that. I am here only to ensure that this envelope is delivered to the proper person. As for the contents, that is between you and our partner, Edward Lutz."

Wanting this whole exchange to be over, I signed my name and grabbed the envelope. "Well consider your job complete. I trust you can find your way out."

I returned to my cubicle and tossed the envelope on top of the random papers that covered my desk. I started to return to my work until curiosity got the best of me. I grabbed the envelope and began to open it. Just then, Paul's head popped up over the wall of my cubical.

"What's all that about?" Paul asked, pointing to the envelope.

"I don't know. Some letter from a lawyer."

"Aw man, you got served! What is it, some kid you didn't know about? Are you a baby daddy?"

"Shut up Paul!"

I pulled the letter from the envelope and skimmed the contents. "It says I may have inherited something."

"Yeah, I get those all the time. Apparently, I am the next of kin to some Emperor in some country I've never heard of. But those all come in email, not delivered by some suit."

"Yeah, but this kinda feels the same. I have never heard of this person and am damn sure not related to her." I tossed the letter back on to my desk.

Paul eyed the letter laying there. "Hartman and Lutz? I don't think that is a fake."

"What are you talking about?"

"Man, Hartman, and Lutz. That is some big firm down-town, not one of these guys you see on late night TV. That's the firm you hire when you have a super giant trust fund and get caught doing coke on the dashboard of daddy's Lambo."

"Yeah well, that's all good, but I still have never heard of this person."

"Let me plug her into some public records databases and see what I can find."

"Don't worry about it, I'm sure it's nothing."

"Like I have anything better to do," Paul said, grabbing the papers from my desk. "Seriously, I'm caught up on work. If I'm not doing this, I'll be wasting my day helping Cedric spy on his family who he thinks is drinking his whiskey. This is way more interesting than a kid sneaking into the liquor cabinet."

I sat in Paul's cube, watching him feverishly type and click through what looked like a thousand windows on his computer.

"Who said hacking isn't a great hobby?" he asked.

The printer on his desk came to life and spat out a page of information. He grabbed it and looked it over before handing it to me.

"The good news is she was a real person. The bad news is she died a hell of a long time ago, long before you were born. So, I'm not sure how you could be listed as part of her inheritance. But here is her name, specifics, as well as the addresses listed as her property. She owned a lot of property, all of them have changed hands since her death, well except one. In looking at this, I would bet that if you are inheriting anything, it would be that property."

Confusion set in as I looked over the paper. She was real,

but she had been dead for over eighty years. Something was clearly not right about any of this.

"To hell with it. There is one way to figure this out." I picked up Paul's phone and dialed the number on the letter.

It rang twice before a cheery woman answered.

"Law offices of Lutz and Hartmann. How may I direct your call?"

"Um, hi. I'm calling about an inheritance. I got a letter with this number on it."

"Okay, sir. Can I have your name?"

"Jim Bauer."

I could hear her rapidly typing on a keyboard and then nothing, silence. When she spoke again her cheeriness was replaced with seriousness.

"Mr. Bauer. I do apologize for the delay. I will put you right through to Edward Lutz, our partner."

Then I was put on hold and forced to listen to some crappy instrumental version of Seal's 'Kiss from a Rose.' A few moments later, the call went through.

"Mr. Bauer, how nice it is to finally hear from you!" said a distinguished voice. "This is Edward Lutz. I am personally handling all these affairs. I trust you received our paperwork?"

"Yeah, I got it all. I'm just not sure what I am supposed to do with it."

"Oh sir, there is nothing to worry about. You are named as the beneficiary in Ida Mansfeld Muller's will, as outlined in the paperwork. All you need to do is set up an appointment to come to my office. You will meet with the executor and me, and we can finalize everything,"

"Um okay. But I still don't understand why I'm a part of this. I've never even heard of this woman."

"Unfortunately, all I can share with you now is what's in

the paperwork you already have. We can go through the specifics when we meet, and I will be happy to address any other questions you have. When would be a good time?"

"Well, I don't know when I'll be able to get some time away from work to come to your offices."

"That is not a problem. These affairs are the top priority for the firm right now, and we will be more than happy to accommodate your schedule. How does Friday evening sound? Say seven PM.?"

I was trying to think of a reason I couldn't make it. But who was I kidding, I had nothing on my personal calendar, and this thing had gotten me very intrigued.

"Sure, that sounds fine," I conceded. "I'll be there,"

"Great. I will have dinner ordered in for us and have my secretary send out an invitation with the details."

"Okay, sounds good," I replied timidly.

"I cannot wait to meet you in person, Mr. Bauer. If there is anything at all you need in the meantime, please do not hesitate to contact me."

I hung up and looked at Paul.

"Strange, yes" he said. "But it still doesn't sound like a scam."

I SLOWED my beat-up truck to a crawl. The sun was blinding on this unseasonably hot day. I passed giant house after giant house that looked like they were all bought out of some catalog for the wealthy. Each massive house had similar long driveways paved with mock cobblestones edged by meticulously manicured lawns with intermittent old growth trees. Some might call them mansions based on size alone, but for me the term didn't quite fit. These houses lacked particular qualities I thought necessary for true mansions. There were no massive grounds or courtyards. There were no guesthouses. These were just obscenely large houses built one after another in subdivided lots. A community for the new elite.

I was certainly a stranger in a strange land. This was truly the last neighborhood I would have expected to be driving through. The entire area made me feel like an outsider. I felt like the stereotypical burnout punk kid wandering into an elite country club. I saw no one, yet I could almost feel the homeowners peeking through the blinds. I looked around in all directions, half-expecting to see a squad car with lights flashing racing up behind me.

"No," I muttered to myself. "I have every right to be here,"

It did nothing to squash my fear, but rather fed into them. It was not that I didn't expect someone to stop me; it was a mere realization that if I were stopped, I had a good excuse to be here. I scanned the street in front of me.

I picked up my phone and glanced at the GPS. Realizing I had a few more blocks to go, I stepped on the gas, deciding to get there as quickly as possible. The old truck roared to life. I cursed its exhaust issue, which caused a terribly loud rattle every time the truck accelerated. Typically, I didn't mind. Right now, I felt as though it did nothing but draw more attention to my presence.

As I continued to drive, the landscape began to change. On the next block, instead of repeated rows of homes, there were only a few followed by a stretch of cleaned lots. I could only assume these plots of land were just waiting for the next mini-mansion to pop up. The street curved right.

As I headed down the street, I could feel the change in the pavement under my truck. The smooth new concrete had given way to a much older and less cared for stretch of blacktop littered with cracks and potholes. The road stretched on for what felt like blocks. There were no houses here. It looked more like a path through a forest preserve than a neighborhood. Both sides of the road were lined with large old growth trees that clearly hadn't been trimmed in years. Wild shrubbery made the forest behind appear impenetrable.

I continued until the road came to an end. There was a large blacktop circle, allowing cars to turn around. As I slowed into the circle, the voice on my phone loudly proclaimed, "You have arrived."

I pulled the truck over to the edge of the blacktop and put it in park. Rolling down the window, I let the summer breeze roll over me. I sat there for a few minutes just looking at my surroundings, assuming this was, as I had guessed, a waste of my time. I picked up the manila envelope from the passenger seat and pulled out the papers. I looked again at the paper Paul had printed for me and compared that to the address on my GPS. "Well, at least according to Google, this is it."

I opened the door and stepped out of the truck. I looked everywhere for some sign of a residence. I spotted an occasional weathered wooden sign nailed to various trees, which surely at one point held a bright orange "NO TRESPASSING" message. I started to walk around the far edge of the circle. I was looking for anything. Something to confirm that this was real and not a stupid scam I'd fallen prey to. Then, I saw it.

Hidden behind the weeds and brush, I could see a concrete slab jutting out. All I could make out was a distinct corner. I walked up to it to get a better look. It was about five feet long lying on its side. From a couple feet away, I knew exactly what this was.

Years before, it must have stood proudly. It was part of an identical pair marking the grand entrance to this property. As I looked ahead, I could see remnants of a rusted chain half-buried in the ground, leading to the piece of concrete. I knew I had found the drive. This was the entrance, although it was clear that it had been years since anyone had used it.

I stood in what I believed to be the center of the aged drive. Now I could see it. The old growth trees stood taller than everything else, and they were all in a neat row like soldiers lined up along the path. I took a deep breath. I had just started to find a way through the weeds when I heard the familiar beeping of my phone.

"Dammit," I muttered.

I quickly retreated to my truck to look at my phone. Just as I'd expected, it was a message from work. I glanced at the time and quickly realized why. My lunch hour was over. I hadn't thought this would take so long. Annoyed with myself, I jumped in my truck and fastened the seatbelt. I drove out the way I came.

———

THE DAYS LEADING up to my meeting with the lawyer were pretty much a blur. I worked as usual, and much of my down-time was spent baffled, trying to figure out what it was all about. I considered calling my mom countless times, but decided that I didn't know anything myself, so, a call to my mom would just end with a lecture on scams, which she often fell prey to. I could think of a thousand things I would rather do.

I wanted so badly to find the connection to me, but I couldn't. I even signed up for ancestry.com to see if I could find some branch of my family tree that may have lived there. At every turn, I ended up with nothing. Rather than tire myself trying to understand it, I decided to see what I could find out about this property that Paul was convinced I would be receiving.

I Googled the address. It gave me nothing of value. Sure, there were a bunch of realty sites that came up, but upon clicking on them, I was only getting information on the other houses in the neighborhood. From the looks of it, they were all those new mansions I drove by. They all were valued at over $2 million. "Well, I guess at the very least the property is worth something," I said to myself.

Google Maps offered no help either. Sure, I could see exactly what I saw from my truck that day but not much else. On the satellite view, I couldn't tell if there was a house on the property. It looked like it was nothing but forest. The only sign of structure I did find was something small breaking out of the trees on the shore of Lake Michigan. It looked like it might be a dock. None of it was helpful at all.

Just before I gave up to trade in my laptop for another beer, a search result caught my eye. It simply read "Muller Home – Illinois". The website was one of those haunting directories that list all the haunted places in the country. When I clicked on it, there was again hardly anything of value. It was a post in their message boards reading:

'Muller Home – Illinois

'Hey! does anyone have info on this house? The big old Muller house on Lake Michigan. Growing up, I heard a ton of crazy ghost stories about it and would love to know if anyone had any experiences there.'

Following that, was a link back to my Google Maps satellite image.

"So there is a house, or at least there was. And apparently it's haunted." Defeated, I shut the laptop. It was time to try and get some sleep. Tomorrow was my day to find out everything.

The next day was filled with anxiety. Going to the lawyer was already out of my comfort zone. The fact that it was for some inheritance no one could explain made it even worse.

The address was of a gorgeous high-rise building right on the Chicago River. I stepped out of the downtown parking garage ten minutes before my meeting was set to begin. The sun was beginning its decline and cast a blend of blinding light and immense shadows across the city. I stood on the riverfront sidewalk, staying close to the edge overlooking the river to remain out of the way of the massive influx of speed-walking commuters. I stood there for a minute and just observed the city. Looking at it from this perspective, I felt a certain disappointment in myself. I mean here I was, 25 years old. I had spent my life within thirty miles of this gorgeous city and could pretty much count on one hand how many times I'd come downtown. I shook it off as I did most of the derailing thoughts I'd been having ever since my birthday.

After a few minutes, I made my way across the street and into the lobby of the high-rise. I was expecting to find a simple directory board telling me where to go but instead found security. The paths out of the lobby were all locked down with electric security gates. I walked up to the front desk. After fielding a bunch of questions about who I was and who I was seeing, I was finally issued my badge. After hesitating a moment, I swiped my badge as instructed. This unlocked the gate between me and the elevator bank. It also signaled the elevator to take me to the proper floor. It was a tad unnerving to enter an elevator with no buttons, only traveling where your badge signaled it to go.

I stepped out of the elevator and into a gorgeous lobby. Apparently, this law firm took up the entire floor of the building. I walked up to the large mahogany desk placed under a huge golden logo of the firm. A woman stood up and greeted me warmly.

"Mr. Bauer, correct?" she smiled while extending her hand to me.

"That's me." I smiled as I shook her hand.

"Right this way, sir. Mr. Lutz is expecting you."

Quickly, I followed her through what felt like a maze of cubicles. At the very end was a wall of large wooden doors. She led me to one set of double doors and stopped. She knocked on the door and then opened it just enough to peek her head inside.

"Mr. Lutz, Mr. Bauer is here," I heard her whisper.

A moment later, she opened the door and led me into Mr. Lutz's office.

The office was massive. On the opposite wall of the door, huge windows overlooked the river and northern skyline. There was a large conference table. Each seat was set up with a leather placemat and ornate lamps. On the opposite side was the more formal office. It was surrounded by carved wooden bookcases, which ran from the floor to the ceiling. In front of the bookcases was Mr. Lutz's desk, carved to match the bookcases precisely. Behind the desk was Mr. Lutz. He appeared to be meeting with a woman who was seated in front of his desk.

He was an older gentleman. Thin with perfectly mani-cured gray hair. He stood up as I entered and gracefully buttoned the top button on his three-piece suit. I couldn't help but notice how everything, including his dress, was the image of perfection. Down to the handkerchief in his breast pocket, probably made from the same fabric as his tie.

Mr. Lutz quickly made his way over to me and extended his hand.

"Mr. Bauer, what a pleasure it is to finally meet," he said while shaking my hand. "Please come and have a seat." He gestured to the chairs in front of his desk.

I walked over to the chairs and sat beside the woman. Mr. Lutz quickly shut the door and walked back over to his desk. The woman was an image of stark contrast to Mr. Lutz and his opulence. She appeared to be at least close to me in age. She was wearing jeans and a red short sleeved sweater. She had long wavy blond hair and incredible blue eyes. She looked over at me with a soft smile.

"Forgive me, Mr. Bauer," he said. "This is Ms. Katherine Schmidt. She will be standing in this evening as executor of the will."

"Standing in?" I questioned, extending my hand to shake hers. "Are you a relative of…"

"Sorry, I'm afraid her mother, the named executor, has fallen ill and is unable to make it here this evening," Lutz interrupted.

She tilted her head appearing to be annoyed by this interruption and then smiled back at me playfully.

"Yes, my mother is the named executor… as Mr. Lutz was so kind to point out," she said with a sarcastic grin. "I'm very glad to finally meet you."

She reached to shake my hand. Her eyes looked me over as her soft hand took mine. She was bold. This was certainly a turn on, especially in that stuffy office. I immediately felt comfortable with her.

"So where do we begin?" I asked returning my attention to Mr. Lutz.

"Well, I have arranged for dinner to arrive shortly. Why don't we take these moments to present the will itself, and then we can discuss anything else about this unique case while we eat."

He shifted in his chair behind the desk and retrieved a thick legal folder. He handed it to me as he took out copies of some documents. He put on a pair of wire-rimmed glasses.

"Normally, we don't read formally read wills. Considering the circumstances of this particular will though, I thought it would be in our best interest if I read for you."

2

"THE LAST WILL and testament of Ida Dorthea Mansfeld Muller, hereafter called the testator, deceased Aug 25, 1932," he started. "Let us skip the other bequests and come to the part dealing with your inheritance." He shuffled a couple of pages. "Here it is. The inheritance is in three sections.

"First, upon acceptance of this will, the beneficiary shall inherit the property at 495 Muller St., Lake Forest, IL under the following stipulations. The property must be held in the beneficiary's possession for a minimum of one year. After meeting this criterion to the satisfaction of the acting executor, the beneficiary can then relinquish ownership in whatever manner they see fit.

"Second, the final balance of the testator's trust fund shall be bequeathed to the beneficiary under the following stipulations. Only ten percent of the final value of the fund can be used for personal expenses. The remaining ninety is reserved for the renovation of the property. Should the property be restored to satisfactory living conditions, in accordance with local laws, the remaining balance of the fund shall be bequeathed to the beneficiary to enjoy in whatever manner they see fit.

"Third, you will inherit the contents of one envelope, sealed by the testator. This is to be presented by the executor of the will, with the family seal intact."

He set the papers down and looked over at Katherine and then back to me.

A sharp pang of concern rose in my gut. As real as this was all becoming, I didn't know what any of it meant. There were so many unanswered questions, especially why. The fact was, this was a very real inheritance, and it most certainly was for me.

I could see Lutz's eyes narrow as he looked at me, awaiting a response of some kind. I took a deep breath and said the only words that came to mind.

"What does this all mean in real English?"

He took off his glasses and a smug smile appeared on his face.

"Well, Mr. Bauer, it means you have just become a very wealthy man," he said.

He turned to the phone on his desk, hit an intercom button, and requested that champagne be brought in. My head was spinning.

"Wait! What do you mean I am a wealthy man?"

"We will get to the real numbers shortly but let me just say the trust fund alone is no small amount of money, not to mention the value of the property you just inherited."

"But why me? I don't know of any relation to this Ida!"

"I understand. I assure you we will discuss the peculiar nature of this will over dinner, but first let us take a moment to celebrate this."

Just then, the door to his office opened, and a man wearing a tuxedo walked in pushing a silver cart. On the cart were glasses and a bottle of champagne. The man began pouring the champagne and passed it out to the three of us.

"Mr. Lutz, do you celebrate all of these meetings with champagne?" I asked.

"Oh, heavens no!" He gave me a discerning look. "But this is a special occasion. How often does a law firm get to bring closure to an open probate case that is almost a century old? In fact, this will was one of the first cases this firm ever took on. Selfishly speaking, it is incredibly satisfying to finally bring it to a close."

"Like I said, this will is almost one hundred years old, and as near as I can tell, I am certainly not related to this Ida lady. I understand this is a big deal for you, but can we please discuss my relation to this all?"

He sat down and offered me a look of surprise. "You are an interesting man, Mr. Bauer."

"How so?" I asked even more perplexed.

"Well, most people in a situation like this, especially people your age, would be fighting to know what they are getting out of the deal. How much money? How much after taxes? But you, your first question is why. Let me tell you what I know and understand of these matters while my staff brings in dinner. Then, we can discuss the legalities over dinner."

He took a long drink of his champagne as he gazed around his office. There was a slight smile on his face.

"I imagine you don't know much about the Muller Mansfeld family, correct?" he continued.

I thought for a moment. The names were slightly familiar to me, but I couldn't place them. I shrugged my shoulders.

"I'm not surprised. I'm afraid their names were not

entered into history in the manner anyone would have expected."

He paused, leaned forward in his chair, and stared directly at me.

"Let's start by talking about Ida. After all, it is her estate you are inheriting."

He leaned back in his chair and relaxed a bit, lightly swirling the champagne in his glass. I glanced over at Katherine. She was also giving Lutz her complete attention. I nodded to Lutz in agreement for him to continue.

"Ida was the youngest daughter of the newspaper mogul Fredrick Mansfeld of New York. Ida married a man named Samuel Muller. Samuel was the only son of his father, who was in many ways the quintessential railroad tycoon of his day. When the two married, it was a big deal. The combination of the richest families in the country. They were constantly in the spotlight. Of course, it didn't help that they were both rather eccentric. Think of them as the Kardashian family of the 1900's. If they went to dinner, it was in the paper. While their public personas were well documented, their private lives were almost completely unknown."

Lutz paused for a moment to let that information sink in before continuing.

"What we do know is that they didn't live happily ever after. They resided in a massive mansion downtown until they commissioned Villa Ortenberg — the estate you just inherited. It was there that they were going to raise their children, away from the city and the spotlight in the very private estate. When built, the Villa was opulent, comparable only to estates held by people like the Vanderbilts. At this time, Ida was the richest woman in the country. Once the estate was completed, things took a turn. They had four children, three of whom survived to adulthood, but a year after the youngest child was born, Ida left the country. She disappeared from public life for nearly ten years.

"Upon her return, she and Samuel divorced. Following the divorce, she lived an isolated existence locked in her city mansion until the day she died. Upon her death, her personal effects were auctioned off and the mansion in the city was sold. All this while the villa sat empty.

"That just about covers the documented history. Now, let me explain part of the story that I personally know a bit more about."

He stood up and began walking through his office. He gestured to a large picture above the conference table.

"You see this photo?" Without waiting for an answer, he continued. "This is my great-grandfather, and here on his desk, this document."

He pointed to a paper on the desk in the photo.

"This is Ida's will. The photo was taken just after signing it. You see, my great-grandfather had been her companion. She helped fund the opening of this firm. Now many said that the two were more than associates, although I have seen no indication of that type of relationship myself.

"At any rate, she wrote this will with his help a few years before her passing. Given the size of her estate, the will was a large undertaking, but the will was not exactly normal. Most would have expected to see her leave her estate to her children. Or maybe even donate it as her father would have done. But no. Her children amongst others were awarded an insignificant amount while the lion's share of her estate was left to you.

"Not to an heir of family blood, but you specifically at a specific time. Do you understand what I am saying, James?"

"I'm afraid I don't," I confessed, letting out a deep breath.

He walked back to his desk and sat down eyeing the papers on his desk.

"Mr. Bauer, her will specifically states that her estate is to be given to one Mr. James William Bauer, born on August 31, 1994, and is to be bestowed upon him following his 25th birthday. Mind you, this was written by her and recorded in 1927."

I SAT THERE in Mr. Lutz's office unable to form a thought. Was he really telling me that, according to this will, she knew I was to be born? Like she was telling the future or something? There had to be an explanation.

Then, I realized what was going on. This was some prank. Surely there was a camera hidden somewhere. Some old friend from school or something would be jumping through the door at any moment.

I drank the entire glass of champagne in one gulp. I was hoping that the alcohol would help me make sense of it all or at least wake me up from this dream. I looked around the room until I noticed that Mr. Lutz and Katherine were staring at me.

"So, you are telling me that I am the next Jesus Christ as foretold by this woman? And you are what — the wise man? I would have guessed a shepherd, but I don't see any sheep."

Lutz leaned back in his seat. His demeanor changed. He looked mad. Well, maybe not mad; frustrated perhaps. I couldn't tell. My head was starting to ache.

"Mr. Bauer, this is no joke!"

"And why should I believe that?" Now, I was getting mad.

Lutz stood up and walked to his bookcase. His finger slowly moved across the shelf as if he was searching for one specific book. Finally, he removed one. After a few moments of silently flipping through it, he dropped it on the desk in front of me.

"There!" he exclaimed. "Read it for yourself if you don't believe me!"

I looked briefly at the page. I really didn't care to read it at all, but the names caught my eye. Samuel Muller and Ida Mansfeld. I stopped and looked up at Lutz.

"What is this?" I asked skeptically.

"This is the legal precedent set by this very will. While I understand how this sounds ridiculous, it is very real." He began to pace. "As one could imagine, Ida's former husband and her kids weren't happy when they learned that most of her estate was to be given to someone who didn't exist and most likely never would. Naturally, they contested. They contested the will any way they could. Even to the point of stating that she was mentally unstable at the time the will was written. The newspapers, of course, had a field day with it. But my great-grandfather fought it tooth and nail. In the end, the precedent was set. Her will was to be executed to the letter, up until your birth date. If you were not born on that day, the remainder of the estate is to be given to the heirs of her children.

"I remember the day you were born. The partners in the firm had all placed bets on whether it would happen. My father's office had become a command center; he had tasked all the secretaries along with some temporary employees to call every hospital trying to find out if you were born. Of course, only a few here understood why we were doing this. I'm sure most here assumed my father had gone crazy. Then it happened. We got word that a birth certificate was filed for you, ending decades of speculation."

We all sat there in silence. No one knew how to respond

or what to say. The silence was broken by the sound of his office doors opening. I turned to see three men in tuxedos walk in. Without delay, they walked to the conference table and started setting up dinner.

Lutz stood up and walked around his desk and came up behind Katherine and me and leaned in-between our two chairs.

"So, you see Mr. Bauer, this is not a joke. What it is, I cannot fully explain or understand. But it is real. Now, let us eat. There is plenty to discuss on the more practical side of this."

For the next couple hours, we dined and discussed the more real matters of the estate. Well, Lutz discussed anyway. I remained mostly silent aside from nodding my head. Katherine also stayed quiet but appeared to be as engaged in the conversation as I was.

From what I understood, the estate was mine. In the years following Ida's death, the estate remained fully staffed and cared for. As years went on, the staff dwindled. The concept of working on a house with no apparent owner caused people to leave. Not wanting to invest time into managing the staff, the law firm decided to use the remaining money to secure the house. However, the security was minimal. It consisted of some chains set up around the entrances and boards to secure the windows and doors. As it was told to me, the house was in dire need of repair. Time and the harsh Chicago weather had taken its toll, and currently, the house was far from being in habitable condition.

Prior to tonight, the law firm had diligently gathered quotes to restore the estate. Lutz mentioned that should I choose to keep the estate, it would be in my best interest to pursue having it listed with the National Register of Historic

Places. While that would restrict some of the restoration options I had, it would also provide me with substantial property tax breaks.

Following the dinner, Mr. Lutz suggested that we formally sign the necessary paperwork. We went back to his desk as he retrieved the documents.

"Katherine, I trust you have the envelope?" he asked.

Katherine opened her purse, retrieved a yellowed envelope. She looked up at me. There was a noticeable change in her demeanor. Her brazen confidence was gone. Her wide eyes showed me a vulnerability she had kept hidden before that moment. She looked back at the envelope. Her hands delicately traced the outline of the wax seal as she silently bit her lower lip. She took a deep breath and handed it to me. I studied it for a moment before looking back at her. She forced a smile, but it looked more like she was about to cry. There was clearly something very important to her about this envelope.

"Here it is," she said. "Just as it was handed to my great-great-grandfather by Ida."

"Much of what I have heard tonight is new information. I know that my great-great grandfather was employed by Ida at the Villa and entrusted by her to carry out this request. While you have described the impact this case had within this law firm, it pales in comparison to just how important it was to my family that this get carried out. I don't know what's in that envelope, but I know that ensuring you got it tonight was the sole mission of my family for the past 90 years."

"James, I would be a liar if I said I do not want to know what's in that envelope," Mr. Lutz said eyeing the envelope. "However, regarding privacy, I feel it only best that you open that in your own time."

I nodded in agreement and put the envelope in my bag.

"Please take a few moments to read through these documents," Lutz said as he slid a few documents across his desk to me along with a pen. "I'm sure you will find them to be straight forward. They simply outline that you have received the envelope as described in the will and that you will be receiving ownership of the estate and the trust."

I leaned forward and scanned the documents. There was a little tab on each with an arrow pointing to the line for me to sign. The first document was all related to the envelope, which I signed and returned. The next detailed the estate and the trust. As my eyes read through it they stopped when I got to the dollar amount of the trust. In a moment of shock, the papers dropped out of my hand.

"Twenty-five million dollars!" I shouted. "Is this real?"

"It is very real, James." Lutz assured me.

Lutz spent the next few minutes outlining exactly where all the money was and what it amounted to. The final amount of the trust was indeed twenty-five million dollars. However, based upon the stipulations of the will, this amount was separated into two different trusts. The first one was mine to do whatever I wanted with. It amounted to two-point-four million dollars. The other trust, containing most of the money, was set up for me to fund the restoration of the estate.

I was in a state of shock. I couldn't even fathom dollar amounts that huge. After reviewing the document again with Lutz, I signed my name. With one simple signature, I had become a millionaire.

3

At the conclusion of the meeting with Lutz, I was given a list of next steps to take. This suited me. There was so much information given out through that meeting that I needed to wrap my head around everything and put in some due diligence. I was still trying to just get over the shock that I was now a millionaire.

After exchanging some pleasantries and setting up upcoming meetings, I was free to go. Katherine and I left together and stepped into the elevator that would take us back to the real world I knew.

I looked at her in the elevator as if for the first time. She had a natural beauty. The way her hair set on her delicate shoulders, the way she carried herself, the way she bit her lower lip in concentration. She was striking. That was when I realized I was staring at her and she was looking back at me with a playful grin. Our eyes met and locked on to one another's. Her eyes were an incredible, silver blue. Not blue like most blue eyes; hers were lighter, whiter and they seemed to just pierce through me.

"Katherine?" I stammered. "So, this envelope was passed down from your great-great-grandfather?"

"Yeah. It sat in a safe at our house forever until, I guess, we realized it was actually time for it to be delivered. My great-great-grandfather was a butler at the villa, and before Ida left, she gave this to him to pass along. I never really got to know all the details, my mom would know far more about it. But this letter was something of a family legacy for us."

"Oh, that's right, your mother. He mentioned she is sick. Is she alright?"

Her face turned sullen a bit as I mentioned it. It was at that moment the elevator dinged and the doors opened to the lobby of the building.

She started to walk out into the empty lobby, and then she turned to face me. "No, she isn't well. She has been battling cancer for quite some time, I'm afraid."

"I am very sorry to hear that. Please give her my best wishes."

I didn't want her to walk away. I wanted to come up with some way to keep this conversation moving. She had captivated me and I couldn't just let her walk away.

"Is there anything I could do to help out?"

She paused and looked at me as if she was trying to read me. Then there was a hint of something more in her eyes, like a spark. She bit her lip again and smiled with an expression of hopefulness.

"Actually, there is something you could help with."

I waited for her to continue, giving her a nod and a smile.

"Well, I know this might sound odd," she paused and chuckled slightly. "I take that back, after what we heard upstairs, I don't know that anything could sound odd anymore. Anyway, could you, at some point, visit my mother? This whole thing has been part of our family for so long, I am sure it would mean the world to her to see first-hand the closure of it all."

"I'd be more than happy to! Besides, that means you would have to give me your phone number." Shit, I thought. She was just talking about her dying mom and I was turning it into some stupid pick up line. "I'm sorry. I was just trying to lighten the mood a little. This whole thing has my head spinning a bit."

To my surprise, she chuckled even more. I guess it was not quite as stupid as I'd thought.

We walked out the revolving doors, onto the sidewalk, and across the street to the river walk. Despite how hot the day had been, there was a cool breeze coming off the river. We walked up to the wall and leaned against it. I felt the warmth of the concrete on my back. I could not stop thinking about how striking she was, how she looked under the yellow light of the street lights, how her hair tossed slightly with the breeze.

"I was serious though," I said. "I would love to be able to come see your mom."

"She would love that." Her expression softened. "So you really walked into that office tonight without having a clue about any of this?"

"Yeah, prior to tonight all I really knew was that I got contacted about some inheritance."

"I can't imagine how shocking this all is. It's a little hard for me to relate since this has been so much a part of my family all my life. Most people I know don't even know the name of their great-grandparents. Yet I grew up hearing constantly about my great-great-grandfather and this mission we had."

"Hey look, this has been a crazy night. You wanna go get

a drink somewhere?"

She shot me a surprised look.

"I mean sorry," I said not even waiting for her response. "I'm sure you have a boyfriend or husband or whatever to get back to."

"What? No...I just..." She trailed off.

"Look, I get it. Can't blame me for trying."

She hit me on the shoulder. "Would you stop! I'd love to get a drink. It's just, with my mom and everything, I haven't really gone out in a long time and the last thing I expected out of this night was to be going out for a drink with someone."

"Well, let's keep it low key," I offered. "Some place we can grab a drink and just hang out for a bit."

"Yeah, I'd like that. Where are we going?"

"I don't have a clue. I couldn't even name a place to get a drink around here. But if we start walking, we are bound to run into something."

WE ENDED up finding a small bar. It was quiet and dark. We found a table and ordered a couple of beers. There, I felt like we were the only people on the planet. The conversation was easy. Most dates I'd been on had felt like job interviews. This was relaxed. The conversation just happened. Talking with her felt more like reconnecting with an old childhood friend than a date.

While her words captivated my attention, I could not stop getting distracted by her looks either. Simple things like how her eyes conveyed so much emotion drew me in. The way she licked her lips slightly before she spoke made my heart race. Her clothes clung to her, accentuating every curve. I often found my eyes start to wander before I forced them back to her face.

The conversation started with her explanation of how she preferred being called 'Kat' over 'Katherine. Soon we were sharing the stories of our lives. She shared a lot about growing up with the stories of her great-great-grandfather and the estate. We laughed, joked, and talked endlessly.

Without realizing it, the simple drink turned into a late night. Soon, the bartender was making the announcement of 'last call' even though it felt like we just got there. I had forgotten that I'd just inherited an estate and money; everything in my mind shifted to the amazing night I was having with her. After the last call, we walked back to the parking garage hand-in-hand. It wasn't awkward. It just felt right.

After a long night, I finally got home and sat down on the couch. Despite everything that had happened, I was thinking of her. I also recognized the absurdity of that fact. Here I was, an overnight millionaire, and my thoughts were of Kat.

I lay there silently with a smile on my face. Thoughts of her slowly let me drift off. I'd nearly fallen asleep when I suddenly remembered the envelope. With a burst of energy, I stood up and retrieved my backpack to pull it out. I got the envelope and turned on the lights.

I sat there for minutes just staring at it. I admired the intricate wax seal and the feel of the paper on my fingertips. Soon, the suspense got to me. I pulled out my pocket knife so I could open it without disturbing the seal.

Inside was a letter. As I pulled out the letter, a pair of keys fell out and clattered to the ground. I picked them up and looked at them for a moment.

They were old and heavy — made of brass. While they were both intricate, they were very different. One resembled a typical old-style skeleton key, only much more ornate. The other was again the same style, but far more elaborately designed. The handle was intricately crafted with branch-like adornments. The loop of the key was not even a loop, but an engraved scene. It almost looked like a picture of a window or a mirror surrounded by leaves. In the center, were some engraved characters I couldn't quite place.

I set both keys on the table and gently unfolded the letter. It reminded me of a historical document you would see at a museum. The paper was yellowed with age and the text was slightly faded but written in a beautiful script. The writing looked more like artwork than actual letters.

Dearest James,

If you are reading this, you have no doubt taken possession of my once beloved estate, Villa Ortenberg. While I am sure this is all new to you now, I am hoping that in time you will begin to feel the memories of my time at the Villa become clear.

It saddens me greatly to deliver the estate to you in this manner, and you must know I had sought for alternatives. However, the forces at the estate from my former husband became far too great for me to overcome. You are the only one who has a chance to make everything right again. Forgive me as I have failed you in life in many ways. I know that I cannot right all my wrongs, but only do everything I can to give you the opportunity to succeed where I did not.

This letter and the enclosed keys are items which I could only entrust dear Edgar with. Please take the greatest care in using them and undoing what has happened. One of the keys is to my parlor in the Villa. I trust that it is still locked and secured. As for the other key, all I can say is you will understand how to use it when you are required to.

Finally, I have put away some of my dearest personal effects into the safe at the Villa. These items are both extravagant in nature but also very important to me. They are yours to do as you wish with them. The combination to the safe should come as no surprise to you:

2 – 27 – 4

Please do all you can to rectify the wrongs I made in life. I look forward to a moment when we can meet again.

Love Always,

Your Mother – Ida

I set the letter down and was overcome with emotion. On one hand, I completely acknowledged how crazy this all was. Hell, she referred to herself as my mother. Yet she knew she was writing to someone eighty years later. At the same time, something tugged at me emotionally. Maybe it was the whirlwind of everything that happened that day coming to some pinpoint in the letter — or something else completely. Whatever it was, it grabbed me emotionally like nothing else.

I AWOKE in the morning feeling oddly relaxed. I started to think about the house and everything I inherited. I really knew very little about the house, just the abbreviated history from the lawyer. I knew more than I wanted to about the will, but mansions like that don't just pop up. There was a story there. A story I didn't know. How did the affluent life end the way it did? I started assembling questions like that in my head. I then realized how I was going to spend my day.

An hour later, I parked my truck in front of an old house. This particular house was home to the area's historical society. I walked through the front door. The inside was set up like a museum. An older woman sat at a desk opposite the door. The door shut behind me with a loud thud. She jumped, startled by the noise and looked up at me.

"I'm sorry, there are not many visitors this early in the morning." She sounded flustered.

She quickly stood up and took a moment to flatten her floral dress.

"I'm Florence," she said, regaining her composure. "Is there anything I can help you with this morning?"

"Hi, I'm Jim." I extended my hand. "I'm researching an older home in the area, and I was wondering if you had anything in your collection that could help me out."

"I'm sure we can help. We have been very blessed to have a lot of things for most of the original homes here. What property are you interested in?"

"I am looking for things specific to the Ida Muller property."

Her demeanor immediately changed. She looked at me with contempt.

"You mean Mansfeld Manor?" she asked with disdain in her voice.

"Uh no, I am actually referring to Villa Ortenberg," I said.

"Same place. Mansfeld is what us locals called it after everything." She still sounded anything but friendly. "I suppose you are another one of those paranormal people trying to dig up something."

"No, I'm not. But I would be interested in understanding why you would suggest that. I am actually the current owner of the property."

"Oh please." She waved her hand at me and rolled her eyes in disbelief. "This is a fine community. The last thing we need is people like you making up stories to tarnish our past."

"Ma'am, I'm sorry, but I assure you that is not what I am looking to do. I am indeed the owner."

"Jim is it? I have work to do, and I don't intend to listen to your lies. Good day." She sat back at her desk.

"I am sorry if I offended you," I said trying to keep from yelling at her, "but I assure you I'm not lying."

She turned in the chair and looked at me with a scowl. "Look, mister, I don't know what you want. I would be glad to help you, but don't come in here telling me you are the owner of Mansfeld. There is no owner of Mansfeld. Maybe if you did your research you would know that no one has owned that property since Ida Mansfeld herself passed. She didn't leave it to her kids. She left it to some unknown heir at some unknown time in the future."

"And maybe if you did your research you would know that the unknown time actually took place about two weeks ago and the unknown heir is me. I would prove it to you, but I certainly didn't expect to you to require proof of ownership in such a fine community as this." I started walking towards the door.

"Wait," she said releasing air from her lungs and letting her guard down. "You're serious. I don't know what to say. It's just, well, no one believed the heir would ever arrive. That is how the papers talked about it anyway."

"Well, it certainly happened. I don't know much of the history that you speak of, but I am the owner." I turned back to face her.

"That's right! I remember now. The original papers stated something like 80 years in the future, which would be right about now! I cannot believe this happened. Well, that and, you must understand, Mansfeld has been a dark cloud over this community for so long. I get tired of people looking to focus on the dirt when there is so much more to this area. Anyway, please accept my apology."

I stopped and looked at her. I couldn't help but notice not only her age but the way she talked about the property — as if she had witnessed everything.

"Florence, how long have you lived here?" I asked.

"Oh dear, I was born here and have been here all my life. Born in 1934, but I suppose I don't remember much from before 1940 or so."

"So, you were here when they closed the estate in 1943?" I asked.

"Yes, I was just a girl, but I do remember that. As you can imagine it was quite a little news story."

"So, are you saying that you are not too busy and would be willing help me?" I asked.

She lowered her head and took a deep breath. "I apologized once — I am not going to do it again, but yes I will gladly help you. But mark my words, if I come to find that this is some ruse... well, do not underestimate this old woman." Her words were stern, and her jaw set tightly. "Please come have a seat in here and let me grab a few things."

She led me to the dining room of the house, which was converted to a conference room.

A few minutes later she returned to the dining room pushing a cart with a couple of file boxes on it.

"Where would you like to start?" she asked, sitting down.

"Honestly, I would love to get some insight from you as to why the paranormal investigators are looking into the property."

"Oh dear, it is mostly folklore I'm sure," she replied dismissively.

"Well, that is even better. Since you grew up here, I'm

sure you heard your share of that folklore first hand," I said.

"It is just wild imaginations of kids if you ask me. But you are right. I was here. In the beginning, it was stories revolving around Samuel Jr. That was Ida's child who died when he was only four. At any rate, when the child of such a prominent family dies for unknown reasons, rumors start to spread. Samuel, Ida's husband... he ended up being truly a wicked man. Then, there was Ida herself. That poor woman. Rumors were she lost her mind and began to dabble in black magic. No one really knows what had happened there. But it was clear, based on the little information the public had, that some terrible things took place. Of course, once the manor was closed, these stories really caught on. Boys would sneak in there at night and come back with horrendous tales of being chased by the ghost of Ida or rabid wolves with red eyes guarding the property. Like I said, all a bunch of mumbo-jumbo."

"I understand. I would like to know as much of the real story as possible. But I also understand that sometimes when there isn't real information to be had, the rumors can help fill the gaps."

"Surely you don't believe there are wolves roaming the estate." Her defensive tone resurfaced.

"Absolutely not," I said, trying to ease her mind. "But I also feel that those stories may have begun with some element of the truth. Why don't we focus on what we do know."

"Actually, there is a lot here. Especially when you consider there were no family keeping these items together. If memory serves me, these files were donated to the city by the butler after the estate was closed."

She put one of the boxes on the table and opened it, slowly taking out items and setting them on the table.

"This box is mostly photos of the estate. Again, with no family to pass these to, the city got them."

The first photo that caught my eye was a picture of a young woman standing in front of what looked like a fountain terrace. I picked it up and looked closer. She was beautiful in a stately way.

"Would you happen to know who this is?" I asked.

"Oh, that is Ida Mansfeld. And from the looks of it, that is a very early photo of her."

I SPENT the next hour or so flipping through the photos. There were a massive amount of them. Most of them were of Ida and the family, but some were of the house. Seeing the gardens and landscape in those photos made it hard to believe this estate was real, and that it was mine.

Florence helped me acquaint myself with what was in the photos. She had a keen eye and was able to quickly identify the people in each shot, including Samuel Muller, Ida's husband, and other notable people from the area.

I picked up one of the last photos on the table. The moment I looked at it I felt a sharp pain in my head. I closed my eyes hard trying to shake it off, and when I opened them all I could see was a bright light. I dropped the photo on the table and pressed the heels of my hands into my temples. After a few moments, the pain started to subside. I opened my eyes and looked at the photo again.

There was Ida. Again, a younger Ida. She was seated, holding a glass of champagne. Next to her was her husband Samuel. They were posing with another man I hadn't seen before. Both men were dressed in suits and had glasses of whiskey in their hands. In the photo, there was a large white stripe across the dark wooden table they sat at. They both seemed to be trying to hold their drinks across the white stripe. I flipped the photo over and noticed there was some writing on the back.

"Cloudland – 1907 – Gen. Wilder"

I flipped it back over. Again, there was a sharp surge of pain in my head. I took out my phone and snapped a picture of both the front and the back of the photo.

Florence gave me a stern look as I took the picture.

"Sorry, I am just trying to capture some of this history to understand the whole story."

She removed her glasses letting them hang from the attached chain. I feared a quick reprimand was coming, but she surprised me by placing her hands on top of mine.

"Is it any surprise to you that we have no exhibits in this building dedicated to your estate or its former owners?" she asked.

"I guess I didn't think about it."

"When it comes to money and status, Ida and Samuel were without a doubt the most affluent residents of this community ever. We are blessed to have a wealth of photos and documents about the estate, and yet, there is nothing on display. This is not by accident, James. Whether you believe the ghost stories or not, there is a reason we refer to the house as Mansfeld Manor. That estate and Samuel cast a dark shadow across this community. When the estate fell apart, we couldn't continue using the formal name, Villa Ortenberg. Mansfeld Manor soon became the name, stripping any relation to Samuel indefinitely. The history books tell of his wealth and his prosperity, but this is not the real story."

"What is the real story?" I asked.

"The real story is far less documented. Buried like the

remnants of that once great home. The real picture of life at the Villa comes to us in fragmented stories. There were stories of excess. As you can imagine, Samuel came off as a bit of a playboy. But there is more. There was a much darker side. Police work wasn't much back then. Combine that with the fact that no police squad would ever dare accuse someone of his prestige with anything, and you get a massive amount of unanswered questions left in his wake. Strange stories, missing people, even dark rituals were commonplace around here. There were tales of families coming to town looking for loved ones who had been visiting Samuel and were then never heard from again. He was constantly hiring new help at the home, but the staff was not turning over...they just vanished.

"I have no doubt that there is a lot of folklore involved. But, as you said, folklore does almost always start with an element of truth. You will never see black and white reports on any of this. The only fact I can relay is that people here were uneasy with his presence. That is, until he disappeared. Shortly after Ida abandoned the house, he just vanished... and this community wasn't exactly concerned about finding him."

I was shocked at what she was saying. Every answered question led to ten new unanswered ones.

"You said wanted to know about the house," she continued. "I feel it only right to tell you the truth. Not all history is good history. Some questions are best left unanswered. Remember that as you continue to dive into this. If I were you, I would focus on the house itself. As for its former occupants, it may be best to leave that alone."

I nodded in response. I wanted to ask more but felt as though she had closed that door.

"I must tend to some other matters. If you need me for

anything else, I will be at my desk." She curtly stood up and left me with the boxes.

The next box contained fewer photos and a lot of papers. As I went through it, I realized that the papers were original plans for the estate. Floor by floor blueprints of the home. Plans for the servant quarters. Even sketches planning the gardens down to the details of what kinds of flowers should be planted where.

After paging through, I stood up and walked over to Florence who was now working at her desk.

"Excuse me, I need to leave in a moment, but I've a question for you."

"Yes, what is it?" she asked.

"I noticed that you have the original plans for the house... or at least some variation of them. As I'm looking to restore it, these would be a tremendous help. Is there any way I would be able to get them duplicated?"

"Of course. Most of our files have already been digitized. But these haven't been touched, I'm afraid. I can arrange to have them added to our next group."

"That would be much appreciated," I said. "And thank you for your time today."

"Just a moment, did you say that you are planning to restore the house?"

"Well, that is the plan. Of course, we will have to see what it'll take to make that happen."

"Oh, that will be wonderful!" she beamed.

As I left there, I still had a very uneasy feeling about her responses. It probably didn't help that my head was throbbing again. What was it now, like four days in a row with these headaches? Yet, aside from my headache, something just made me feel very unnerved.

I brushed it off and headed back to my apartment.

4

THE REMAINDER of that weekend was spent trying to learn everything I could about the owners of the estate. My mind continued going over Ida's cryptic letter and how she'd referred to herself as my mother. I had no relationship that I could trace to Ida... nothing that I could explain anyway. Her story was all I cared about. It felt as though an invisible cord connected me to her.

I took the warning Florence had given me about digging into the past and used it as my jumping off point. If she was correct about Samuel, it certainly was a history that was hidden... and hidden well. Everything I came across was different renditions of what I'd already learned from the lawyer. Even Samuel's disappearance wasn't really covered. I couldn't find any articles about it. It was as if he not only disappeared, but no one noticed or cared about his disappearance.

When I walked into work on Monday, Paul was eager to find out what happened. I relayed the short version of what happened with the lawyer.

"So, you're gonna take the money and run, right?"

Paul asked.

"What do you mean? Most of the money is set aside for restoring the house."

"Aw man, forget about that. You said it yourself, the house just needs to be livable. Do the minimum to meet that criteria and sell the house. The property alone is worth more without the house. Why would you want to deal with that mess? Take your money and let the house rot. Go live on the beach and never worry about it again."

Prior to this moment, the thought of just getting what I could out of the house never crossed my mind. Now that it had, I realized it was not a thought I could entertain in the slightest. That was the easy route for sure, but it felt completely wrong. I thought of the house as my home. The place where I wanted to live.

"I don't think I can do that. I looked up pictures of the place. It was amazing, and it just feels like this is something I need to do."

"Need?" he asked. "You don't need to do anything. How much of your life are you gonna give up by taking this on?"

"I think that is the point. What life am I giving up? I show up here day after day, return to my shitty apartment, and maybe go work out. That isn't life... that is existence. I don't have a family. I have nothing important to me. This could give me something more than existing."

I felt a sense of pride wash over me as I spoke. This was something I could be a part of. It was a life that was more than just existing. It was a purpose.

"Now, that is nuts. Your life can begin on the beach." He apparently didn't see things the same way.

That simple conversation seemed to make everything clear to me. Gone were the days of a boring mediocre exis-tence. For the first time in as long as I can remember, I had a purpose. I had something I wanted to accomplish... something that was mine... I had an estate.

I blew off a meeting I had scheduled that morning. Instead of working, I found myself sitting in my truck in the parking lot. I called Lutz and informed him of what I wanted to do. He set the wheels in motion to provide me with the research his firm put in to restore the property. Additionally, he informed me that the trust which was set up for my personal use had been successfully transferred to my account.

I sat there with a new-found direction in life and a very full bank account. I walked back to my office. There was a small voice inside me telling me to be rational. I ignored this voice as I asked my boss to meet with me. I promptly quit, packed up my desk, and left that job far behind me.

I was beaming as I got into my truck and smiled at the small box of items from my desk. I was unsure of what to do next. Sure, I had purpose and direction, but this was a long journey. I wasn't ready to go to the house yet. I decided to just enjoy the day. I started the truck and drove to the first car dealership I came across.

A couple hours later, I walked out with the paperwork for the brand-new truck I'd ordered. It was an experience I had always dreamed of. I literally walked in and ordered the most expensive, fully loaded truck I could. As the salesman began to roll his eyes, bringing up the fact that he needed to get me approved for financing, I just got out my checkbook and paid it in full.

Fueled by the exhilaration of the day, I decided to go for broke. I picked up my phone and called Kat. In an atypical conversation, I simply told her that we were going out for dinner. Much to my surprise, she not only accepted but sounded excited at the prospect. I was a new man.

Over the next few days, with no more job to go to, my mind was free to run. The obsession with the house began to consume me. Unfortunately, everywhere I turned I seemed to run into dead ends when it came to gathering information. The only thing luring my attention from the house was Kat. We'd spent every evening going out together. Our relationship grew quickly. Like the house, the onset of my feelings for her came fast and with unbridled intensity.

There was something about her that connected with me in an extreme way. If I wasn't with her, I was counting the hours until I could see her. I would endlessly play with my phone, hoping I would get another text message from her. The concept of being so enthralled with her frightened me... yet there was nothing I could do to stop or even slow my feelings for her.

That Friday, I arranged to make good on my promise to her and visit her mom. No matter how comfortable I had become with Kat, meeting her mom unnerved me. I'd fallen head over heels for her daughter and that fact made this meeting scary. Although the premise of the meeting was really about the house, I was concerned about how she'd react to meeting me.

I'd received a call that my new truck was ready for pick up. So, I distracted myself from thinking any more about Kat's mom by picking it up. I drove to the dealership and bid farewell to my old truck. Moments later, my new one pulled up in front of the showroom. It was white with red stripes and every upgrade possible. As I drove home, I couldn't help opening the windows and turning the stereo up as loud as it would go. Yes, this was a great day. I got home and took a shower. I put on some new clothes and headed out the door.

Soon, I was pulling up to her house. Kat's car was

already there. Her mother lived very close to my new estate. I couldn't help but wonder if that was a coincidence.

I walked up to the door as nervous as a teenager on prom night. I took a few deep breaths to relax as I pressed the doorbell. In the distance, I could hear the chime ring, followed by footsteps, then the lock of the door. Kat opened the door and let me in, giving me a quick hug. My God, she felt so good in my arms.

"Jim, I'm so happy you made it!" She smiled brightly.

"I wouldn't have missed it." I smiled back.

"Here, come into the kitchen and sit down for a minute." She led me down a hall into the kitchen.

We sat on stools around the island counter.

"Listen, I wanted to talk to you before you go up there. My mom... well... it is just that since she has been sick..." She hesitated as if she was choosing her words carefully. "Sometimes she talks kinda strangely."

She was sitting facing me, looking at me with those piercing eyes. It took me a moment to even realize that she had started holding my hands in hers.

"I don't know. It's just weird. A lot of the time she's my old mother the same as she always was. Then other times... I feel like I don't even know who is talking to me."

"I'm sorry. I get it. It'll be fine, don't worry."

She hung her head as she gently squeezed my hands. Then, she looked back up at me.

"I'm just saying if she starts sounding crazy, go along with it. Okay?"

"Well, after that meeting we had with the lawyer, I would be more shocked if she didn't talk crazy," I replied.

Still holding my hand, she walked me upstairs to her mother's room. The house was silent and smelled like a hospital. In the room, there were machines beeping around the bed. As we approached, I was shocked at how young she looked. Sure, she was Kat's mother, but I was expecting someone who more resembled a feeble 80-year-old.

"Mom, James is here to see you. He wanted to come by and speak with you."

The woman sat up in her bed and looked at me. She had the same piercing blue eyes as Kat. She eyed me cautiously for what felt like minutes until a smile appeared on her face.

"See Katherine, do you feel it?" she asked looking at her daughter. "My mother always told me that I would be able to feel it when he arrived, and she was right! Come sit down here where I can see you clearly. I must speak with you."

I walked over next to her bed and sat down on the chair. She reached for my hand and grabbed it, pulling it close to her.

"I am so thankful you are here. I now know everything will be right."

I glanced over at Kat and gave her my best attempt at a smile.

"Tell me, have you been to the Villa yet?" she asked.

"No ma'am. I have not. It's a bit overgrown so I have only driven by it. I'm hoping to head out there tomorrow for the first time."

With that, she looked at me and seemed to breathe a sigh of relief. She covered my hand with her other hand. "Katherine? Please go to my desk, and open the top drawer."

Without a word, Kat headed across the room to a desk and pulled open the drawer.

"What do you need mom?" she asked.

"Please get my smudge stick, and give it to James," she replied.

"Smudge stick?" Kat asked while she was digging

through the drawer. "I'm afraid I don't know what you want,"

"Katherine!" she said with some agitation. "You must know! It's the bunch of sage. In the back of the drawer."

Moments later, Kat came back holding what looked like a pile of dried weeds tied tightly together. When her mother saw it, a large smile crossed her face.

"Yes! James, please take this with you to the Villa. Before entering the house, light this on fire until it starts smoking. Then walk the perimeter of the house, dousing it in smoke. Let them know you are there in peace and you are there to right the wrongs. It will not have any long-term effects, but at the very least, it will give you the ability to enter without any disturbances." She squeezed my hand.

"Of course, ma'am, I appreciate this very much," I replied.

Then, within a matter of seconds, she peacefully fell asleep. Her eyes closed, and her hand slipped out of mine.

Kat reached over and placed her mother's hand gently at her side. She then grabbed my hand and softly whispered, "C'mon. Let's go downstairs."

"See, I told you she could get a little weird on us," she said once we were back in the kitchen. "I appreciate it though. It means a lot to me for you to do this...Are you really going there tomorrow?"

"Yeah, it's about time. I figured it is supposed to be a nice day. It'll give me a chance to truly see what I'm in for. It's so overgrown that it might be a struggle to even get my truck in there."

"Well, I don't know how you feel about it, but I am free. That is... if you don't want to go out there alone. I can even help you with this smudge stick." She shrugged, holding up the dried sage.

"You really want to come with?" I said, giving her a look of surprise.

"With everything I've heard in this last week, how could I not want to see this mystical estate?" she said with excitement. She looked at me with a cheerful smile and then looked down at the floor. After a few moments, she looked up at me with softer eyes. "Well, I would be lying if I said I just want to see the house. I mean, of course I do, but it's more that I just want to spend time with you." She moved closer to me.

Her eyes, still soft, were staring like they were going to burn a hole right through me. I couldn't think. It was as if my entire being was put on some sort of autopilot. I wrapped my arms around her and pulled her tight into me. I just held her. I held her for what felt like an eternity. Eventually, I moved my lips to her ear and whispered, "Please. I want you there with me."

As I headed home that night, I began to think about Kat coming to the house with me. Kat was wonderful, and I truly wanted her at the house with me. I wanted her everywhere with me. I was enthralled. What confused me was the fact that she also wanted to be there with me. I was so accustomed to being the one who longed for a relationship and connection far beyond what any woman wanted from me. Yet with Kat, it felt mutual. It felt like we were on the same page. I was stepping into uncharted territory with her. I was scared, but it felt so right I overrode my fears and just went with it.

I spent the remainder of the night shopping and packing my truck. I had no idea what we were in for. I wanted to be prepared as much as I could. First, I got a toolbox full of basic hand tools, a chainsaw, and other yard tools to help clear a path if needed. Next, I packed a large duffel bag with flashlights, lanterns, and candles. Finally, I packed a large cooler full of beer, water, and some food.

After I finished packing, I got a beer and sat on the couch. Thoughts of Kat were battling with thoughts of the estate for priority in my head. The struggle was that right now, neither was winning. As a result, I was unable to think clearly about anything. Just as I took another pull from the beer, my phone rang.

It took me a second to figure out who could be calling. Then, it dawned on me. It was Friday. My mother always called me on Friday night. I'd missed her call last week. So, I had to answer before she freaked out. The worst part was, now I had to tell her everything. I took a deep sigh and picked up the phone.

The first few minutes, we talked about nothing, just the typical. Finally, I found a way into the conversation and simply asked if she knew anything about an inheritance I'd received. She went dead silent.

"Mom? Are you there?"

"Jim, I completely forgot! I mean... you know... I didn't believe it was real! I just assumed it was some prank or something... are you okay?" She sounded panic-stricken.

"Yeah, I am fine. What are you talking about?"

"I don't know. I never did know... I just knew it wasn't right... His voice, the way he talked. I wanted to pack up and move you far away when I heard his voice!" She sounded increasingly alarmed.

"Mom! What are you talking about?"

"When you were born... I don't know, it must have been about a week after you were born. We were at the house and your dad had just left for another supposed job interview, which I knew meant he was sitting at the bar. Anyway, you had just fallen asleep in your bouncer when the phone rang.

I picked it up. There was this man on the line. I remember him being super formal saying something like: 'Mrs. Bauer, we understand you gave birth to James a few days ago. I am calling you to give you a warning. When James is twenty-five, he will be contacted about an inheritance. There is nothing but danger surrounding this. Please ensure that he does not accept this inheritance as it will be a curse.'

"The words may not be exact, but I will never forget that voice! I cannot believe you are twenty-five, and I haven't thought about it since! Please tell me you did not accept it!"

Her voice was pure panic.

I was in shock. "Mom, it's okay. I am fine. No, I am good actually!"

"So, it's real then?" she asked.

"Yes, it is real, but it's all good," I pleaded.

For the next half hour, we talked about the will. I kept out some details like the crazy letter from the butler and things that I thought would only alarm her. Eventually, she calmed down. We ended the call in a composed place... although I could tell by her voice, she was far from satisfied. She was scared but also realized there was nothing to be done now.

The last thing she said to me was, "Be careful Jimmy. Please! Be careful!"

5

KAT and I pulled up to the property at around nine the next morning. It was a beautiful day. The sun was bright, and the sky was clear. The ride there with her had been a relief. It was light-hearted and playful, exactly what I needed to clear my head. I pulled up to the same spot I parked my truck last time and parked again. We got out and walked up to the same dilapidated entrance. We slowly walked up to the remnants of the toppled gate.

We stood there staring off into the wooded entrance. We were holding hands, and it felt like we were about to start a great adventure. We quietly entered the property.

A few steps past the gate, we got behind the brush that blocked the view from the street. The trees were completely blocking out the sun. About fifty feet in, we were finally able to see where we were. There was a clear cobblestone drive leading up from where we were. It was overgrown and in horrible shape, but it was there. We could see the Elm trees lining the drive as it extended. This was without a doubt, the true entrance to the estate.

We silently walked down the path, our hands intertwined. It was dark, and a cold wind traveled through this corridor in the woods. We were surrounded by sounds of birds chirping and animals rustling in the trees. Soon we could see the outline of the house. It stood as the centerpiece of the drive. From that distance, it looked like an immense dark wall. It extended far beyond our view in both directions. It was a dingy gray stucco building covered with planks of weathered plywood, no doubt covering the windows. To say it was massive was an understatement.

"Oh my God!" I exclaimed. I was in awe of the sight. "I have never seen anything like it!"

She stood there silently, mouth agape, and squeezed my hand.

"Well, we should probably get the truck up here," I said without looking away from the structure. "That path is completely overgrown, but I think the truck should be able to make it."

She agreed, and we walked back to the truck. When we exited the woods, the bright light of the day hit us and, I immediately realized that I had yet another headache. The light shot right into my skull. I squinted as we got back to my truck.

After a few minutes of very cautious driving, we got the truck into the clearing and then drove slowly up to the front of the house. It was so dark on the path that the truck's automatic headlamps turned on.

We slowly approached until we were about ten feet from the entrance. I parked the truck, and we got out. Now, close to the house, we could see it for what it truly was. The mammoth front face seemed to glare down on us. The stucco was merely the tattered remains of a once beautiful house. In some places, it had been overtaken by the ivy that hid anything underneath. In other places, the stucco had fallen from the face of the house leaving only the brick underlayer visible. The windows were secured with plywood that was far beyond its expected lifespan. In the center was a large granite entryway which appeared to be intact aside from the plywood covering the opening where a door should be.

Standing in the front of the house, even though sunlight was again forcing its way through, it felt dark. The cool breeze was chilling despite the heat of the day. As we crept towards the doorway, the ominous caw of a crow, sitting atop the entrance, echoed. I jumped. It sounded incredibly loud, and the booming sound sent a surge of pain through my head. A feeling of foreboding took over my body. Then, the crow took flight, leaving us alone at the doorstep of Villa Ortenberg.

I shook off the foreboding and turned to Kat. "Well, I knew it was a bit of a fixer-upper. I guess I have work to do."

"I can't believe the size of this place! I feel like this isn't even real!"

"Oh, it's real enough," I said as I walked into the entryway. There I could see the plywood was set up as a door complete with hinges and a weathered Master lock keeping it secure.

"I never thought I would be walking into my first house using a padlock key, but I guess it's my only option."

I reached into my pocket to find the keys I'd gotten from the lawyer when I felt the sage Kat's mother had given me. I had never been superstitious. Yet it felt like I should heed her advice. At the very least, it would be a considerate gesture.

I pulled it out of my pocket along with a lighter and looked at her.

"So how does this work?" I asked.

"Seriously?" She chuckled. "You don't have to do that. Like I said, my mom can get a bit weird about stuff."

"No, for real, it was important to her, so I figure maybe I should listen. Besides, it isn't like it'll do any harm."

"I have never done anything like this before. All I know is what I've seen my mom doing." She reached over and took it from my hand. She eyed it cautiously for a moment. "I remember she would light it on fire and then blow the flame out. It would start smoking kinda like a stick of incense. Then she would kinda wave the smoke around. That is really all I know. I always thought it was pretty silly."

"I think she said I have to talk to the house too, which sounds really strange now standing here with you, but what the hell. Let's give it a go."

I took the sage back from her and lit the end of it. In a few moments, the flames started to die down and I blew them out. Immediately, a stream of smoke came from the top edge of it. I walked to the door and waved the smoke on it as if I was painting it, covering it in smoke.

"I come here in peace," I said. "Please bless this home and watch over us as we come to restore this home and to right the wrongs of the past."

The first time I said it I laughed and looked over at Kat. Then, I did it again. The second time, I forced myself to close my eyes and tried to focus my attention on the house. With each word I spoke, I felt the pain in my head subside. I grabbed her hand, and we slowly walked the perimeter of the house constantly waving the smoke and saying that we had come in peace. With every step we took, it started to feel warmer and warmer.

As we walked, I began to take in the enormity of the estate. The broken and overgrown lily pool on the south side of it was still impressive. The immense courtyard and terrace facing Lake Michigan on the Eastern side was nearly destroyed but still held beauty. Finally, as we turned toward the northern side of the house, we saw the vast outbuildings and garages. Eventually, we made it all the way back to the entrance. Directly in front of the entrance was a large crumbling planter. There, I extinguished the sage and placed the remainder of it in the planter.

I smiled at Kat. We had walked the perimeter in silence aside from my talking to the house, and now again. For a moment I realized how embarrassed I should have felt walking around telling the house that we come in peace like it was an alien in a movie. Yet, it wasn't embarrassing, it just felt right.

"So, is it safe to walk inside now?" I asked.

She laughed. "Well, definitely as safe as it was an hour ago. There's really only one way to find out."

I walked up to the front door and unlocked the padlock. Once the lock was removed, the plywood door creaked open. Behind it was the massive original front door of the house. It was beaten up but still relatively solid. I started to panic for a moment as I did not have a key to this one. When I grabbed the handle, I realized it was unlocked. It didn't move freely, and I had to put some weight behind it before it finally swung upon. Daylight crept into the estate for the first time in years. With the door open, I gingerly stepped inside, hearing the floor groan with each step.

It was dark aside from the triangle of light coming through the doorway. It was surprisingly cool and completely silent. I didn't realize just how loud the wind and the forest were until I stepped into the house's utter silence. I looked back at Kat as if to say, 'I guess this is it'.

She stepped in behind me and lightly placed her hand on my shoulder. We didn't walk any deeper into the house.

We just stood there. I was trying to take it all in. It was hard to really make everything out in the darkness, but the enormity of the foyer was hard to grasp. Against the walls was furniture draped in dusty white sheets, giving it a true haunted house feel. The ceiling was adorned with a crystal chandelier, surrounded by wood. Dust particles drifted in the sunlight shining in. It appeared to drape everything in a sheet of twinkling lights. I noticed something on the floor. It was dusty and dirty, but it was there... the large 'M' monogram that was on my envelope inlaid into the marble floor.

"We can't see a whole lot with the windows blocked," I said, breaking the silence. "Why don't we grab some lights from the truck, so we can really see this place."

We went to the truck, and grabbed some water and my bag of lights. As we stepped into the house again, I turned on a lantern and set it on the center of the floor. The stark white light lit the entire room. It was immense and beautiful. The intricate woodwork throughout the foyer, though worn, was incredible. There were open doorways to both the left and right and a double door leading to the main hall directly in front of us.

We ambled into the main hallway. As our lights bounced around the interior, I noticed the ceiling was made of glass. The entire hall ceiling was a skylight. Now plywood covered it from the outside and much of the glass was broken. Clearly, the plywood protecting this was less than adequate as the flooring and walls clearly suffered from water damage.

Slowly we prodded along, feeling the floor sink slightly under our weight. My light caught the double doorway on my left, and we entered cautiously through it. It was a room unlike anything I'd ever seen. In sharp contrast to the dark wood in the rest of the house, this room was bright. The wooden flooring transitioned to white marble. The room was large and long with Roman-style columns framing the space. On the far end stood a shallow marble pool with what I could only assume was a statue or fountain in the center, now draped in a sheet. The far wall was rows and rows of windows with a double door in the center.

"Have you ever seen anything like this?" I asked in awe.

"Not in real life. It looks like a museum or some monument from Washington."

The mood lightened entirely in this room. We both let go of the silent caution we had before and began to explore with more abandon. I walked up to the shallow pool and yanked the sheet off. A cloud of dust erupted, causing me to cough. Beneath the sheet was a three-tiered fountain, which looked like it belonged in some Italian park. I put my hand on it, feeling the cool marble. Then something caught my eye.

IN THE POOL AREA, at the base of the fountain, I saw something shiny reflecting the light from the lantern in my hand. I knelt to look at it and saw it was a coin. I reached for it and picked it up. It was a penny, a silver penny. It was immaculate like it just came from the mint.

"Kat! Come take a look at this!" I handed her the penny. "It was in the fountain like a kid threw it in, thinking it was a wishing well."

"Oh my God!" She gasped as she looked at it.

"What... what is it?" I asked.

"It's a penny... a 1943 penny; they made them from aluminum to save copper for the war. But..." She trailed off staring at the coin.

"But what?" I asked, concerned.

"It's silly. Don't worry about it." She handed it back to me.

I put my hand on her shoulder, gently brushing her hair back.

"No, what is it?" I asked.

She let out a sigh and put her hand in her pocket, pulling her keys out.

"It's just strange." She held up her keychain for me to see.

There, on her keychain, was a pendant of sorts. As I looked at it, I realized there was an aluminum penny mounted into the pendant.

"Wow, I don't know that I've ever seen one of these. Now two in one day."

"Well, yeah. They're kinda rare...but that isn't it!" She shook her head and looked me in the eyes.

"That penny on my keychain was my great-great-grandfather's. He had it put into this pendant and it has been passed down in our family. I remember my mother giving it to me, telling me that as long as I had this, I would always know who I really was."

I didn't know what to say. It was an odd coincidence, yes. But I didn't really know that it could have been anything else.

"My great-great-grandfather," she said finally. "The one who worked here."

I looked at her and then back at the penny. The date on the penny stood out to me now. 1943.

"And that penny was minted long after the estate was abandoned except for the staff," I said looking at her. "So, he left this here."

"Like I said it's silly. But the penny feels different. When

I touched it, I felt connected to it if that makes any sense."
She paused. "Wait! Put it back. Back in the fountain."

I looked at her quizzically.

"Why do people put coins in a fountain? They make a
wish. What if this was his wish? We need to leave that there
for now."

I nodded my head and knelt to put the coin back where I
found it.

"You know, I think you've watched the Goonies a few too
many times." I smiled as I stood up next to her.

"Stop!" She smiled and punched my shoulder playfully.
"I told you it was silly. Why can't you just follow along?"

"I'm always game to follow along." I smirked at her.

She lifted her head and she looked up at me.

"What if I do this?" She stepped closer to me and put her
arms around me. "You still going to follow along?" She
stared into my eyes.

"How could I not?" I pulled her body into mine.

A moment later with our eyes still locked on one
another, we kissed.

We spent the rest of the morning going through the
rooms on the first floor. The house was immense. There was
another room around every corner. I was amazed at how
intact everything was. It was dirty and needed some help,
but most everything seemed to be solid or at least struc-
turally sound. It was clear that someone took great care in
trying to preserve everything that was there. Every large
fixture or piece of furniture was covered and thus remained
in remarkable condition. One thing that bothered me a bit
was that there were no items outside of the furniture. In the
library, the furniture was there, the ornate bookcases were
there, but there wasn't a single book. I couldn't help but
wonder what happened to everything. Despite everything

being in better condition than I expected, the lack of these items made it feel terribly cold and vacant.

Having Kat with me for this turned out to be better than I anticipated. There was the obvious mutual attraction, but there was something else. It was like she was my best friend from childhood or something. We laughed and joked. We paraded around the house like it was a clubhouse. We pretended to be aristocrats prancing into each room as if we were invited to a ball. I simply couldn't think of another time in my life when I was so relaxed and free.

When we finished exploring the first floor, we decided to get something to eat. We stepped out the front door and were immediately blinded by the sunlight. We sat down on the steps to the entrance and let our eyes adjust. After a minute or two, I stood up and walked to my truck. I opened the cooler in the back and grabbed two beers, a couple sandwiches, and a bag of chips. I sat down next to her and handed her an opened beer.

"Well, now this tops it off," she said eyeing the stubby bottle of Coors Banquet. "If someone told me that one day I would spend my Saturday sitting on the steps of an abandoned turn-of-the-century mansion, drinking a Coors, I would have sworn they were nuts."

"Well, if someone told me that one day I would inherit an abandoned turn-of-the-century mansion, I would have said they were nuts," I said taking a sip from the bottle.

"Yeah, I guess this isn't a typical situation," she agreed. "So, what's your take on all this?"

"I dunno, what do you mean?" I said.

"I guess, we haven't really talked about it aside from the general 'this is strange' thing. I don't know, I mean this has got to be crazy for you. One day you are just living your life and the next you're meeting a lawyer for the strangest meeting ever, meeting my insane mom, and then this is your new reality on the steps of this house, your house."

I sat there for a moment staring off into the overgrown courtyard, thinking about the question.

"Wow, I guess I haven't fully processed it yet." I looked at her. "I mean, this last week, I have kinda been on autopilot, I suppose."

I took another sip of beer as I got up and walked towards my truck.

"You know what? I haven't thought about it. I haven't reacted to it at all really. Before I met the lawyer, I was totally into figuring out what this was all about. From that point on, I have just been obsessed with trying to understand the story behind the house."

I looked at her sitting there in the sunlight. She smiled at me.

"Well...I guess there is one other thing that has occupied my mind," I said.

She got a mischievous smirk on her face and stood up. She walked towards me with conviction. She stood there for a moment staring at me with those clear blue eyes. She pushed me back against my truck and grabbed my arms, pinning them against the truck. Her motions were forceful but playful at the same time.

"And what would that be?" she finally asked softly.

Without another word, she leaned in and kissed me. Her hands still held my arms against the truck. It was like we were melting together. Every touch between us contained an aura of magic. It was consuming. For that moment, nothing existed except the two of us.

6

WE STAYED THERE for what felt like an hour, just holding and kissing each other. She started to move away from me at one point and I wrapped my arms around her waist and pulled her back so that my head was resting on her shoulder.

"So, was it that obvious that I was interested in you?" I asked.

She turned to face me, grabbed my hand, and started leading me back to the steps.

"No my dear, you are far from obvious," she said.

"It's kinda like... if I try to think about you, about what you're feeling, what you're thinking, I am clueless. But then, when I don't think, we just seem to be in sync."

We sat down, and I thought about that for a moment. I realized that was exactly how I felt. Yet, something seemed wrong. I mean this was my house, yet she was here following along with everything like we were partners.

"Why are you here, Kat?" I asked. "Surely we could have seen each other elsewhere. Gone on dates like normal people do. But, you are here with me."

"I guess you're right." She rose and walked towards the door, stopping in front of it. "Maybe there is more to it for me than just seeing you." She turned to face me. "Think about it. Here I am, thrown an opportunity to really understand my own history, the story of my family and why we were obsessed with ensuring this house went to you and that we delivered that sacred letter. So, hell yes, I am drawn here. It certainly doesn't hurt that coming here means spending time with the one person who hasn't left my thoughts since he awkwardly walked into my family's lawyer's office. Is that wrong?" She sounded hurt.

I walked to her and wrapped my arms around her.

"I'm sorry, I didn't mean it like that," I said, holding her.

She looked up at me. For the first time ever, I saw apprehension in her eyes. She looked vulnerable.

"Jim, look. There is a lot going on here. I like you a lot. In a way that is so different than anyone I've ever met. And honestly, I'm scared. I just want to make sure that you take care of this place. I don't know how to explain it. I mean I have never been here, but I feel like I need to make sure it's taken care of. I didn't really think about it at all. I just really wanted to be with you. Then, when you found that penny, it was like I just felt this panic."

"Okay, let's step back a minute. You're right. There is a lot going on, and none of it needs to be figured out today. Let's just forget about it for now and enjoy the day together."

We finished our lunch as we tried to push off the serious conversations for a bit. It was already two in the afternoon. We quickly realized if we wanted to have any chance of exploring the top floor today, we had to start now. We grabbed our lights and walked back into the house. Past the main hallway, we reached the grand staircase. It wrapped around the room, ending in a balcony overlooking the room where we stood. I started up the stairs, and at about the fourth step, I could hear the wood groan beneath my feet.

"You think it's safe?" I asked, suddenly second-guessing the decision to go up there.

"Oh, don't be such a scaredy cat," she said as she casually walked past me.

It was amazing how easily we were back to the playful banter of friends. Despite her teasing reassurance, I was not one-hundred percent confident the stairs would support my weight.

The upper level of the house was laid out in a large square going around the sunken area where the skylights were. There was bedroom after bedroom. Some were connected by an internal hallway. Others were just larger bedrooms by themselves. As we made our way towards the front of the house, it was clear that the house was preserved almost as well upstairs as it was downstairs. There were spots here and there where the plaster from the ceiling had collapsed, and clearly the roof was not flawless. But all things considered, it was in better condition than I had expected.

In the front of the house, there were only two doors in the main hallway. These were the master suites. The first was a massive room, with a smaller parlor and bathroom attached. The second was a mirror image of the other except, instead of the smaller parlor, there was a small hallway around to the south side of the house. The hallway led us to a locked door. We had explored almost all of the house, but this was the first locked door we'd encountered.

Kat walked up to the door and turned the knob, trying to force it open, but it wouldn't move.

"How is it possible for this to be locked so tightly after all these years?" she asked.

"I have no idea," I said looking at the door.

I ran my fingers along the door frame. There were several spots along the frame where you could tell someone had attempted to pry the door open with tools.

"Look at this!" I said. "Forget about still being locked tight! This door has been attacked with tools and hasn't moved! That's impressive!"

"That is so strange," she said." I don't know what to make of it. So how do we get in?"

"Wait!" I exclaimed as I walked backward down the hall a few steps. "If those are the master bedrooms, then that would make this a parlor for the master bedroom, right?"

"Uh yeah... I suppose so... why?"

"I know how we get in!" I yelled, excited. "Come with me!" I grabbed her hand and started running towards the stairs.

"Hold on!" she yelled back, but her tone held warning rather than joy, as we ran to the back of my truck.

The sun began its descent, casting a warm orange glow onto the face of the house. I jumped into the back of my truck and began rummaging through things. I grabbed an empty backpack and opened it.

"Don't think that I'm going to stand here and let you force your way through that door with whatever tools you have back there," Kat said seriously.

"Stop." I smiled at her. "The last thing I'm going to do is break down a door."

"Then what the hell are you doing?" she asked.

"I'm going to get us in," I replied while pulling beer bottles from the cooler and putting them in the backpack. "It's that simple! But if this is what I think it is, we are both going to need some supplies."

I closed the backpack and jumped out of the truck.

"Here, hold this for a second." I handed her the back-pack and placed a quick kiss on her cheek.

"Um... sure, we could both use a drink, but will you just tell me what is happening," she pleaded. "How is this going to get us in there?"

I leaned into the passenger door of my truck, opened the glove box, and grabbed the envelope Kat had handed me at the lawyer's office. I walked back over and took the backpack from her.

"It's not. But this is." I held up the envelope to her.

"Are you serious?" she said, grabbing the envelope.

She opened it and looked inside. Then, she pulled out the keys and held them up.

"So wait... for the last seventy years or whatever, I am the one who had the key?" she asked.

"I believe so, which is precisely why we need this," I said, holding up the bag. "You ready for this?"

"Uh, I think so," she replied.

She stopped and looked in the envelope again.

"Can I read this? I mean, now I'm just curious." She looked at the letter inside.

"Go ahead, maybe it'll make sense to you," I replied.

We sat there silently as she read the letter left by Ida. I couldn't help but notice how gorgeous the house looked right now. The glow of the setting sun seemed to block out all the imperfections. It was as if I could see the house without the plywood covering it. The way it had been then. I was almost in a trance looking at it when her voice broke me out of it.

"Holy shit!" She folded the paper and returned it to the envelope. "Okay. You're right. I have no clue what any of that means. Why does she refer to herself as your mother? I mean, she was writing this knowing when it would be delivered. Clearly, she knew that wasn't possible."

"If this started weird," I said. "I think when we go through that door, this shit is gonna get surreal in a big way."

"So, maybe you should get a little distracted before we go in there," she said, playfully.

"Um, maybe I should get just a little distracted," I started playing with her hair.

She smirked as she looked at me. "You're lucky I like you."

"Why is that?"

"Because...if I didn't, I wouldn't do this," she said as she kissed me.

She then stepped back from me, holding my hand and pulling me, a teasing smile on her face.

"Was that enough distraction for you?" She chuckled.

"Fuck." I sighed. "Enough... not enough... I do know it was something though."

I started to walk with her back into the house.

Within a few minutes, we were standing at the door again. Kat handed me the keys and shot me a hopeful look. I don't know why, but there at that door, I felt so frantic. It was odd that it was locked tight all those years, but I was standing there like I was about to open a treasure chest. I had no idea what we'd find inside. I could not shake the feeling that it would be something big. Something to help connect the dots in this crazy story.

I took the simpler of the two keys and slid it into the lock. I took a deep breath and tried to turn the key. The key felt as if it was resisting me as I turned it. Then, there was a loud mechanical thud. The sound was eerie. It wasn't the typical click you hear while opening a lock. It was loud, low, and seemed to echo throughout the silent house, making the hair on my neck stand up. I turned the doorknob and leaned into the door with my shoulder, expecting it to give resistance. The door swung free with just the slightest squeak of the hinges moving for the first time in decades. The room was silent and dark. As I grabbed the lantern and stepped inside, I was immediately struck by the scent of something pleasant. This room smelled like freshly cut flowers. Kat followed behind me. Once both of us were inside, our lanterns lit the room enough to see everything around us.

The whole room contrasted with everything else we'd seen in the house. Room after room was solid and decently preserved but also filthy with signs of age. This room, though, was pristine. As if, just yesterday, it had been cleaned. In the other parts of the house, there were no personal effects or anything smaller than furniture. Still, this room remained set up and decorated. On a vanity sat perfume atomizers and a silver mirror and brush. Not set there for storage but because that was where they belonged.

On the far wall were old wooden crates. They were stacked in perfect rows. There had to be twenty of them stacked floor to ceiling. They were out of place in this room and clearly didn't belong.

I looked around the room, taking a deep breath. I smelled flowers. I looked again at the far wall, but the crates were suddenly gone. No longer was the room dimly lit by lanterns. I could see the last rays of sun beaming through the windows. The vase on the mantel was filled with wildflowers.

I shook my head and blinked. The sun was gone, replaced by the dark plywood covering. The crates were there again. It was all back to the way it had been when I walked in. But that fragrance was still there.

"Do you smell that?" I asked.

"The flowers? Yes. How is that even possible? I thought it was my imagination."

From behind me, I felt her reach for my hand and hold it in hers. My eyes drifted over to the beautiful white marble fireplace. On the mantel was a vase. But there wasn't a bouquet of wildflowers. There were the remains of those flowers, all shriveled and dried.

I walked towards it and picked up the vase, bringing it to my nose, expecting it to smell like fresh flowers. It didn't. As I set the vase down, I noticed a folded piece of paper sitting on the mantel. I picked it up and slowly unfolded it. I walked closer to the lantern to see it better. It was a letter.

April 30, 1943

Master James,

For the past fifteen years, I have kept my agreement with dearest Ida and followed her requests to the letter. Yet, today I am writing to ask for your forgiveness for the liberties I have taken. As per Ida's request, this room was to remain locked to everyone but I, and to remain precisely as it was on Ida's last day here at Villa Ortenberg.

However, in the past weeks, the staff has begun closing the house, transitioning from maintaining this fine house to preserving it. With that in mind, I understood that this room would be the only place in the house truly secured from outsiders. Therefore, I took it upon myself to pack up many of the smaller personal effects in the house and bring them here to keep them safe.

You will find the crates on the eastern wall of this room. In each one, I have enclosed a document explaining which room each piece belongs to and the precise placement it had. Again, I apologize for this intrusion to this sacred room.

I leave here today for the last time. I am saddened that I will not be able to personally transition the estate over to you. Seeing you in this house is something that, like Ida, my heart will always long for. As my time here ends, and I move on to devote my life to my other love, I bid the Villa farewell. I wish many blessings upon you and this house, Master James.

Warmest Regards,

Edgar Ludwig Stein

"That's my great-great-grandfather!" Kat yelled as she grabbed the letter from my hand. "He was here, and he knew you! He wrote to you too!"

"Yeah, apparently everyone knew about me. Why does everyone from a hundred years ago know more about me than I do?" I rubbed my eyes with my hands. "And why the hell does this room smell like flowers?"

Kat didn't respond. She sat down on the floor with her legs crossed, her eyes glued to the letter. I sat next to her and pulled a beer out of my backpack. I opened one and took a long pull from the bottle.

"Fuck!" I said, taking another swallow. "Why does everything have to be so damned cryptic? Like a secret code or something. At least a secret code I could look at and know I can't read it. But this, this is just fiendish. Can no one just write something that makes sense? You know, 'Hey Jim, here's the deal. This shit went down, and a crazy wild-eyed scientist hopped out of a DeLorean and told me I had to leave this house to you, or Darth Vader would melt my brain.'"

She gazed at me with compassion in her eyes. She set the letter down and wrapped her arms around me. She felt so warm. It was comforting, but I wasn't finished. Now, with her head on my shoulder, I continued more softly.

"I mean, don't get me wrong, life before this wasn't exactly great. It sucked, actually. But as much as it sucked, at least I knew what was going on. I knew where I was going. Now, I just feel like I'm in some Twilight Zone episode. Am I fucking crazy? Is that it? None of this is real, right? I'm gonna close my eyes and open them to find myself sitting alone in an abandoned house I broke into, right?"

"Jim, you know this is real. I'm here too. I don't know how or why any of this is the way it is, but right here and right now, we are both here." She squeezed me in her arms.

We sat there for a long time. I closed my eyes and just felt her. Slowly, the feeling of comfort and peace I had in her arms overtook the madness I was feeling. Soon, everything was just peaceful. She lifted her head and backed away just a hair. I opened my eyes and looked into hers.

"I'm sorry, I just let all that shit build up in me. That letter kinda pushed me over the edge."

"Jim, don't apologize. For chrissake, this is an impossible situation. Besides, I'm a big girl. I can handle you blowing off some steam."

She placed her hands gently on the sides of my head. Her thumbs lightly rubbed against the stubble on my face. She looked at me, biting her lower lip.

"Besides, I should be the one apologizing here," she said.

"What do you need to apologize for?" I asked.

Suddenly, I saw that mischievous smirk on her face again.

"Well, obviously, I've not done a very good job of distracting you," she said as she leaned into me.

Her eyes were locked on mine. She moved in to kiss me and stopped short. She was so close I could feel shallow breaths on my face. She bit her lower lip again and then lightly touched my lips with her tongue. Again, her lips were so close to mine. She held that position for what felt like hours, every so often touching my lips with hers ever so lightly. Everything swirled around me. Just when I realized that there was no way I could stand this game for even a second longer, she kissed me. It was not just a kiss, it was like a tornado of passion that for an instant focused every ounce of its energy on that one kiss.

There in the parlor of that long-forgotten mansion, we completely submitted to one another and made love.

7

LATE THAT NIGHT I laid on my couch. Part of me was cursing myself for being there in my apartment alone. The last thing I wanted was to be away from Kat. Yet, it had been a long day, and the house was in no condition to stay in. It was the right choice even though I knew neither of us was entirely happy with it. We had decided to go to the estate again tomorrow when we would explore the rest of the grounds. I should have been asleep hours earlier, but I was too keyed up. I knew that if I had any hope of sleeping, I shouldn't think about the house... I shouldn't think about her. I just needed to let go and sleep.

Finally, around two in the morning, my eyes started to drift shut.

Instantly, I was transported back to the house. I could feel the house but had no clue where I was. I looked behind me at the terrace wall and fountain, not overgrown, but perfect. The flowers planted around it were perfectly manicured. In front of me was a majestic staircase leading down to the lakefront. In the center of the stairs was a long intricately carved waterway. A fountain ran the length of the staircase, exquisitely carved in marble. Everything was pristine and beautiful. Everything except for the sky.

Dark clouds converged over the lake, as if they were going to run into each other with a cataclysmic crash. Watching the clouds move, I felt the wind howl up from the lake and almost knock me over. I grabbed onto the fountain for support, as the wind sliced through me with pure coldness.

"Jim!" I heard from behind me. "There you are!"

It was Kat calling to me. I turned to go up the stairs when I saw her turn the corner, coming down to me. She was walking hand in hand with another woman. I realized the other woman was Ida. She looked exactly like the photos I had seen of her. The two walked up to me and stopped. Ida reached out and put her hand in mine.

"It's time, Jim," Kat said to me.

Ida led us down the stairs. She walked in between us, holding each of our hands, as we slowly descended the stairs. With each step closer to the lake, the storm worsened. At the lower landing, we were still about twenty feet away from the lake. Below us was a majestic white marble swimming pool. The water in the pool swirled like an ocean amid a hurricane.

Ida turned to face me and placed her hands on the sides of my face. "Dearest James. I am sorry it happened this way, but you did it! You did a fabulous job! These last steps I must take on my own James. I'm sure you understand. Thank you so much."

She stepped up and gave me a strong hug. She then turned to Kat.

"My dear," she said as she hugged Kat, "if only Edgar were here today, he would be so proud of you. Please take care of James for me."

Without another word, the woman turned and started walking down the curved staircase to the pool and lake. The wind worsened. Drops of rain were carried on the wind and they felt like spikes as they hit my skin. But the woman didn't falter. She walked stoically down the steps. Right there before my eyes, she disappeared. As soon as she did, the clouds dissipated, and the wind stopped.

By the time I turned around, the clouds were gone, and the sun was shining. The sound of the howling wind was replaced by the gentle chirp of birds and the sound of waves rolling onto the shore.

Kat turned to me and gave me a huge hug. Pulling back, she looked at me with her placid blue eyes and said, "Welcome home."

I OPENED my eyes at the blaring siren of my alarm. I grabbed my phone to silence it and tossed it aside. I sat up on the couch and squinted at the morning sunlight, coming in through the windows. I immediately clutched the sides of my head with my hands. My head was throbbing with an excruciating headache. I made my way to the kitchen and took some ibuprofen. I glanced at the clock and saw it was 8:30 in the morning. Kat was expecting me to pick her up in an hour. I had just enough time to take a shower and pray that the water would take the edge off my headache.

By the time I got in my truck, the headache had subsided. I drove straight to Kat's mother's house where Kat had been staying ever since her mom got sick. I parked my truck and got out to see Kat already coming out towards me. She looked spectacular. She was wearing jeans and a black

V-necked t-shirt, and she looked beautiful. She quickly walked up to me and gave me a quick kiss on the cheek.

"Good morning sunshine!" she said with as much pep as a cheerleader.

"Mmmmm, it certainly is now," I replied.

We got into the truck and started the short drive over to the Villa.

"So, what is your master plan for today?" she asked.

I looked at her with a smirk, and she playfully responded by hitting me on the shoulder.

"No, I mean the house. What are we going to do today?"

"I have no plan. There is far more to explore than we have time to see today, from the garages and outbuildings, to the pond and gardens. What peaks your interest?"

"Well considering we have sun today, let's start with the grounds and see what happens," she replied.

Soon, my truck was exiting the quiet road onto the rough overgrown drive of the estate. I parked in front of the house again. We got out of the truck and decided to start in the back of the house on the lakeshore side. We wandered through the terrace courtyard behind the house before we found the steps down to the lake. The steps were so overgrown I could barely see them. As we turned the corner, I immediately knew where we were. The wall and the fountain were there, exactly as I had dreamed them. That was, aside from the decrepit state they currently were in. For as well as the house itself was preserved, the grounds were nearly destroyed.

I eyed Kat walking towards the center stairs down to the lake. She stopped and knelt, looking at what remained of the fountain channel, which ran the course of the stairs.

"Oh my god!" she said. "Have you ever seen anything like this?"

I approached her and looked at it. My eyes traveled down the steps. You couldn't even see the landing. It was as if the fountain extended down into a complete forest.

"Actually, I have. I've seen this... Well not like this. But this fountain, the way it originally was."

"What do you mean?" She looked at me, intrigued.

"I mean this. I saw this. But perfectly clean. Walk down the stairs. I bet you anything, you will find a marble pool along the lakeshore down there."

She put her hands on top of mine. Her eyes were a storm of concern.

"What do you mean? Did you see photos online or something?"

"No! Fuck no! That would be logical. You're right. I have never seen anything like this. Until last night. Last night I was here. Hell, you were here. We stood right here!" I snapped back.

"Jim?" she asked, squeezing my hand.

"It was a fucking dream! But not like a normal dream where you wake up and only remember blurs or a couple snapshots. This was more vivid. And we were here! Right here! But it was perfect. I can remember the details. Look at that wall." I pointed to the crumbling wall behind us. "Did you know there are lamps that should be on either side of that fountain? Large black iron lamps, exquisitely forged, each with a white glass globe on them?"

She just looked at me with that concerned expression.

"Look, I have never seen this before. I have never been down here. I had only seen a photo of it at the Historical Society. But last night I dreamt of it with perfect clarity. I played it off as some crazy dream inspired by the photos I looked at. But here, standing here... I know it was more than the photos."

We sat down on the steps. I told her my dream and every detail I could recall. After I finished, she put her arm around me and kissed me on the cheek.

"I will say, normally I would be excited to know you were dreaming of me. Well, I guess I still am. But this is a bit much to wrap my head around. So, is it wrong that I kinda want to go see if there's still a pool down there?"

"Why? I didn't see you bring a swimming suit." I smiled.

She stood up and started slowly making her way down the steps.

"Who said I would wear one if I did?" she said over her shoulder.

I quickly followed her down to the landing. There, we fought our way through the brush to get to the stairs on the left.

"Holy shit!" she yelled as she continued down. "There is a pool! Well, there was a pool, but it's gonna take a hell of a lot of work for you to see me swimming in that anywhere but your dreams."

She was right. The far wall of the pool was only a few inches higher than the water level of Lake Michigan. The gentle waves of the lake rolled up and crashed onto what remained of the pool's wall. The brick terrace behind the pool was nearly destroyed. The ground below shifted to the point it looked more like the grounds of a fun house. The large granite pool house was covered with spray paint and resembled a building you would see in photos after a bombing in World War II.

"I don't think we are gonna get in there anytime soon," I said.

"Yeah, this is pretty depressing looking, but imagine what this had to be like back then," she said dreamily. "You wake up, get a cup of coffee, stroll down to this incredible terrace and sit poolside without a care in the world."

"Well, I guess that is how I am supposed to make it again. But damn, I cannot even comprehend the amount of work that will take." I felt defeated.

"I know what you are supposed to do, but are you really going to live here?" she asked.

"I really don't know. I mean I haven't even talked to anyone to see what it would take to make this place livable. But there are two things I guess I need to consider. First, financially speaking, I would be a complete fool not to do this. It's kinda like, live in this fabulous mansion and then you will have enough money to do whatever you want for the rest of your life."

"You don't really strike me as someone who is purely motivated by money," she replied.

"What do you mean?" I asked.

"Sure, we need money to survive and there is a certain amount of crap we have to do to ensure we have some. But beyond that, I don't really see you being focused on it like your only goal is to get more money. You... well, I just think you are more likely to do what feels right to you and let the chips fall where they may."

"I suppose you're right about that. But that kinda assumes I know what feels right. Sometimes I just... I dunno, I feel like I am wandering through life with no real direction."

"Maybe you just haven't found your path yet. I'm sure there is far more that you've done that you just don't see. Anyway, what's the second part?"

"Do I have a choice?" The simple question rolled out of my mouth with no thought.

Hearing myself ask it made my body tense with anxiety.

With the inheritance, yes, I was receiving a lot, but it felt more like I was being thrust into a new life, a life not my own. A preset path I could not deviate from. The worst part was, I couldn't even comprehend why I'd been chosen for this forced path.

"What do you mean? Of course, you always have a choice. But what does that have to do with the second part?"

"That is the second part. Look at it. You were there when they read the will to me. That whole thing was designed so I didn't really have a choice. Sure, I don't have to fix the place up. I can ignore the massive amount of money secured for restoration while this place sits unable to change hands until I die and lawyers figure out what to do."

She turned away from the pool to face me and grabbed my shoulders. "You're right. You cannot just walk away and be a millionaire, but you were not one before any of this. You can forget about this house and just be you."

"I don't know that I can. This is too ingrained in me. It's really my birthright. They knew me fifty years before I was conceived and I'm pretty sure no one held my mom at gunpoint when she hooked up with my dad. There were no special doctors who ensured I would be delivered on the day I was. Nobody forced my mom to name me James. They knew me. She knew me. I don't really see what choice I have."

"Say you're right. Say for some reason she did know you were coming. She had some vision of you being born or whatever. She knew where you began. But only you can choose where you go. It's still your life. It is no different than an overbearing dad forcing a kid to go to medical school or to play football. Those kids still have a choice. This Will is your choice. Sure, it's what she intended and what she wanted. But what about you? Maybe this is your path.... But maybe it's not either, and you are the only one who can make that choice."

Hearing her say those words made me realize that even if I had a choice, I really didn't. There was something growing inside me. I was a part of this house somehow, and there was something for me to accomplish here.

WE SPENT the rest of the day exploring the grounds of the estate. The grounds were absolutely massive. The garden area alone was the size of a football field.

Beyond the gardens, on the southern side of the property, was a pond. The entire area was sectioned off from the immense gardens. The overgrown shrubs separating this area were nearly impenetrable. We struggled to break branches and clear enough of a path to even get close to the pond. As we neared the edge of the growth, we finally got a glimpse of what lay before us.

The pond was more of a wading pool than a pond. It was a large oval, surrounded by short concrete walls. The image reminded me of an elaborate fountain in a park. A fountain where you could sit down on the edge and enjoy the day. Even from a distance, it was clear that this pond had suffered greatly from time and weather.

The pond itself was intact more than all the fixtures surrounding it, but even it suffered. Statues that once surrounded the area lay half destroyed under the brush. On the far southern end of the pond was another building. It was like a large open-air patio shelter. It was immense. Roman-inspired granite walls rose up from the ground. The corners were marked with crumbling pillars. In the center was the entrance, a rounded doorway large enough to fit a car.

The granite walls were covered with spray paint and it was difficult to even imagine how it should have looked or how it fit into everything. Despite the state it was in, it was clear that the entire area had once been just as majestic as the house itself.

As my foot stepped out of the brush into this area, I froze. A cold wind howled through the trees and sent a chill down my spine. I couldn't place it, but something there felt wrong. Every other area of the house seemed to welcome me, but here, I almost felt forbidden to enter.

I squeezed Kat's hand and looked at her. She didn't say a word, but I could see in her eyes that she too felt the same thing. The previously comforting look in her eyes had changed to terror.

"Uh...You know, there is a ton of ground to cover on the property. Maybe we should check out the other side before it gets too late." I tried not to show my looming apprehension.

"You don't have to make an excuse for me. This place is damn creepy!"

We stepped back towards the house. Almost immediately, the winds died down. The hot sun again overtook the day.

"Okay, I don't have any clue what that was, but you felt it too, right?" I asked.

"The wind? Yeah. If the house had felt like that, I wouldn't have come back today. Something isn't right there. You must have missed that area with my mom's sage yesterday." The edge of her mouth rose up in a smirk.

"If sage can make that place feel comfortable, I will be converted into a true believer," I said.

Back at the front of the house, there was another drive, extending to the north side of the property. We casually walked down the drive. About fifty yards past the edge of the house, the trees opened, revealing a giant garage structure. I marveled at the size of the structure. There had to be at least ten garage doors, plus there was a second story. A line of boarded-up windows extended across the top of the building.

The garage building was intact but looked far less stable than the main house did. The roof sagged horribly, and there were visible holes in it. The fact that it looked as if it could fall with the slightest breeze made us decide that we would tackle that on another day, probably sooner than the pond though.

For the most part, we had fun exploring the place together. It gave me a better idea of just how vast this property was. I realized that restoring the house was one project, but restoring the grounds was an even larger undertaking. Beyond all the gardens and structures, there were acres upon acres of densely wooded land. It felt like it would take over a year for me to simply see every part of the property.

Despite the rather serious conversation we had on the lake-front, the rest of the day was light-hearted. With every step we took and every conversation we shared, I felt closer to her. It was difficult for me to step back and think of it as a relationship. The word relationship to me had always conjured thoughts of frustration and awkwardness. With her though, everything felt so natural. I didn't have to think about what to say or do. I was just me. For the first time in my life, it felt like being me was the right thing.

As the sun started to set, we decided to call it a day. As I drove her home, I realized it was Sunday. That meant she would have to return to work, putting an end to our day-long explorations of the house, at least until the next weekend. Instead, we decided to meet for dinner on Monday and just see where everything went.

As I dropped her off, we kissed, and I wanted so badly to keep the night from ending. The only way I could let her walk out of my truck was knowing in my heart that today was just the beginning. I knew there would be many more days with her.

8

WITH KAT AT WORK, I was able to focus on the house. I was hesitant to start calling the contractors for the renovation though. When I was there, I realized there was something beautiful about the undisturbed nature of it. I knew that once the renovation started, nothing would remain untouched. It was all a game in my head. I knew that soon enough I would be calling contractors and they would roll in, but right now I was at peace with everything the way it was.

I decided to take another stab at my own research into the property. Unfortunately, I quickly discovered that I had exhausted everything I could find on the internet about it. Unsure of where to go next, I called Paul.

Knowing Paul's uncanny skill for finding information that no one else could, I figured he would be my best bet. With a short conversation, I'd given him his mission. He already had the address and Ida's name. I added Samuel to the mix and asked Paul to find absolutely anything he could about him.

When I hung up the phone, I was left once again with

my own thoughts. I felt like a caged tiger pacing back and forth. I knew it would be some time before Paul came back with anything. It wasn't thoughts of the house tormenting me, but thoughts of Kat. I couldn't stop thinking about her.

After a few minutes of obsessively thinking about her, I decided I needed refocus my mind. The only thing I could think of to shift my thoughts away from her was to work out. I couldn't bring myself to drive to the gym, so I opted to go for a run. With the wind blowing against me, and my headphones blaring in my ears, my thoughts drifted away. With every mile my feet carried me, my thoughts became clearer.

The next thing I knew, I was in a different place completely. The small forest preserve I was running in was gone. The lush gardens of the house now surrounded me. Everything was pristine. The change startled me. I stopped abruptly. I looked behind me and could see the house in the distance. The spot where the lush gardens succumbed to the forest beyond, lay only steps away. The music was still playing in my headphones, but I was hearing something else. Beyond the thundering drums and low guttural guitar riffs, was a voice.

"Discover his secrets and bury him with them."

The voice repeated over and over. Each time the phrase was stated it became louder and louder until the music was drowned out. As soon as the shock of the scenario passed. I ripped my earbuds from my ears. Instantly, I was back in the forest preserve as if nothing happened.

I trudged back to my apartment, constantly looking over my shoulder. I didn't know what to think. Was it a blackout, a dream, or had I gone nuts? I walked into my apartment where the blast of cold A/C nearly dropped me to my knees. I grabbed a towel and dried the sweat from my body. Then, I heard the alert from my phone. It was an email response from Paul.

The thoughts of whatever had happened on my run disappeared as I read Paul's email.

He stated that he hadn't been able to find out much about the house beyond what I'd already learned. However, when he got to Samuel, there was a massive amount of information. Most appeared to be benign, typical things like parents, when he was born, marriage and divorce dates, etc. His email went on to talk of Samuel's disappearance. It was like Florence had stated. There was news about him missing. There was a police report filed and a full investigation. According to the report, he was last seen talking about going back to the Villa despite no longer being welcome there. There was also a comprehensive search of the Villa's grounds for him and interviews with the staff, all yielding nothing.

What I found even more interesting were the large number of police reports filed for missing persons. These reports all seemed to align with what Florence had mentioned. In almost all the reports, Samuel was interviewed, and the location of interest was the Villa. In every single one, the investigation just stopped following the interview with Samuel. Either Samuel was completely unlucky that all these occurrences randomly happened near him or there was much more to the story.

I opened the last attached file. It was titled Samuel Leopold Muller and was about the death of Sam's and Ida's son. The file included numerous newspaper reports, as well as more formal reports. Tales ranged from the typical to the outrageous. There was no autopsy done. Today that would have been considered suspicious, but for those times it seemed as though it could have been innocent. Yet this opened the doors for the news to run wild with speculation. There were accounts of Ida attending a dinner party when she was told of the news. Her response was nothing more than a stoic nod while she continued the party as if nothing happened. Other reports showcased the exact opposite in her response.

Some articles stated that no cause of death was confirmed, and that his body displayed nothing out of the ordinary except his bloody eyes. There was speculation of drowning, strangulation, and even a morbid tale stating he was brutally murdered for his organs. There was so much information here, but it was so scattered. It was impossible to come to any realistic conjecture. The only certainty I took away from the files was that that the situation in that house was nothing short of tragic.

Meeting Kat that evening gave me the opportunity to stop thinking about the house. Seeing her was both intoxicating and refreshing. I didn't bring up the house, and while with her, I was able to not think about it at all.

Once I returned home, I started researching again. As I pulled out my laptop, a memory popped into my head. It was the memory of Florence referring to the house as Mansfeld Manor. All my previous searches had revolved around the name Villa Ortenberg.

I started to Google 'Mansfeld Manor'. The result was listing upon listing of haunted directories. Some were simply directories of haunted places while others allowed users to submit their stories. I spent hours reading every story I could find. Most of these were in line with the tales Florence had referred to but with much greater detail. The more I read, the more I was able to identify many similarities between them. First, no one writing any of these had been in the house itself. They all referred to the grounds of the Villa.

The pond I had felt uneasy at was the center point for most of these tales. Many of them included some sort of wolf or rabid dog that appeared near the pond. At which point the wolf would urge the person to follow them and would slowly walk to the forest edge near the pond. Some people ran away at that point. Others brave enough to enter the canopy of trees found the wolf urging them on to a clearing. Once there, the wolf would vanish, and everyone reported blacking out and waking up hours later.

My mind wandered back to my run. Seeing the house, then the pond, and finally the forest. A shiver ran up my spine. That voice echoed through my head. "Discover his secrets and bury him with them."

I hardly believed in ghosts, but this all felt uncanny. Was it really possible for me to visualize the exact spot where all these hauntings supposedly took place? I forced my thoughts away from that question. I tried to impose logic. I understood that all these reports were probably written by the same person, who had never been there, but heard the story on the playground. As much as I tried to qualify it all, it was impossible to deny the fact that it was the same spot.

Intrigued, I decided to look beyond the haunted directories. There were a couple of message boards for urban explorers. Those, however, had no information aside from wanting to know if the place still existed. Then, I found multiple listings pointing to the same site. As I clicked through, I found a site completely dedicated to the estate.

That site's navigation was divided into three sections; The Estate, The Grounds, The Ruin. Each section was filled with photos of the estate. The first two sections were mainly composed of photos I had seen at the historical society. There were some additional ones that looked like scans of newspaper articles. The section titled, 'The Ruin,' contained a massive number of photos of the estate in its decay. It started with old black and white photos taken when the estate looked perfect but boarded up. As I scrolled down, the photos transitioned in time until I reached a set that looked very recent. The decay of the estate mirrored what I had seen with my own eyes.

On the left side of the site, there was the story of the estate. The author went from the family's background, to the planning and construction, all the way through to the court cases about the will and the final closing of the estate. Clearly, whoever owned this site understood more about it than anyone. I looked at the bottom of the page to find a contact button.

I then came across a link to comments. I clicked on the link. There were about one hundred comments. I scanned through them. Most of them praised the author for chronicling the property. A few mentioned always wanting to know about the house and never knowing the details. Then, there was one that stood out.

"A very conservative chronicle of this estate. I wonder though, in all your research did you not see the darkness covering the estate? These are the stories we all know, but what about the real stories? PM me: ParanormalArchaeology@gmail.com"

Without even thinking, I opened my email and typed a message to him.

Hi,

I saw your comment on the website about Mansfeld Manor. I want to know the real story. Can you help me?

Thanks,

Jim

I hit send. I wondered for a moment why I was so quick to reach out to this one person in particular. I had seen countless posts from people claiming to have first-hand experience while this person had none to speak of. I couldn't come up with an explanation. It was just a feeling. When I read this comment, I felt I needed to speak to him.

The next evening, Kat and I decided to go to a quiet little pizza place where we could just sit down and be together. I walked in a couple minutes late and immediately spotted her across the dimly lit restaurant. It had been less than a day since I saw her last, but I had missed her. I made my way over to the cozy booth and sat down. She started to talk about her day and her job. It was nice just to exist for a moment without being consumed by the house. That was until she asked me about my day.

"Kat, do you believe in ghosts?" I asked.

"Wow, nothing like diving right in." She stuck her tongue out at me sarcastically.

"Seriously, do you?" I asked.

She paused for a moment as if thinking about how to respond.

"I don't not believe in them. I think there's a lot we don't know. But at this point, I haven't ever seen anything that would make me say I'm a believer... This isn't a random question, is it?"

"Of course not," I replied.

"Is this about that dream?"

"I don't know. I mean sure, that plays a part but no different than anything else about the house. I mean, I guess I just thought it was all really strange and inexplicable."

"And now something is making you rethink that?" she

said, interrupting my words.

I talked through everything that had happened; the blackout, the research Paul provided, then the online information, and the comment I replied to.

"I guess I don't really know what to think. Even your mom obviously feels something, giving me that sage to burn and everything."

"That's kinda just my mom. I mean she has always done stuff like that. I never really thought anything of it other than that it was a little odd."

"Yeah, that's all I really thought at the moment. But now... It just seems like there is too much improbable stuff to not believe something is happening."

I glanced up at Kat and was relieved that she wasn't rolling her eyes at me. She looked genuinely interested in what was on my mind. This gave me the courage to ask more questions.

"Did your mom ever go to the house? I mean, there is obviously a connection there. Maybe she went and felt something."

"I have no idea," she said with a sigh. "I mean, it wasn't like it was dinner conversation at home."

"I suppose not," I said.

The waiter came by with a pitcher of beer and two frosty glasses. He couldn't have come at a better time. I so needed to change the conversation. I felt like the more I talked, the worse it was getting. Kat immediately started pouring the two glasses.

"You contacted him, didn't you?" she asked handing me a glass.

"Who?" I asked.

"The ghostbuster guy you found online who knows about the house," she clarified.

I smirked and took a swallow of beer. "Of course I did."

"Okay. Why?" she asked.

I looked at her in silence for a moment. I really didn't know why. I just did it.

"I guess I'm just looking to understand everything. Who knows. He might have some insight. Why? Do you think it's a bad idea?"

"No. I just don't want to see you jumping down some wormhole wearing a tin foil hat. Information is good. Stay open-minded but know that everything you hear may not be the truth."

"Oh, so now you are telling me Big Foot doesn't even exist?" I asked with a chuckle.

"No! Big Foot is real. He hangs out in the forest by my house. I'll ask him if he has ever seen anything strange over at the villa. Seriously though, do you want me to talk to my mom and see what she knows?"

"Yeah, if she's comfortable with it. No sense working her up though."

"No, I think she'll appreciate it. She's still beaming from when you came by."

We spent the remainder of the evening just talking and laughing. We were genuinely having a great time together. One pitcher turned into two. Time raced by, and soon we were the only ones in an empty restaurant. Then, my phone beeped. It was an email response from that paranormal person I'd contacted. Without realizing it, I'd started staring at my phone.

"What is it?" she asked with a concerned tone.

"Um well, you remember how I said that I wanted to learn everything I could about the house? I guess this is my shot." I put the phone down, letting her read the message.

It was a simple response. The paranormal archaeology

person only replied with a phone number.

"Wanna call it with me?" I asked.

She looked around the restaurant seeing that it was deserted.

"What the hell?" she said. "Let's see what he has to say."

I dialed the number and set the phone on the table, turning the speakerphone on. He picked up on the second ring.

"This is David," said the voice on the phone.

"Uh...yeah... I got this number in an email," I said stumbling over my words.

"Ahhh, Mansfeld," he said interrupting me. "Is that your site?"

"No, I just came across it. I would like to know what you were referring to though."

"Look, I do this for a living. Mansfeld Manor came up in some research I was doing for another client. I kinda posted that hoping I could get a gig investigating that place."

"Well, tell me what you know," I said. "Maybe I'll hire you to investigate the place."

There was a long silence on the phone. I saw Kat shrug her shoulders.

"What have you seen?" he asked.

"Listen, do you know anything or not?" I was getting irritated.

"Oh, I know plenty, but I want to know what you have seen. Like I said, I haven't been there. I haven't investigated it. I know about some dealings that took place involving it and seeing as the place was just left to rot, there has to be some residual energy there. So, I ask again, what have you seen?"

"Just dreams," I reluctantly offered.

"Okay, tell me about these dreams." He silently waited

for me to continue.

I gave him the full account of the dream I had. Then I talked of the daydream I had while I was running. Kat shot me a look when I mentioned that. I must have forgotten to mention that part to her.

"Look, I'm just trying to understand everything," I said.

"Okay, okay," he said. "Do you know anything about the KGC?"

"I have no idea what that is," I replied honestly.

"Figures," he said with disdain in his voice. "Listen, I'm not here to give you a history lesson. Why don't you research that a bit? Then, give me a call back when you know the basics." He paused. "Who are you anyway? I mean, what are you really looking for?"

"Well, I own the property. I'm just trying to put the pieces together."

"Wait! From the will?" Now I had his attention.

"Yes. I inherited the estate."

"Well, that certainly changes things. How about I drive up there this weekend, and I can go through everything then?"

"Well yeah, why not," I said. "We can even meet at the house."

"No. Not at the house. Not yet. You need to understand everything before we get to that point. I will email you some info and we can set this up. In the meantime, learn your history.... or at least the public history. Research the KGC."

"I will," I said.

"Okay, talk to you then." He hung up the phone.

"What the hell was that about?" I asked.

"I have no idea, but you're gonna to find out I think."

I reached for her hand.

"No, we're gonna find out."

9

THE WEEK WENT BY QUICKLY. I dove into researching the KGC, which felt like a homework assignment. It was interesting, sure, but I didn't really see anything in it at all connecting it to the Villa. From what I found, it sounded like a Confederate secret society. This made no sense to me as we are in Illinois, the Land of Lincoln. I couldn't imagine any ties to a Confederate society here.

In addition to my KGC research, I decided to weed through the quotes I was provided for restoring the mansion. This felt like an insurmountable task. There were many different aspects to tackle from the grounds to the swimming pool, to the house itself. Each area had quotes from different local specialists. In order to keep my head straight in making sense of all those, I decided to first focus on the house. Ideally, I thought I could first get the house habitable. Then, I would be able to focus on things like the grounds.

When it came to the house itself, there were again certain parts of the project quoted by different specialists. I called and met with them all. After what felt like a hundred meetings, a plan started to form. The first priority was working on the foundation. Every other effort was on hold until that could be completed. Following the foundation repair, we would be fixing and rebuilding the roof. From there, the windows could be replaced. Of course, by the time we got to that point, it would be time to work on everything else. Plumbing, electricity, etc.

Based upon the initial inspection, the foundation was not in bad shape. The house, despite its neglect, was very solid. The foundation work we would be paying for was not intended only to make sure it was okay now, but to ensure that it would be for decades to come. It was estimated to be a three to four-week job. So, I signed on the dotted line and scheduled work to start in two weeks.

I also began the process of trying to get the house listed as a historic landmark. This was important since it would dictate any of the upcoming renovations. Fortunately, because the foundation only involved solidifying the existing structure, it could be done with no repercussions on achieving landmark status.

As I tried to plan out everything on a timeline, I realized that one of the most expensive parts of the renovation would be the swimming pool. It was so cost prohibitive to restore that when complete, it would easily become one of the most expensive pools on the planet, even though it was still a simple swimming pool. As I learned, the reason for this had nothing to deal with the pool itself, but with the location. First, being on the lakeshore, where erosion had overtaken it, meant there were massive environmental hurdles involved in trying to give it a new life. Secondly, the location was next to impossible to get equipment to. These quotes called for a barge to float the needed equipment to the pool area. I felt the importance of bringing the Villa back to its original state. However, when it came to areas like this, I struggled with justifying such efforts. It wasn't that I didn't want to move forward with it. It was just insane to me to spend more money on a pool then I made all last year working.

Of course, the bright side of the week was spending every night with Kat. Every evening, we had dinner together and ended up talking all night long. It was a bit surreal. I usually struggled with knowing how to act, what to say and what to do. Yet with Kat, on top of the pure attraction I felt towards her, there was also a comfort.

Saturday morning, we were scheduled to meet the paranormal investigator. I picked Kat up, and we headed to the Holiday Inn he'd set as the meeting place. We were both silent as we drove there. I think we were both a little unsure of what we were getting into. As I pulled into the parking lot, she leaned over to give me a quick kiss.

"You know, if there's a camera crew waiting for us here, I'm leaving," she said.

"You and me both," I agreed.

"I still don't get it. You randomly find some ghost hunter on the internet that supposedly knows everything about your house, and we can only talk to him by meeting him in private. Did you even Google him?"

"Eh, no. You were there when I called him. It just kinda happened."

"Alright, but if he turns out to be one of these Craigslist killers, I fully expect you to be using those amazing muscles of yours to protect my ass."

"Oh stop. I am sure he's harmless. He will definitely be super weird, but that is it."

We walked into the hotel and headed to the elevator. I started getting nervous as we walked down the hall to his room. I hesitantly knocked on the door, half expecting it to swing silently open to reveal a man in a black robe standing before an altar with red candles. I immediately regretted not fighting to have this meeting in a public place like a coffee shop.

THE DOOR OPENED, and I was almost surprised to see a normal hotel room. Instead of a black hooded host, there stood our investigator. He was short, about 5'7" and slightly overweight. He wore jeans and a Baja poncho. From the looks of things, he clearly hadn't used the hotel's shower nor the complimentary bottle of shampoo.

"David?" I asked, extending my hand. "It's Jim and this is Kat."

"Yes! Come in and sit down." He led us to the chairs on the far side of the room.

As we walked over, I saw him peek his head into the hallway and quickly look both ways before shutting the door. He then walked over and sat on the edge of the bed.

"Whoa, you really did inherit that place. I can feel it, man." He stared at me intently.

"That is what the lawyers tell me anyway," I replied.

"Right, let's jump right into it."

He pulled out a large blue binder, like the ones a kid would use for school. I noticed the word 'Cloudland' was scribbled onto the front with a red pen.

"So you did the research?" he asked. "You know, the KGC?"

"Yeah, I read up on it," I said. "Some Confederate version of a Freemason type society. Right?"

"Well... that is what they want us to believe," he replied.

"Alright bro. Let me tell you what I know about them... So, everything everyone talks about involving the KGC includes two things, well three really if you are looking for treasure, but that isn't what we are here to talk about. So, we will leave it at two things. Yeah, everyone knows two things about the KGC. They were Confederates, and they were a secret organization. Right?"

"Yeah, that is about what I found out," I agreed.

"Wrong!" he snapped back. "Well, wrong on one point anyway."

"Okay?" I was confused.

"See, it's like this. They were hell-bent on creating a new nation. A better nation. More like a better nation for them only. And that is where everyone gets it wrong. They assume because it happened around the civil war, and because it was about rising against the government, that it was Confederate. It wasn't Confederate. Sure, there were a lot of castles in the South, but they had some in the North too. Anyway, even the name, the Knights of the Golden Circle... Everything we know about the organization is from the perspective of the knights. Well, a knight isn't just a rogue force. They take orders. And who do you think gave orders to this army of knights?" He waited for an answer.

"Um, the leaders?" I said reluctantly.

"Yes, the leaders. But they are never mentioned anywhere. They were only referred to sparingly as the Sovereign Lords. Now, these dudes were bad. They put together five of the most powerful people in the country, and they called all the shots for the army of Knights. These five guys specialized in everything they needed for a nation. You had one who controlled oil. One who controlled steel production. One who controlled the cotton trade. There was one who controlled all the rail lines in the country. And finally, one who controlled industrial manufacturing."

"Hold up," I said. "What does this have to do with anything?"

"It has everything to do with everything. You gotta know this to understand anything else, bro. Here, let me get to the point. So, there are two things you gotta remember about the KGC. First, is that you cannot go join them. It's a heritage. Membership is passed on from generation to generation. Second, they are alive and well no matter what anyone says. All I'm saying is, stay clear. You go in trying to mess with them, and you are in for some serious trouble."

"Okay, I got it. I think." I really didn't have a clue what he was getting at.

I looked over at Kat who had a smirk on her face and was rolling her eyes. Clearly, this meeting was going nowhere.

"Wait a second," I said. "Can you tell us exactly what it is you do?"

"Yeah! I am a paranormal investigator who specializes in residual energy."

"Residual energy?" I asked.

"Yeah, it's kinda like this. Every energy has a ripple effect. Like, if you were to get pissed off, and you punch the wall, the energy of your anger is transferred into the punch. But it doesn't end there. You mess up your hand, you mess up the wall. Next thing you know, you are paying the doctors to fix your hand, and you are spackling the wall. This is all residual effects of that energy transfer. If you don't fix your hand or the wall, the effects linger on. Now, understand that you cannot see or feel all energy. Spiritual energy gets released but some of it sticks around and lingers like that hole in the wall. That is the residual energy. It is why you feel a chill when you walk into a morgue. Or why when you step onto an old battlefield you feel that energy. Sometimes there is a lot, and it manifests itself into trapped spirits. Sometimes, it is just a bad feeling from a place or object."

"Okay, I think I follow," I said.

"So yeah, I specialize in this residual energy. Ultimately the energy needs to be released and cleansed. The only way to do that right is to understand why it got there in the first place."

"Got it. Now, what about my estate?" I wanted to get something of value out of this meeting.

"Yeah, the infamous Mansfeld Manor. A few years back I get a call from a client. This rich dude who built this spectacular cabin in the mountains. Anyway, his wife was all into antiquing and shit. She picks up this table to use in the dining room. Then, all of a sudden, shit starts going down. They are fighting. The wife is seeing shit everywhere. Electricians are all up in this house trying to figure out these random electrical problems. I go to check it out, right?" He paused to make sure I was following. I nodded. So he continued. "I get there, and I walk in, and I can feel it. There is some nasty energy in the place. And the table is just kinda weird. It is like this super fancy ornate turn of the century table, but it has this giant white stripe painted down the center of it."

"Wait a second!" I yelled.

I pulled out my cell phone and started flipping through the photos until I found the one I took in the historical society. I handed David my phone for him to see.

"Is this the table?" I asked, now feeling like we were getting somewhere.

A giant smile appeared on his face as he looked at it.

"For sure! That's it. That photo was taken down at Cloudland, and that is one of our lords!"

"Our lords?" I asked, showing my confusion.

"Yup, Samuel Freidrich Muller, prince of the railroad and second-generation Sovereign Lord."

We all sat there in silence for a few moments.

"Man, way to kill my big reveal." He looked disappointed but continued.

"Alright," I said, "so the original owner of my house was one of these Lords and even ate at that table you have been cleaning. How does this relate to the house at all?"

"That is what I am telling you!" He was clearly frustrated.

"How about starting with the super dumbed down version?" I asked hopefully. "Then we can start going into the details."

He just stared at me for a minute with an overwhelmed look on his face. He looked over at Kat and narrowed his eyes slightly.

"Wait, who are you?" he asked.

"This is Kat," I replied. "She's helping me with all this."

"Nope!" he said. "She is connected." He eyed her suspiciously while he rubbed his chin. "You are very connected Miss. But what I don't feel is how. What side are you on?"

"Side?" she asked with a look of frustration on her face. "What are you talking about? I just want to help Jim with the house."

"Hmmmmm," he said. "Maybe you don't know. At least not yet."

"Listen, can you just give us the super dumbed down version," I said, "and then we can just go from there?"

"Alright, here is the short version. Your man Sam there. Let's just say he was one evil mother fucker. Like I'm not even talking your run of the mill bad guy. He was straight up evil. So, he works a deal to hook up the Cloudland with a railway line to get people there. That meant the owner owed him. In exchange, Sam gets the run of the place one week every year. It becomes like the clubhouse for the Lords...You with me still?"

"Yeah, I guess so...So there is some hotel somewhere. The owner of my house is some asshole who takes over the hotel with his friends and basically has a frat party?"

"See, you are paying attention," he remarked back.

"Uh okay, just get on with the story." I was still confused but needed him to get to the point.

"Great! So, Evil Sam also has a bit of an issue. See, he needs to pass on his seat with the Lords. He needs a son. Problem is, the son he has ain't his. Seems the missus was having some fun behind his back. Now, he knows he cannot pass on his position to a kid that isn't his blood. But he is also super well known. So, it isn't like he can exactly walk out and start fresh. If he were a normal dude, there were a thousand ways this could have ended, but he was Evil Sam. He goes down for his week in the mountains alone with his Lords. They bring in some backwoods warlock and then shit goes down. Long story short, the boy ends up dead."

"Wait, you are saying first, that their first child was not his?" I asked. "Then, you are saying Samuel, being all-powerful and evil, used a warlock to kill the kid off purely to pass on membership to his club?"

"Well, when you put it like that, it sounds kinda juvenile." he said.

"Of course it does!" I said. "You're reading some twisted comic book plot to me, and you expect me to take it seriously?"

"Hey, you came here looking for information about the

house," he shot back. "I drove my ass up here to give it to you. Did you ever stop to think why I would do that? I mean it is not like you are paying me!"

"Okay fine. Why are you here?"

"I'm here because this shit is real," he explained. "You don't have a clue what the hell is going on, and it would be way bad karma for me to just watch you walk in without warning you."

"I'm sorry. Can you please just tell me how this all goes back to the house?"

"I really don't know. Like I said, I have not really investigated it directly. So, these are all educated guesses. But, what I do know is this. Across my client's table, Evil Sam and his buds conjured some wicked shit to off this kid. I am talking wicked enough for the residual energy on that table to be stronger than most legit haunted houses. I say that because the brunt end of the energy they conjured goes straight back to your house. So, if you think for a minute that a table, which played a minor role, can become one of the most haunted items I have ever seen and that house of yours, which was ground zero, does not hold some wicked energy, you are dead wrong!"

He took a deep breath and laid down on the bed as if he'd just finished running a race. Kat and I just stared at each other, not sure what to say or do. A moment later, he sat up and looked at me.

"You are connected, I can feel it. You are the light power. That also means you will be the first one under attack." He was pointing at me again. I wished he'd stop doing that.

While still pointing at me he turned to look at Kat.

"And you... you are just as connected. I cannot feel darkness in you... yet, I cannot feel light either."

David continued to take us through everything he knew.

Most of it was an in depth history lesson which lauded his efforts and findings around that table. Despite his craziness, by the end, I kinda liked him. I still held my reservations about all that he said, but for some reason, it all felt like it fit. David's lore was off the wall, but the connections he drew fit better than any other explanation I had heard. For the first time since this all started, I was hearing something that felt right. Kat loosened up to him as well. The whole thing was so surreal. Soon, the three of us were talking like old friends.

When he finished talking about what he knew, I suggested that we all go out to get a drink. I knew I needed one. We ended up going to the little sports pub connected to the hotel. The place was quiet except for some truckers on the far side of the bar, playing some variation of a legal slot machine. We sat down in a booth and ordered some beer.

"David, how do you know all of this?" I asked. "I mean, it started with a table for you. Did you see visions or something?"

"Nah man. I am not a clairvoyant. Like I said, I specialize in residual energy. I can feel things. I can't see them or hear them."

"That is a lot of detail to learn from feelings," I said.

"Yeah well, it all kinda starts with the feelings. The feelings direct me, but a lot of what I do is historical research. Of course, when I need to, I work with Linda, a partner of mine. She is a straight up legit clairvoyant. But she needs to focus. She cannot walk in and sit at that table and get the whole picture. I research what I can and then that gives her areas to focus on. In the end, when we combine everything, we typically have a pretty clear story."

"So what is the history of that table then?" Kat asked.

"Honestly, if it didn't have the stripe painted on it, I would have been totally lost. When I saw the stripe, I was kinda like, 'Who would paint that on a table worth more than my car?' But, then I remembered it. Me and my buds used to hike the Appalachian Trail a lot. Anyway, I remember being up there in the mountains and reading this plaque about a hotel that used to be there. It was built right on top of the Tennessee and North Carolina border. It was kinda this big deal. They painted the state line on the table and the floor in the dining room. Supposedly you could only drink on the Tennessee side and there would be some cop up there waiting for you to cross the line with your drink. Anyway, that was the table."

He stopped to take a long swallow of beer.

"See, objects are hard to translate once they are outside of their surroundings. I mean, a place is easy for me. I can look up property records, police reports etc. But a table? I got lucky with that one. Had it not been for the stripe, it would have been about a month of researching it before being able to figure where it came from."

"So, do you want to come out to the estate and feel it for yourself tomorrow?" I offered.

"Does that mean you're hiring me?" he said with a hopeful look in his eyes.

"Why the hell not?" I replied with a smirk.

10

AFTER LEAVING THE BAR, Kat and I decided to head back to my apartment. It was all a little much, and we really needed some time together. As we started driving, I noticed she was unusually quiet. When I glanced over at her, she was absently staring out the window as if in a daze. It had been kinda a crazy day. So, I just looked past it, thinking that if there was something she wanted to talk about, she would.

When we got to my apartment, she immediately curled up on the couch. She still had that same listless look to her, and when I looked at her eyes, it was like the crystal blue clarity was gone. They were clouded over.

"You okay?" I asked.

When I spoke, her head twitched a bit, and she blinked as if I had awoken her from a dream.

"What, yeah. Sorry."

I sat on the couch and slid my arms around her. I could feel the tension in her body.

"Seriously, what's bothering you?" I asked.

"It's nothing...just David," she admitted.

"Well, yeah. I admit it isn't like this is conventional, but the pieces he spoke of kinda fit well."

"Jesus Jim! That isn't it." She glared at me.

"What? If you want me to call it all off with him, that's fine. I just thought it was interesting. He clearly knows more about this house than I do. It was nice hearing some of what he had to say." I thought that would help smooth everything out.

I looked at Kat and she just continued to glare at me. Now, she looked pissed. I was so confused. On instinct, I decided I should keep talking and try to dig myself out of whatever hole I'd fallen down.

"I get it. You don't like him. I honestly don't care about him. If he makes you uncomfortable, then forget it."

Her gaze didn't waver. "You really think this is because I didn't like something about him. I am not that petty!"

"I know you're not. I didn't mean it like that. Just tell me what's bothering you, please!"

"What side do you think I'm on?" she asked, her curt words cut through me even more than her icy stare.

This was that point where I realized she had given me one of those questions where it doesn't matter how you answer.

"Kat, stop. Just because he didn't feel something doesn't mean shit. I feel where you are. I know there isn't even a part of you that would bring harm to me or that estate or anything else."

"Why? Because you dreamt of me? Or are you just being nice because we slept together?"

"What are you talking about. That has nothing to do with it. Whether we slept together or not, from the moment we met, I felt I needed to be close to you."

I tried to pull her close to me. I was confused. I was also

pissed off and scared. She tore my arms off her and pushed me away from her. I just sat there looking at her, not sure what to do or what to say. Her feet pushed her deep into the corner of the couch. That is when I saw the tear. A single tear slowly running down her cheek as she stared off into the distance. I wanted so badly to wipe it off her cheek. I wanted to be the one to comfort her, but I didn't know how. So, I just sat there, confused, looking at her. The silence was suffocating. Finally, she stood up and abruptly darted to the door.

"I have to go," she said as she was walking out the door. "I need space to...".

I stood up to follow her and got to the open door. She was already about twenty feet away.

"Kat! Please wait!" I yelled.

She continued walking, not even acknowledging my words.

"I drove you here! At least let me give you a ride home!"

"I will call a cab...just stop...let me be!" She never turned to face me.

I SAT THERE for about an hour, in shock. I replayed the night over and over in my head. The words that were spoken. Her pushing herself into the corner of the couch. Her tear. In my mind, her tear sparkled like a diamond, unable to be ignored. I felt like my world had collapsed. Eventually, I got up and made it to the kitchen where I found a dusty bottle of Jim Beam. I poured a large glass and walked outside. I sat there on the patio drinking and staring into the sky.

An hour later, I was still on the patio. The bottle was empty. I pulled out my phone, as I had a thousand times that night, hoping to see a text from her. As usual, there was none. I typed out the only message I could think to send, "Worried about you. Call me!"

I grabbed the empty bottle and threw it as far as I could. I could hear the explosion of glass hitting the parking lot when it landed. I stood up, a bit wobbly from the alcohol. I made it over to my couch where I lay down and closed my eyes.

I opened my eyes to find myself standing on the garden terrace of the Villa. The sky was dark, and there was a cold wind that cut right through me. A light fog blanketed the ground. It looked as if the fog was battling the lights on the terrace. The fog forced the light to be constrained into a small area, like glowing orbs in the distance.

Without a thought, I started to walk. My destination was unknown to me. Yet, I walked with purpose as if following a command. I walked down the steps and through the center of the garden. The loose gravel crunching under my foot was the only sound. I continued walking until I reached the path towards the lily pond. As I turned to enter the lush park surrounded by hedges, the rain began to fall.

The rain was overwhelming. Sheets of water poured from the sky. Still, I continued forward. Driven by an inexplicable force, I approached the pond. The entire garden was lit only by the lights under the water, creating an eerie glow with the surrounding fog. I reached the far end of the pond and stopped. The angelic statue in the center of the pond cast wild shadows across the pond. I felt like the statue was moving. I could feel it coming closer to me. I stood paralyzed by fear.

That statue looked as if it was within only a couple feet from me when the lightning struck. A single strike of lightning with an immediate boom of thunder crashed just behind the pond. The ground shook from the thunder, causing me to wince. Then, for that split second, with the sky illuminated by the lightning, I saw his face. It was not the angel statue. It was Samuel, and he was coming up to me. There was a devilish grin on his face as he approached.

"Master James, did you really think you could win?" he roared.

"I will win." I yelled back. "Your reign is finished!"

"Is that so? For I would think that if that were the case, I wouldn't even be here right now."

He took a step back and raised his arms. As he did so the rain instantly ceased. Now, I could see him clearly from the glow of the pond.

"As you see, I am still very much in control." He confidently stared me down. I could feel his dark dead eyes sizing me up. "Not just that, but here you are. The one who challenges me, and I feel nothing but fear from you. You are not the worthy adversary I waited for all these years."

My fists clenched in rage. Yet, I was paralyzed. I was unable to move, unable to speak. He turned his back to me and walked up to the angel statue in the center of the pond. The sound of the water sloshing around his feet, as he waded through the pond, made my stomach turn. In front of the statue now, he turned to face me again.

"Master James, leave here at once! You do not belong here! Should you choose to stay, we both know your fate!"

He immediately turned to the statue and shoved it. As if in slow motion, the statue fell into the pond. It landed with a crash. A plume of water rose around the toppled statue. He was gone. The statue lay broken as a cloud of red surrounded it. The blood-like cloud grew until it swallowed the entire pond. Unmoving, I stared out at the crimson glow of the now blood-soaked pond. In the distance, I saw something.

I turned my head, Kat stood at the far end of the pond. There was a wide smile on her face as she looked at me. It was not a smile of joy at seeing me. It was joy at seeing him torment me.

Another lightning bolt shot through the sky and blinded me for a moment. I closed my eyes.

When I opened them, I was back at my apartment. It was bright and sunny. My head throbbed with pain. My hair and my shirt were drenched in sweat, despite the fact that the apartment was cold enough to make me shiver. I picked up my phone to look at it. There were no messages. That was the moment where the memory of last night overtook me. In my head, I started playing the slow-motion video of her crying again. Then, there was the blood of the pond and her laughing.

I pounded my fists on the coffee table.

AFTER A HEALTHY DOSE of coffee and ibuprofen, I finally felt alive enough to face the day. I sat for several minutes staring at Kat's number in my phone. My finger hovered over the call button. I took a deep breath and pressed it, hoping that after sleeping off the day she would talk to me. After two rings, the automated voice of her voicemail came on. Frustrated, I hung up the phone, grabbed my keys and left.

Soon, I was at the hotel picking up David. I didn't know what to expect today. Really, I didn't know what to expect when I had planned this with Kat. Now, without her, I was lost. I hadn't ever even been to the house without her. I sat in the parking lot and sent David a text. Then, despite telling myself not to, I sent Kat a text.

"Heading to the house. Would love to see you there. Meet me if you can."

A moment later, I saw David walking toward the truck. He looked the same. He was wearing the same poncho, same jeans, and the same worn out Converse All-Stars. He was also carrying a large backpack with him.

I got out of the truck to greet him, and he shot me a look.

"Whoa, looks like the party didn't end after you left me here last night. You know, if you were holding, you could have shared."

"Hell, I just had a nice long chat with my friend Jimmy Beam last night," I admitted.

"Looks more like an all-out barroom brawl with Jimmy if you ask me," he chided.

We got in the truck, and I started pulling out on the road.

"Where's Katherine?" he asked.

"Oh, something came up...she couldn't make it," I replied weakly.

We drove a few miles in silence.

"You know what is really funny about being in tune with feelings and energy like I am?" he asked looking at me.

"No, what is it?"

"When people feed you a stream of obvious bullshit and expect you to believe it," he replied. "You don't have to go telling me all your shit, but have some consideration."

"What are you talking about?" I asked defensively.

"Really?" he asked with an overly mock surprised look. "C'mon, you want me to pretend that something didn't blow up between you two last night? That you didn't go hitting the bottle because it was the best idea you could come up with?" He paused to look at me with intensity. "And you had another dream!"

"So what if you're right?" I asked.

"Just saying, it is pretty silly to watch you try and act like nothing happened."

I ignored the comment. I just focused on driving. This day was looking like it was going to be far more frustrating than I had imagined.

"I can't say I am entirely disappointed to be doing this without her," he said quietly.

Now I was just pissed. Sure, this guy was annoying but up until now, it was just that, annoying. Now he was crossing the line. I realized that I was either going to turn around and just drop him off, or I was going to keep driving knowing full well he might push me over the edge to the point I hit him.

"Don't be mad," he said. "I don't mean it like that, bro. It's just that there is some stuff I need to talk to you about without her."

"Like what?" I asked, still fuming.

"Yesterday, I was trying to be as considerate as I could be with my words, but I have a very bad feeling about her. Like I said, I feel things. I don't get a vision or anything, just a feeling. But, in getting them all my life, I have become pretty good at interpreting them. With you, there is definitely a super strong light power. But her. It isn't light. It's not dark either. It is more she is in the middle, both equally light and dark. Most people don't stay that way. They either consciously or unconsciously find themselves going to one side or the other. As they do, the other fades away."

"What the hell am I supposed to do with that? Do you ever just speak English?" I was no longer able to hide my irritation.

"That is my point," he warned. "There's nothing you can do. At some point, she will move one way or the other. That will be her choice. But if she goes dark, I fear that could be trouble for you."

"Gee, thanks for the warning," I said sarcastically.

"You don't get it, do you?" he asked with concern in his voice.

"No, I don't get a damn thing about any of this!"

"Look, if there is even a fraction of the residual energy in that house that I think there will be, it will be enough to swallow up the strongest of men. You will be going to war, my friend. A war like you have never even imagined. How well do you think you will fare if the person who consumes your thoughts is fighting on the other side?"

We approached the circle drive in front of the property. I slammed on my brakes and parked the car. "It isn't a fucking war! It's a house! Great! There's the oogie boogie man in the closet. You can come in and toss some holy water on it and we'll move on!"

"I wish it were that easy. Tell me, you ever just get a bad feeling about something?"

"Yeah, everyone does."

"Okay, when you get that bad feeling, don't you typically make decisions based off that feeling?" he continued.

"I 'spose. Why?" I was now slightly more composed.

"Because that is exactly what this is like. Take a bad feeling or a good feeling, whatever. They affect you by influencing your actions, your thoughts, your perceptions. It happens to everyone everywhere. But now imagine yourself living in this house, surrounded by these feelings of such intensity that it consumes everything. You think you will make good decisions then? We live in a world where one action can affect the rest of our lives. Take the guy who gets pissed off and drinks. He isn't a typical drunk, but he has a bad night. He then jumps in his car and the next thing you know someone's poor kid is getting put in the ground. Yeah, he got drunk and drove. He hit the kid. That is what he is punished for. But the reality is, that is the end product of the chain of reaction. It all started with him getting pissed off. That is the energy that led to the end. Because he didn't have the strength to overcome that one simple energy. The energy, I believe is at this house, will make all of that look like a little pond compared to the Pacific Ocean."

I sat there for a minute. I didn't want to admit it. What he was saying kinda made sense. I really didn't buy into the idea that this house was the bottomless pit of hell thing, or the light and dark, but in concept, I saw what he was saying.

"So, with all your feelings, you know why she isn't here, don't you?" I asked.

"No, I really don't. Why isn't she here?

"I dunno. She kinda flipped out last night about you saying that she needed to choose sides. That's all I really could get out of her."

"Oh! She does know then."

"She knows what?" I asked.

"She feels it too. She knows she has to choose once and for all. I hope for her sake, and ours, she is staying away to choose the path she knows is right."

"So, how do you want to do this?" I asked. "Do we have to walk from here so you can feel the whole place, or can I drive up to the house?"

"Man, I can take it all in as we go," David replied. "Let's roll up there. If I feel something, we can come back to it."

I drove the truck into the estate. I watched David. He just sat there like a kid amazed at the world around him. When we arrived at the house, he got out, walked up to the front door, and placed his hand on the house. His eyes were closed. Then, he turned around and approached me, setting his backpack down on the ground.

"What is it?" I asked.

"This is absolutely unreal." He shook his head in awe.

"What?" I asked again.

"This house is just like Katherine in a way. It isn't dark. It isn't light. Here outside, I feel the darkness just oozing everywhere to the point it is like the house is just covered in black sludge. But the door... the white light inside is forcing its way out. It is like they are equal powers converging on one another. Deadlocked in a battle for all eternity."

"Soooo gray? I can live with gray, right?"

"No, it isn't like a color wheel. They don't mix. There is light and dark. Out here is the most overpowering darkness I've ever felt. But the house itself is protected by what I can only imagine is an equally powerful light power."

Then he looked up at me.

"Locked in a battle for all eternity until..." He trailed off and started rummaging through his bag.

"Until what?" I asked.

"Until something changes. You own this house now. You change the environment. I need to feel more. Let's go inside." He grabbed some electronics from his bag.

We walked inside the house. David walked slowly, holding some sort of a meter with flashing lights. I was curious what he was doing but could not bear to be reprimanded for not knowing. So I let him just do his thing. We walked through the house much in the same way I did with Kat. It was far less enjoyable this time. Instead of laughing and trying to envision the grand house as it had been, we went room by room feeling things and listening for beeps on his machine. The only thing that broke the monotony of it all was when we entered the room with the fountain. He immediately walked up to it and gave it a curious look.

"There's something here," he said. "There's protection here."

"That's a good thing, right?"

"Well, it is better when there is no need for protection. But for now, yes. It is a very good thing."

Looking at the way he examined the fountain, my mind shot back to that moment with Kat. How she lit up upon seeing that penny. Despite everything, my mind was on her. While I partly understood what he was feeling about her, I felt I needed to stand up for her.

"You know, I am not going to pretend to feel things like you do, but I think you are wrong about Kat. Maybe she is confused right now, sure. But I walked through the house with her. You say that fountain is protected. It's protected by her great-great-grandfather. I saw her feel that connection."

David stopped and set his meter down, looking at me with a stare. "Look, I'm not sayin' she is a bad person or anything. I get it better than you know. I've no doubt she could feel something in here. It is one of the main reasons I could feel she was connected, back at the hotel." He stroked the stubble on his chin. "Hear me out. We have barely begun going through this house. Everything I've felt in here has been about protection. Yet outside, I know there is something far darker. Something battling this protection. While she connected with her family in here, how do we know she doesn't equally connect with the darkness outside?"

I stood there not knowing what to say. Inside, I loathed the fact that he made logical sense to me. I really wanted Kat back regardless of what side she was on.

"I get it," he said. "You care about her, and you want to fight for her. Just please be open to learning what this house has to say to us and where Katherine fits in. Besides, we don't have much of a choice today. Just give me a chance."

As much as I wanted to fight him on this, he was right. We didn't have a choice today. So, I tried to shrug it off and to see what David had to say when we were done.

We continued our walk through the house, eventually making our way upstairs. We walked through all the rooms and the corridors in silence. When we approached Ida's parlor, his meter lit up like a Christmas tree. He stopped and slowly ran it along the hall and then the door. The second it would be in front of the door, it would light up again.

"Here! Right here! What's this room?" His eyes widened.

"I believe it's the parlor," I said.

"Whoa, this is insane. I have never felt this much in one place! This door is... no... there is a sentry guarding this door. For real! You can't see him, but he is right here guarding the door! I can feel it!"

"That door was locked. It was the only one locked when I first came into the house. Look at the frame. You can see where people tried to get in."

"But no one could because of the sentry!" he yelled. "This is amazing!"

"Wait 'till you go in." His enthusiasm was rubbing off on me.

"It is well...you'll see," I said as I put the key in the lock and opened the door.

He slowly stepped into the parlor. When his foot hit the floor inside the room he froze. He didn't move. He didn't speak. He just stood there with his eyes wide. He turned to look at me, and I was shocked. He had gone completely pale.

"Shut that door!" he yelled as he backed out. "Lock it and stay out!"

"What's going on? I've been in there. It's peaceful and smells like flowers."

"Look again! Don't stay! Don't go in! Just look in and then lock that door!"

I rolled my eyes and peered through the door. The room was the same but completely different at the same time. It wasn't bright and clean as it had been. The inviting smell of flowers was gone, replaced with what smelled like smoke. I closed my eyes and shook my head before looking again. When I did, I saw what David had seen. The far wall of the room, which had been a very pleasant yellow color... was now red. Blood red. It looked wet as if it were sloppily painted only minutes before. I clenched my fists, and I turned to David.

"What the fuck did you do?" I fumed. "You think this is a joke?"

"Me? Just please lock that door! Now!"

I grabbed the front of his shirt. I was enraged.

"Stop!" he yelled. "Just lock the damn door!"

I winced in pain from my head. As if someone had just stabbed my temples. I let go of his shirt. The second I did, he bolted over to the door, slamming it shut. He then grabbed the key from me and locked the door. He grabbed my arm and started pulling me down the hall.

"You are going to have to wait to kill me." he yelled wildly. "Right now, we need to get the hell out of here!"

Within moments, we were outside the front door of the house. Oddly enough, even in the time it took to run through the house, the intense pain in my head had subsided. I looked over at David. He looked terrified. I wasn't sure if he was scared of the house or scared of me. Honestly, I didn't really care which it was. I grabbed David by the shirt again and threw him against the planter.

"You thought this would all be a funny joke. Make a mess of that room so I think there's a spirit for you to catch. After my bank account is empty, you run back home. Nice system you have running here!"

"Jim! It's nothing like that! I swear!"

"Talk!" I spat at him.

He held up his hands, waving them at me. "I don't know what you think I did. I was just here like you, seeing this all for the first time."

"Why should I believe you? You know more than you say. This bullshit about your feelings and light and dark.

Hell, this whole paranormal investigator crap is all a front. What do you want from me? Money?"

"Why would I fake this? Besides, you're the one who called me. What even makes you think I did something? You were in that room already. You were the one telling me there was something strange in there. And you are the only one with a key to that room."

"Strange yeah, but not like that! That was just straight-up horror movie fucked up!"

"Alright, why don't you tell me what you saw the first time you went in there?"

"Uh well, it was peaceful and serene. The red paint on the wall wasn't there. That's for damn sure! Everything was perfectly clean. It felt bright. It even smelled like freshly cut flowers."

"This room is telling us something. What's different about today from the last time you were there?"

"Well... you, and last time I was with Kat," I said.

He just stared at me. And then it was as if a light bulb went off in his head. He stood up.

"I was wrong!" he shouted.

"Um okay, how so?" I asked.

"Yes, Katherine needs to choose her side, but I'm afraid if she doesn't choose our side in this, we will not prevail."

"Yeah, I'm not following again," I said.

"See, the house is showing us. It is reacting to the situation it is put in. And that room, for some reason, that is ground zero for all the energy in the house. But when you walk in with her, it responds to that. And responds well... welcomingly. Without her, it shuts down as if giving in to the darkness. She is definitely connected but far more than I ever estimated."

He sat down again and took a deep breath.

"Tell me, what is her connection to this home?" he asked.

I went through everything I knew about her. I talked about her lineage, the letter for the will kept in a safe in her home, my visit with her mom, even the whole penny in the fountain thing.

"We are both missing something," he said. "If she was here, maybe she could fill in the gaps, but maybe even she doesn't know. By all logic, if she was the child of the butler, then she would be light. He protected this house and ensured its future. There is far more to this story. And for now it appears, without her, we may be stuck."

"So, what do we do now?" I asked.

"Well for starters, I am staying out of that house until I understand more."

"Great, so you are leaving me to fight this solo?"

"No, no, no!" He shook his head adamantly. "But we need a better interpretation before we go disrupting things even more."

"Yeah, well interpret this for me." I stood up and turned to face him. "We have talked about Kat and her 'connection.'" I made air quotes with my fingers. "But you know what we haven't talked about? The one damn thing that's more important than anything in all of this despite everyone not paying attention to it or trying to understand it."

"What is that?" he asked.

"Me!" I yelled, staring him down. "How about my connection or lack thereof? How did I even get connected to this damn place? You talk about me as if I'm the white knight, but I have no blood in the game. The only thing I know is that I was selected to inherit this house seventy years before I was even conceived. Years before my mom or my drunk ass dad were even born. Does no one find that at all strange or worth looking into? How can I put together the puzzle of this house without even knowing who I am in relation to it?"

I sat back down. I was exhausted. I was simply tired of being the main player in a ghost story without knowing why. I didn't want to disturb those ghosts. Hell, I would have never even known they existed without inheriting this place. But I did care about it all. I did feel close... or so I thought. At that point, I didn't know if this was just crossed lines in my head regarding my feelings for Kat.

"You're right bro," he said. "You want my take even though it's only a guess?"

"Well, that would at least be someone finally talking to it for a change....so yeah, let me have it."

"I know a couple things that bring me to this conclusion. First, we know Sam was one hell of an evil dude. He was tied up in everything from murder to witchcraft. Serious dark art shit from what I can understand. People don't dive that deep solo. It's a progression, like a religion or anything else. It starts with interest and intrigue. Then it progresses. My point is, there seemed to be many happyish years of marriage prior to when this shit fell apart. There is really no way I can believe that Ida was not on some level exposed to this. Perhaps they even shared an interest. Anyway, it is completely plausible that she dove into some of this world too. At that time period, especially for women, involvement in witchcraft was almost exclusively focused on speaking to those who have passed on and trying to predict the future. You know your typical crystal ball and seance shit."

"So you're saying Ida grabbed a crystal ball, and it told her about me?" I asked.

"Not exactly. But also, kinda yeah. I mean the strange thing is, historically speaking, things like that have been less than reliable when it comes to details. A typical medium rarely gets the whole story. They may see images, places, and times. They can feel the emotions of people. Sometimes they get a name. Sometimes they get a date range. But for a medium of any sort, as I understand, it would be almost unheard of to get a specific name and date for someone to be born, especially someone with no direct lineage. Clearly, there was no prediction of just some random person. So, the connection is what we are missing. Why you? Did your great-great-grandfather have an affair with one of them? Who knows? It doesn't even have to be like that. For all, we know you are the descendant of the kid selling newspapers she walked by every day, and she decided to help him out far in the future. Either way, there must be something."

"So, how do we figure out my connection?" I asked.

"Man, that is the tough part. I mean, sure, we could spend the next month putting together a super-comprehensive map of your lineage and look for areas it could have crossed. But real info will only take us so far. Even the most documented families can only give enough information for the basics. I feel this one is more obscure than that, even if we had all the facts."

"So, you're telling me I'm shit out of luck?" I asked.

"No! I'm telling you that understanding this is going to require research of another kind." He looked at me with a curious expression. "I believe you were found by a medium back then. I think it's time we use one to help us understand why."

I hung my head. "Seriously, why can't just one thing be a simple answer?" I asked, not expecting a response.

"Well, if it helps, I really think we can get somewhere with the right help. I mean, you're not walking in the dark. You are already dreaming. That is a big plus. You're dreaming, I'm feeling, and we have a ton of historical data. Linda will be able to connect a lot of these dots I hope."

"If you say so.... So, what do we do now?".

"For now, you go home. I'll go home and meet with Linda. For the most part, let's continue what we were doing. But in the meantime, I do think it would be best if you could get in contact with Katherine, even if it is by putting feelings aside. She is tied in here somehow, and I fear we need her."

He stood up and walked over to the entrance of the house and put his hand on the pillar. Then he looked back at me.

"Actually, I have one other thing for you to do," he said.

"What?"

"Not today, emotions are too high for anything to be accurate, but at some point, I would be very curious what that parlor would look like if you walked in there alone. If you have a chance, go in, look. But be careful and do not stay. Just look. And be sure to do it with a clear mind. That room seems to respond to you."

PART II

REQUIEM

12

SEPTEMBER 7, 1927 – Villa Ortenberg

The large clock in the entryway had just struck for the twelfth time. The echoes of the sound reverberated throughout the corridors of the empty and silent mansion. It had been a week since Madam Mansfeld had indefinitely left the estate. Edgar was used to her absence from the Villa, but this time was different. Prior to that week, the staff would be hurrying around, making meals and ensuring everything was perfect in the off-chance she would happen to arrive without notice. That was protocol. If she arrived at the Villa at 5:50 PM, she would be seated in the dining room at 6:00 PM expecting her formal dinner. There were of course other occasions, when the Villa would become the playhouse for Samuel and his partners in her absence. Fortunately, these had become a rarity in recent years.

Now, however, Edgar had given the staff a reprieve. He knew there was no reason to make dinner as Ida would not be arriving. Likewise, following the divorce, Samuel was never to set foot on the property again. That was one point Edgar was pleased with. He could never stand the man.

One would expect that in the absence of the Madam the staff would have the run of the home. Edgar would never tolerate such indulgences. His priority was the estate and ensuring it was exactly as the Madam would have expected.

On that day, the house was silent. Edgar walked slowly up the staircase, carrying a vase of freshly cut flowers in his hand. As he approached the end of the hall, he reached into his pocket to retrieve a key. He unlocked the door and entered her parlor, shutting and locking the door behind him. This was the first time he'd entered the room since the Madam's departure. He walked across the room to the fireplace. He picked up the vase of now wilted flowers from the mantel and replaced it with the vase he carried. He walked over to the chaise in the center of the room. He unbuttoned his coat and sat down. He sat there for a few minutes, silent and motionless, his hands resting in his lap.

He then reached into his pocket and withdrew the envelope Ida had given him. He ran his fingers across the unbroken crimson wax seal and lifted the envelope to his nose. He inhaled, closing his eyes. He could smell the unmistakable scent of her perfume still lingering within the fibers of the paper. He opened his eyes and looked at the envelope. He retrieved a small pen-knife from his pocket and cut open the envelope. Inside was a letter.

Dearest Edgar,

I apologize for my delivering this letter to you under the pretense of it containing my instructions to you. You may remain in my employ, but you are far from my servant. I know that your priorities remain with the Villa as they have all these years. For that, I want to ensure that you will be well compensated. However, I do not forget the past. I know better than anyone the sacrifices you have made. I know this house has robbed you of the future you dreamt of.

I am sincerely sorry for that, and you must understand it is a fact which pains me as much as it does you. I have spent the last number of years trying to rectify the pain of the past in hopes that it may brighten the future. I humbly realize now that such things are not within my control.

There is another matter I wish to discuss with you in hopes that it will bring you some peace moving forward. Please do not think that in my absence I have been blind to the events that have transpired at the Villa. I know that Lucinda is with child. I also know that the father of that child is Samuel. Edgar, I fear for that child's future. You know that Samuel is evil. The only thing worse than simply being born of his evil blood would be to grow up knowing the evil that created her.

If you see fit, please take the child and raise her as your own. Let her never know the truth about the evil she will undoubtedly carry in her veins. Please think of her as your future. Raise her to value the love and compassion I know you have. You were once robbed of the opportunity to raise a child. The world was robbed of having that child grow up within it. This is your opportunity to overcome that past along with stamping out the evil that Samuel has done.

Your duties to this house will soon come to a close. The coffers used to maintain this house will run dry. I have arranged for a substantial amount of money to be bequeathed to you that you may live on independent of this Villa. Please trust me, dearest Edgar, peace will come. The sun will shine upon the Villa once more. It will not be in either of our lifetimes, but it will come.

I will always love you my dearest Edgar,
Ida

Edgar slowly folded the letter and placed it back into the envelope. He then placed the envelope back into his jacket pocket. He clasped his hands together and sunk his head down, resting his chin in his hands. He let out a long sigh and sat there. A single tear rolled down his cheek.

13

A COUPLE WEEKS WENT BY. Work on the foundation of the house had begun. A crew had come in with excavators and all sorts of machinery. They dug out a trench on all sides of the house where they were going in to reinforce and rebuild portions. I stayed out of their way. Actually, the only time I went to the estate was on the first day when the crew arrived. They had cleared a bit of the entrance brush and set some rock on the drive to make it possible to bring their trucks in. I arrived to give some personal instruction about the project to the foreman. For me, the most important thing was to disturb as little as possible in this process. Considering it was the first step, it would be easy, at least in my mind, to damage another part of the estate making the restoration more difficult. I had also asked that the crew keep their eyes open for anything out of the ordinary, be it an uncovered artifact outside or anything else.

The foreman updated me at the close of every workday. I was thankful that so far there was nothing in the updates other than work as usual. All things considered, this project was moving along with ease.

David's work on figuring out this puzzle was proceeding far slower than I had hoped. His trusted medium was out of town. He continued to dive into every ounce of historical information he could get his hands on. While that was interesting, it didn't really yield anything that helped either of us. Even if he had found anything tangible, he was hellbent on waiting for Linda before sharing it. The next morning, we were scheduled to finally meet with Linda. I was actually driving down to Tennessee to meet her. At first, I thought it would be more logical to meet at the house. However, I didn't really fight David on the suggestion to meet in Tennessee. I thought it would be good to remove myself completely from everything for a couple days.

Besides the construction crew and David, I had a very quiet couple weeks. It was a nice break to not spend every waking hour focused on the house. Still missing though, was Kat. I had texted a couple times. I had even worked up the courage to call. With no answer, my courage ran out before I could leave a voicemail. For me, Kat consumed most of my thoughts for those weeks. I wanted more than anything to just drive to her house or her work, and just show up. I felt that face to face, she would be more willing to at least say something. Although, that was probably the exact reason I didn't. It was easier to just think about her and wallow in my loneliness than it was to see her and hear that maybe there wasn't any hope.

I was finishing my packing when I heard my phone ringing. I looked at the clock, realizing it was far too early for the foreman to be calling with an update. As I picked up my phone, I saw it was her.

"Kat? Are you okay?"

"Jim... um look, I don't know what to say."

"Kat, don't worry, whatever it is, it doesn't matter," I said.

There was silence. All I could hear was a deep sigh. I wanted to reach through the phone and hug her more than anything.

"Listen, I need your help." Her voice was cold and direct.

"What do you need?" I replied matching her tone. "Just tell me."

"It's my mom. She wants to talk to you. That's all."

"Of course. What's wrong? Is she feeling worse?"

"No, it's just... Jim, I tried to talk to her. I wanted to ask her about the house, to find out..." Her voice trailed off.

"Find out what? What is going on?"

Then, I realized I was talking to no one. She had hung up. She was gone as fast as she came.

"Fuck!" I yelled.

I couldn't think. So I didn't think. I grabbed my duffel bag, packed, zipped it up, and ran out the door, throwing it in my truck. A normal person would have probably called back. A smart person would probably just relax and wait for her to call back, whenever that might be. Clearly, I was neither of those. I spun the tires of my truck and hit the road, driving straight to her mom's house.

I spent a few minutes driving as fast as I could. My heart was beating out of my chest. Finally, I composed myself enough to call her back.

"Jim?" she answered.

"Look, I don't care what's going on! I will help you!"

"Jim, I'm scared." I could hear in her voice that she was crying. "I didn't want to call you. I swore I wouldn't, but my mom. She demanded it."

"Why would you swear not to call me?" I asked.

There were a few seconds of silence. I didn't know what

to say. Without thinking I just said the only thing that I truly felt.

"Katherine, I love you!"

"Don't say that!" she yelled. "Just don't! You don't know me!"

"No, you stop!" I yelled back. "I love you, Katherine. I don't care who you are or what you have done. That doesn't matter. I just love you, and unless you can honestly say you don't love me, just stop."

She said nothing. The only sounds were sniffles.

"I will be there in a couple minutes, and we can talk. If you really want nothing to do with me, then I will leave, and you will never hear from me again. But I need to hear you say that. I need to see you look at me when you tell me that."

A moment later, the line went dead again. I threw the phone across the inside of the truck and slammed my fist into the passenger seat. I couldn't drive. I pulled over on the side of the road and put my truck in park. I was furious with myself. I had no idea where my words even came from. It sounded like the perfect way to ensure I'd never see her again. I spent about ten minutes screaming at myself. I was trying to compose myself. After taking a few deep breaths, I pulled out onto the road again. At the very least, I had to stay the course at that point. I hadn't lied to her. Granted, I certainly hadn't expected to say what I did, but I couldn't for a second pretend it wasn't true. There. I'd set the table. Now, it was her move.

She was sitting on a bench next to the front door of the house as I pulled up. She was curled up in a large hooded sweatshirt. The image of her reminded me of that last night in my apartment. My heart sank seeing her like that. I took a deep breath and walked out of the truck. I walked up to the house. When I got within a few feet of her, she looked at me.

Her eyes were bloodshot. She wiped the tears from her face with the sleeve of her sweatshirt and then looked back at me with this half smile. It was the kind of smile that says, 'I am horribly depressed and kinda wanna kill myself, but seeing you still brings me some joy.'

She stood up and wrapped her arms around me. Her body trembled. I felt her crying on my shoulder. We stood there for minutes until her body relaxed and the tears stopped. There was a large sniffle, and she let go of me wiping off her face again.

"Well, if you want to tell me to fuck off, you are missing your opportunity," I said.

"Come in and talk to my mom. Then, you can decide to do what you want." The tone of her voice was depressed.

She led me into the house and up the stairs to her mother's room. We walked in and her mom was sitting up looking far more alert and more spry than she had the last time I'd seen her.

"James, thank you for coming," she said.

She welcomed me over to the side of her bed. Kat stood behind me and rested her hand on my shoulder.

"You know why I asked you here?" she asked.

"No ma'am, I don't," I replied.

She nodded. "I see. Well, Katherine asked me a question, and I realized you needed to be here to hear the answer too. You remember the letter that was given to you with the will?"

"Of course," I replied.

"That letter was kept safe in this family for you. It was never opened. There were implicit instructions from my great-grandfather to deliver it to you and only to you. That story you know, I'm sure."

I nodded my head in agreement.

She leaned back and sighed. There was a bit of a mischievous grin on her face.

"What you don't know..." She paused and looked at Kat. "Well, what neither of you know, is that there were actually two letters passed down from him."

There was a slight pause.

"Unlike the one you received, the second one had less specific instructions. The instructions on that one simply said to be opened when necessary. Katherine told me about your friend. She shared with me her concerns about who she was and how it may hurt you."

"Ma'am, please do not read into that," I said. "I assure you his comment was not intended to cause any stress."

She raised her hand with her palm facing me, signaling for me to stop talking.

"Let me tell you my story before you foolishly jump to any conclusions for yourself," she said in a stern tone. "I would consider my life to have been normal. I was raised in a family surrounded by love. My grandmother would always share stories of that house. Like is the case with most families, we had stories that were like folklore within our house. She spoke very fondly of the lavish estate her father once worked at. They were just stories. Then, when my father passed, I was next in line to carry on this task of caring for the letters. I hadn't put much thought into them. My grandmother was long gone, and her stories were just a simple memory. But I was curious. Then one day, curiosity got the best of me. It was just after I found out that I was carrying Katherine. Her father was at work, and I was bored. The maternal instinct in me wanted to pass down to Katherine our family's story. I don't remember why, but that day I felt I needed to see it for myself. So, I drove out to the estate."

She stopped to take a drink of water and then adjusted herself in the bed before continuing.

"I stepped out of my car in front of the house, and the sky turned black. A cold wind blew, and rain began to poor. I never got any closer. Of course, I didn't need to then. I knew I was not welcome there. It was as if the house itself had pushed me away. I was scared and drove straight home. Now, I suppose most of this probably sounds as if I am just some old lady telling ghost stories. But you... well... both of you I think, can relate to this a bit more than most."

I nodded my head, and I could feel Kat's grip on my shoulder tighten.

"I drove straight home and locked myself in my bedroom. I had never felt a fear like I had that day. Katherine, your father came home, and I refused to open the door. I think he eventually assumed it was pregnancy hormones or something. But I stayed in that room for hours sobbing and hiding under my blanket like a child. It was then I decided to open that letter."

She looked at Kat and asked her to open the safe and bring her the letter. Kat silently let go of my shoulder and walked over to the closet. A minute later she came back and handed the letter to her mother.

"Let me read this to you," she said.

To whom it may concern:

I fear I cannot address this letter to anyone in particular as I do not know when or by whom it will be read. I only hope that it is being read by some descendant of mine in a time period in which this letter serves as nothing but historical information, which has no effect on their life.

My name is Edgar Ludwig Stein. For many years, I was the butler and head of staff at the Villa Ortenberg estate. When my employer, Ida Mansfeld, left the estate for the last time, she left me several strict instructions to ensure that, in her passing, the estate would end up in the hands of the proper heir. In addition to that, she also requested that I take a child to raise as my own.

Jeanine Ida Stein, my beloved daughter. She is not my daughter in blood. However, I formally adopted her and raised her as if she was my own. The fact of her bloodline is a matter in which Ida Mansfeld had sworn me to secrecy. It was her belief that the bloodline alone could define who she became. I have learned this to be untrue. I have loved and cared for Jeanine and watched her grow up to be loving, caring, and respectful in her own right. For that reason, I am writing this. To explain the circumstances in which I was entrusted to care for her and her own true heritage.

During my tenure at the Villa, I had much interaction with both Ida and her former husband Samuel. Samuel was a despicable being. He seemed to live only for his own benefit. He only came to the Villa, in the later years, to drink and wreak havoc. It was on one of these nights when he sought the company of a female. Lucinda Mary Rosenberg was a maid at the Villa. She became his victim that evening, as he forced her to be his companion for the night.

Being an unwed, soon-to-be mother whose only employ was that of an estate soon to be shuttered, she had no option but to give the child up. This was when, at the request of Ida, I adopted her child. She lived only knowing me as her father and the lie that her mother had passed in childbirth. The truth of the matter is that she was born of Muller blood.

Please understand the reasons for which I kept this truth silent. Samuel was an evil man, and I sought to break that curse. Even though Muller blood runs through your veins, I believe the love and compassion in which you were raised overshadows that.

Today, I shuttered the Villa for the foreseeable future. In that act, I left a token reaffirming my vow to the estate. Enclosed in this letter is the same token for you, my descendant. It is to be a reminder of the vow I made to you to protect you from the evil of that home and the Muller bloodline. I lived my life serving first the Villa and then Jeanine. In both rights, my purpose was to protect from the evil that lurks around every corner. Let this token serve as a reminder that I am always there protecting you.

Love Always,

Edgar.

She folded up the letter and handed it to Kat.

"Katherine, the token he spoke of is the penny I gave you. While I admit, I was far too logically minded to submit to the ideas of curses and ghosts, there was a power I felt at the Villa, unlike anything I have ever experienced. There is no doubt in my mind that it was nothing but pure evil. That night, when I held the penny in my hand, I felt peace. That is why I kept it with you throughout your life," she said.

"Mother, what difference does any of this make anymore?" Kat asked.

"Logically nothing. You are my daughter. You are exactly who you should be. Just as I was. I saw evil at the Villa that day. I fear that there is something there that knows the truth of our bloodline."

She looked over at me for a moment, then continued.

"James, your friend said he felt a connection between Katherine and the Villa. Is this correct?"

"Yes, it is," I replied.

"There you have it. This is our connection. I know not what it means or the effect it will have on anything. But it is there, and I fear it cannot be denied or hidden on a piece of paper any longer. James, you were sent here to right the wrongs of the past. Please do your part and lift this curse which runs through our veins."

After we finished the conversation with Kat's mom, we

went downstairs to the kitchen. For the longest time, we just sat there not talking. Her swollen eyes were just staring off into the distance. I tried to decide what I was feeling. The fact was, I cared for Kat no matter what her last name was.

"You know, none of that matters, right?" I looked into her eyes.

She looked back at me shaking her head. Her eyes looked confused.

"How can you say that?" she asked.

"Because nothing in that conversation changes who you are or what you mean to me. I met you and knew nothing about you, and I was attracted to you... the you that is sitting here. Nothing changes that."

"Tell that to David!" she snapped.

I stood up and grabbed her hand, pulling her up.

"I will tell him that, and you know what, you will be there with me. Let's go and tell him that now."

"I can't," she said.

"You can't, or you won't?" I asked.

She just stood there staring at me. She was clearly on the verge of tears again.

"You don't understand Jim...," she started.

"No, you don't understand. I don't care what David says or thinks. I want to show you that. I want you to see that it doesn't matter to me. If your presence angers spirits or whatever, so be it. There is no point in me doing any of this if you are not with me."

She sat back down and buried her head in her hands.

"Kat, I care about you. Hell, I love you. I need you with me. I need you to stand next to me through this no matter what that means." I put my hands on her shoulders. "Look, I am driving to Tennessee to meet with him. I cannot force you to come, but I want you to. I want you there with me so we can deal with this together. Besides, it gives us a hell of a drive where we can talk this all out."

I sat down next to her and gently grabbed her hand. She looked up at me sadly.

"Please come with me, Kat."

14

AFTER SOME TIME, Kat reluctantly agreed to come with me. She went upstairs to pack and clean up, and shortly after that, we hit the road. The first hour was excruciating. We sat in silence, with her blankly staring out the window. What concerned me most was that I really had no clue why she was reacting so strongly about any of this.

I teetered back and forth from being mad at her to being mad at myself. On one hand, I was still completely pissed at myself over what I'd said to her earlier. Sure, I might have been rough in my conversation with her, but the part that really pissed me off was that I dropped the 'L' word. Hell, I said it a couple times even. It wasn't that I didn't mean it. It was that I'd said it. I remembered how a friend had once told me the loneliest feeling in the world was to say that and to not have it said back to you. Just as I would start to feel sorry for myself, anger at her would kick in. I mean fuck, she could at the very least respond with something, or even acknowledge that I said it in the first place. Just when I would be done condemning her, then I would look over at her sitting there.

It broke my heart to see her like that. So completely upset, and the best I could do at consoling her was to keep my mouth shut. I hated overthinking shit like that. That was one of the things I liked about her in the first place. I had always just been me around her. With her, I never over-thought anything. We just kinda fit together without thought. Yet, here I sat.

We had just turned onto I-65 and had what felt like a million miles to a drive south with absolutely nothing to distract me. Kat hadn't moved. The silence was killing me. I weighed my options, which were minimal as I really sucked at dealing with stuff like that. I could turn on some really angry music, or I could try talking to her. Granted, talking to her was the scariest option, especially in my current mind-set. I could see myself lashing out at her, saying too much again, or something else. Really, that option seemed just plain stupid... and was probably exactly why it was the option I chose.

"I'm worried about you Kat," I said while I placed my hand on her leg.

She closed her eyes and slowly shifted in the seat until she was looking at me.

"You know...you can talk to me," I stated.

"What do you want me to say, Jim?" she asked.

"I just want you to let me in. Even if I can't help, maybe just saying it would make you feel better. I just want to know what is going on."

"I just care about you, okay?" She struggled to speak. "I care about you, and I don't want to hurt you."

My heart dropped. I was convinced the next sentence out of her mouth was going to be something about being friends. Jeez. I didn't know how I would survive another eight hours of driving with her if she was going to say that.

"Holy shit, are you seriously breaking it off with me right now?" I blurted.

"Stop! That isn't what this about," she said. "Look, it's just been rough with my mom, then all this stuff with the house and that letter. I mean, think about it. Everything everybody has been focused on is in the past, and I am directly connected to that past in a pretty shitty way. Then there is you. You come out of nowhere into my life, and yet I feel like I have been with you forever. I wasn't supposed to meet someone at the will reading. I was supposed to hand the cursed house over and be done. But it's you, and no matter what I do, you are there with me in my heart."

Now she was crying again. I was pretty sure I was about to cry. I focused on the road as it was the only way I knew to keep my composure.

"I don't care about the house, not if it is going to upset you like this," I said.

"That's what you don't see. You can't. You cannot escape it. Listen to my mom, hell my whole family. The house is cursed. My ticket out was finally passing it along. Not only did I mess that up, but I tied you to it. If I had any clue..."

"Any clue of what?" I didn't give her a chance to respond. "It doesn't matter. You did exactly what you needed to do. I get this house has been hanging over your family's heads, but it isn't going to hang over mine. It's a house. I am not going to let it take me down. I will fight it, even if I have to burn the fucking place down, and I am sure as hell not going to let a house come between you and me."

She stopped crying and looked at me with hopeful eyes, grabbing my hand.

"Seriously, you think a stupid curse is gonna keep me down?" I smiled.

"I hope you're right, Jim."

Following that conversation, I gave up on thinking. I didn't know if she loved me or not, and I couldn't think any more about it. I was curious about the way she spoke, as if there was some master plan that I'd stepped into. It was all just too much for me to wrap my head around. I just stopped thinking. I turned on the radio to break up the silence and then just tried to talk about nothing. The last thing I could handle was any more talk of the house or the curse or whatever.

It took a bit of time, but soon Kat loosened up. Eventually, we were just enjoying each other's company again like we had before. It still felt as though there was a cloud hanging over us. The way she'd spoken earlier unsettled me in a strange way. I began to wonder if there was something I didn't know about her, as if I had been too quick to trust her as much as I had. I fought to push those thoughts away. If anything, I knew that the only way questions like that would be answered was in time, and right now, I needed to try to hang on to what I had.

Soon, we were about halfway through the trip. The sun had set, and the road was wearing on me. I looked over at Kat, and despite the chipper turn our conversation had taken, she looked exhausted.

"I don't know about you," I said, "but I need a break from the road. Wanna stop off for something to eat?"

"Oh my God, I'm starving. But where are we even? Can we find a place to eat out here?"

"Well, I'm sure we can grab a blue plate special at the Flying J," I said.

"Wow, you really know how to show off for a girl," she laughed.

I turned off at the next exit and headed straight into the largest truck stop I could find. We pulled in and parked under the glow of a giant yellow billboard with red text that boasted Fireworks, Cigarettes, Adult Books.

"This should do the trick, I think," I said.

"Hmmm, so are we getting food, or just picking up enough fireworks to burn down that house?" she joked.

We walked in and took a seat in a brown vinyl booth. We silently thumbed through the menus. Kat dropped the menu on the table and reached across the table to grab my hand.

"I can't believe I'm ordering country fried steak at a truck stop," she said. "Should I post a picture of this meal online?"

"I guess that depends if you are washing it down with a proper sweet tea or not," I said.

Soon, we ordered. She looked over at me and let out a sigh.

"Okay look, I know this has been a rough topic, but if I am going to be there with David tomorrow, you gotta update me on what's going on," she said.

"Yeah, I s'pose I owe you that much," I said, trying to lighten the mood, "but if this conversation means you are gonna freak out on me again, you are getting the bill for dinner."

We spent the next hour eating and talking through what had happened over the last two weeks. I told her everything I could remember. The only detail I failed to dive into was the part about David's concern about her and her need to choose a path. I did, however, mention the fact that he had been convinced, based upon the parlor, that she needed to be involved in this.

The conversation as a whole went very well. She didn't freak out or disengage at all, which was encouraging. It started to feel like we were pushing past everything.

By the time we got back to the truck and started driving,

everything seemed to be back to normal. She spent a lot of time apologizing for the break between us, but we also spent a lot of time just talking and being us.

After a couple hours the talking started to fade. I glanced over to see her sound asleep in her seat. Her hand was still holding mine. She was beautiful and completely at peace.

Still, there was an uncertainty nagging at me. I understood everything she said about why she walked away and I could justify all of it. Certainly, with her mom and everything else, this was stressful. What I couldn't rationalize though was why she just walked away without trying to talk to me about it all. There was something about it that was unsettling.

As the miles piled up, so did my apprehension. I couldn't qualify it or even come up with a reason why, but something was off. I felt it in my gut. I loved her, I cared about her, and I wanted more than anything to be with her, but she frightened me. She frightened me in a way I had never felt.

I had finally shoved all those feelings aside by the time we got close to Erwin, Tennessee.

I pulled my truck into the Mountain Inn at just after one in the morning. The parking lot was dimly lit by a few lamps, and it was completely quiet and peaceful. As I put the truck in park, Kat woke up. She stretched and rubbed her eyes.

"We made it. How was your nap?" I asked, kissing her on the forehead.

"Sorry, I didn't mean to sleep," she said.

"It's okay. You had a long day," I replied. "I suppose we should check in. Oh, you know I didn't know you were coming with when I got the reservation. So, I only booked the one room."

"Mmmm, I wouldn't want it any other way," she replied sitting up to give me a kiss.

I woke up the next morning to the sun shining through the sheer curtains of the hotel room. Kat lay next to me appearing completely peaceful. The sheet was wrapped around her body like a giant snake leaving only one leg and one arm exposed. I put my hand on the soft skin of her thigh and drew closer to her, giving her a kiss on her cheek. She sighed and stretched a little before kissing me. We were both wide awake by the time the alarm went off.

"Do we really have to get up?" she asked.

"Yeah, I think we do," I said, kissing her. "You know David. He will be texting me a hundred times a minute if we aren't there on time."

A half hour later, we were in the truck, driving to the address David had given me. We drove right through the main street of the quiet town. After turning down a side street, we pulled into the small parking lot of a one-story brick office building. The building was simple. It looked like it had been built in the seventies, and it had no markings on it saying that it was a business of any kind.

We walked up to the front door, carrying our to-go cups of hotel coffee. When we opened the door, there was a clang of a sleigh bell attached to the door. Seconds later, the interior door of the foyer opened, and there was David.

"Jim, I'm glad you could make it," he said, his eyes moving toward Kat with visible surprise. "Katherine, I didn't expect to see you today but welcome."

"Yeah, we figured we'd give you a surprise," I said.

He walked us into a large fluorescent-lit conference room.

"Welcome to the home of Murderous Mary!"

"Murderous Mary?" I asked. "Who is that?"

He waved his hand at me.

"You know I'm not gonna tell you. You gotta do your homework. Nothing to do with you... that I know of. It's a local thing. But don't go asking people in town about it. They will not take kindly to some Yankee bringing up that past."

"Um... okay, noted," I looked at Kat and shrugged my shoulders.

"It is a crazy story really, but I am obviously more into it than most given it was one of my first real cases. Anyway, have a seat." He motioned to the chairs surrounding the conference table.

We took our seats at the table. On the opposite side of the table was a massive whiteboard covering the entire wall. Taped on the whiteboard were several photos and lines connecting everything.

David sat down and took a seat across from us.

"Okay, Linda will be here in about an hour. I figured I would take this time to update you on what I've uncovered." He gestured to the whiteboard.

He spent the next half hour explaining everything. In the center of the board, was a crudely drawn cloud with a photo of the Cloudland Hotel. From there, there were several lines drawn across the board, connecting to other sections. Most had to do with other members of the 'Sovereign Lords'. Then, he got to the line drawn to Samuel. Next to the photo of Samuel was a photo of Ida. Underneath was a photo of a child, their child.

Most of it was a recap of what we already talked about in regard to his theory about Samuel killing the child. The child being of another father and so on. I wanted to tell him about Kat actually being Sam's descendant. I looked over at

Kat and held back. This was her story and I hoped she would bring it up.

David picked up a book and tossed it on the table. "This is what we have been looking for. Well, I mean it isn't black and white of course, but it at the very least tells me we are on the right path."

I picked up the book and started thumbing through it. It was old and looked to be written in German. I didn't recognize any of it, including the name of the author.

"I don't follow," I said. "What is this?"

"Okay, remember I said that we already know there is a shit ton of evil power at the Villa thanks to Sam? But there was another power there pushing against his. Like an equal but opposite power. So, it was time to look into Ida. This is my start." He picked up the book. "Long story short, I told you how Ida was in the social spotlight like no other? Just like today, you have paparazzi and all that stuff following celebrities. This is the 1930s version of that. Just after having her last child, she up and went overseas for like seven years. This book was written as an exposé...memoirs of her chauffeur while she was in Germany. Granted, like any exposé, it cannot be fully taken as the truth. There are certainly embellishments within this."

"Okay, so what did you find in there?" I asked.

"I don't speak German. So, I have only been able to translate a bit. But here, this is really interesting. It talks about him being required to drive her deep into the Black Forest where she would go off for days at a time. She would return like three or four days later no differently than if she had just gone to the market."

"Yeah, not following...so she liked to go hiking in the woods," I said.

"Jeez, did you ever take the time to learn anything about

history?" he shot back. "Okay okay, I'll dumb it down for you. The Black Forest in Germany is not like your local forest preserve. It has forever been the center point for many of the witchcraft practices in Europe. Think of it like Jerusalem for the black arts. On the surface, there is a lot of folk legend type stuff around areas of the forest, ghost stories and such. But to anyone who has truly studied witchcraft, much of what we know today originated in that forest. So, if even a shred of this exposé is true on that front, I fear our Ida was developing her own set of supernatural skills."

"So we are dealing with two ghosts then?" I asked. "That's fine, I think Ida likes me."

He leaned in and whispered in a suddenly serious tone. "It isn't ghosts that are the trouble. Ghosts are easy. It is almost certain that Ida is there as a ghost, but this is so much more. We are talking about demons, possession, and curses here."

Just then, we were interrupted by the clanging of the sleigh bell on the door.

"Excuse me," David said as he stood up.

Moments later David led a woman into the conference room.

"Jim, Katherine, this is Linda," he announced.

15

Linda walked into the conference room and greeted us. She looked like she was about sixty years old. She was round, short, and had long gray hair, pulled back into a ponytail. She had a brightly colored scarf wrapped around her. She bobbed back and forth as she walked in and sat down. She remained silent for a few moments as her eyes scanned the room.

"James, how great it is to meet with you," she said warmly. "And I believe this is Katherine. What a pleasant surprise."

"Thank you for agreeing to work with us on this..." I started.

Linda held up her hand gesturing for me to stop.

"Please, do not speak. I am trying to get a feel for you both."

She slowly continued to look back and fourth between Kat and I. There was a stillness in the air as we anticipated her next words.

"Before I get started, just to minimize interruption, does anyone have any questions?" she asked.

"I am just curious as to why we are doing this here as opposed to having you come to the house," Kat replied. "I would think it would be easier to feel everything going on at the location."

"After visiting the house, I realized there was a tremendous amount of power at work there," David said. "I set this up here so that we could take a slower approach and really understand everything we are feeling. When there is so much power concentrated in one place, it is often difficult to break it down and really tell what is all at play. Here we can understand the foundation to help us when we go to the house."

"Have you brought the items, James?" Linda asked.

I reached into my backpack, pulled out a folder, and slid it across the table to Linda. The folder contained both the letter left on the mantel by the butler and Ida's letter that was presented to me with the will. As David had instructed, I had to bring something related to the house and the people so that Linda could leverage the residual power of it.

Linda carefully opened the folder and laid the two letters out before her. She silently looked them over. A moment later, her head jolted up, and she looked frustrated.

"There is more here," she said, giving Kat an icy stare. "I feel that you have brought with you another item connected to this house. Please, show me what you have."

Kat glanced at me with a look of confusion on her face.

"I'm sorry, I didn't realize I was supposed to bring anything."

"My dear, it isn't what you were supposed to bring," Linda said. "It is what you *did* bring. I can feel there is more here,"

Kat didn't say a word. She reached into her pocket and retrieved her keys. She took the penny off her key ring and tossed it to Linda. There was an unspoken feeling of trepidation in her motion. She looked over at me.

"This was my great-great-grandfather's, is this what you were talking about?" Kat said.

Linda held it tightly in her palm and closed her eyes before responding.

"Yes, this is exactly what I felt. Thank you."

She pulled out a worn, leather-bound notebook and a pen, setting it on the table. She looked over at David.

"Let us begin," she said solemnly.

Linda closed her eyes and gently moved her hands to each item and then began writing in her notebook. I looked over at Kat, who seemed to be concerned, and shrugged my shoulders. We spent the next hour in silence watching Linda. Not a word was spoken. Linda offered no reaction at all. She closed her eyes and rested her hands on one of the items for a few minutes and then wrote in the notebook. This process repeated multiple times. I caught David a few times looking distracted. He would look back at the whiteboard behind him and then back at the letters.

Finally, Linda closed the notebook with a loud snap that echoed in the silent room.

"We are finished," Linda proclaimed.

She gracefully slid the penny across the table to Kat and then carefully put the letters back in the folder and slid them across the table to me. David nodded and then looked at Kat and me.

"Okay, we need to give Linda some time to process everything and reflect," David said to us. "Please come outside with me,"

David stood up and opened the door showing us out. He walked outside leaving Linda in the conference room by herself.

"Whoa, that was intense!" David said as we got outside.

"What was that?" I asked. "What is going on?"

"It is just her process man. It takes a lot out of her. We just gotta give her some time to work it all over, and then she will tell us what she saw."

"I don't know what is going on, but that was kinda creepy," Kat said. "And what was that with my penny? How did she know?"

David put his hand on Kat's shoulder. "Do not worry. They are all pieces of the puzzle. She is the best there is at this. She will see everything we need, whether we want her to or not."

"So what? Are we just supposed to sit out here until she is ready and calls us back or what?"

"Nah man, it will be a while. Why don't you guys go grab some lunch for a bit? I will call you when she is ready. Head to the Dari Ace down the road a piece. Get a taste of Erwin."

We agreed and walked over to my truck. As the truck started up, I looked over at Kat.

"You alright?" I asked.

"I'm fine. I just...it's just... this unnerves me a bit. The fact that she knew about the penny was just unreal."

She looked up at me with a bewildered look that I hadn't seen before.

"I can't understand it, but there is something to it," I said.

"Do you think we should bring up the fact that I am really a descendant of Sam's?"

"I thought about mentioning it in the beginning, but I didn't. I guess I was kinda scared about how you'd react to it if I did."

She squeezed my hand and looked at me with a soft smile.

"Thank you," she said. "But I'm fine. It's like you said, I

am me, no matter what my lineage says, and I want to solve all this too."

I gave her a kiss.

"Maybe we should hold that card back a little," I said.

"What do you mean?"

"I mean, let's not bring it up. If Linda can identify something, sure, we'll confirm it. But right now, I am kinda curious to see if she can."

"Are you serious?"

"Hell, yeah. Look, I don't think it is doing any harm if we hold it. If they can identify it, great. Besides, it would be kinda fun to throw out an explanation for why David was so confused by if you were dark or light."

After a few hours, Kat and I were called back to the office. We walked back in unsure of what was going to come out. But we were together, and comfortable. The unknown didn't seem as frightening as it had before.

We sat down and were ready for David and Linda to tell us what they had learned.

"Okay, we are getting somewhere now," David said, wasting no time. "There are plenty of gaps, but I think we understand the basics of what happened there."

"Let's start with Samuel," Linda said. "As you know, he is at the root of many torments. From what I've learned, his motivation was purely the pursuit of power. Power he had with the KGC. The problem with that was this power was not immediate. The KGC was hell-bent on taking over the country in a very long game. In order to maintain this power, the most important thing for him was to produce an heir... an heir worthy of his seat of power. Essentially, an heir he could trust to lead the new world.

"The trouble all really stemmed from Ida. Ida was not a woman who could be controlled. Her marriage to Samuel was the last decision she made under someone else's influence. Here you have a strong-minded woman married to a power-hungry tyrant whom she does not love. So, she stood up for herself."

Over the next hour, Linda explained how throughout the strained marriage Ida fell in love and conceived a child with her lover. Samuel Jr. was their offspring. Samuel was enraged and killed the child. This action created a rift between the two like never before. Ida became hell-bent on keeping herself separated from Sam in every way. Sam was of course still driven by needing an heir.

At this point, Linda and David still did not know the details, but Ida was forced to conceive children. She was subdued via black magic and raped by Sam. Additionally, Sam, enraged by her conception of Sam Jr., put a curse on her and her home. He made her life a living hell, until she finally conceived a son for him. Shortly following that, she devoted all of her energy to doing everything she could to separate herself from Sam and keep the house from falling into his possession or even into the possession of her own children. She fled the country. Upon returning, she used witchcraft of her own to fight back. Ultimately, that house had become a battleground for the supernatural.

"Which brings me to Katherine," she finally said.

I felt my fists clench beneath the table when she said this. She looked directly at Kat with a very emotionless stare. It unsettled me a lot. I wanted to jump from my seat and just walk out with Kat. Yet, a part of me also really wanted to hear what she had to say.

"While I can say for certain there is a lot of energy around you in relation to this house, I cannot place it. Your great-great-grandfather, the butler... well he was in love with Ida. From what I can tell, that love lasted all of his life.

Despite that, his role in the elements that plague the estate today seems to be minor. I believe he was both aware and understood what was happening and did everything he could to assist Ida in her activities. Yet, these curses are really between Ida and Sam."

I could see Kat smirk. I was impressed that Linda could indeed pick up on the fact that there is more then what was on the surface. At the same time I was hesitant to buy into everything. After-all we knew that Kat was really a descendant of Sam's, a point Linda could not see.

"The curses are certainly between Ida and Sam," she repeated, "but you are far more than a bystander. I wish I had a clearer understanding of how or why, but right now, I really do not."

Kat looked like she was about to speak and spill her little piece of news on this when the ever-eager David jumped in.

"There is one more thing I discovered," David said.

His voice hung in the air. I felt as though I was going to be dealt a crushing blow.

"One thing we have not been able to understand as of yet is the question of why you," he said staring down at me. "Obviously there is a lot of supernatural activity, leaving many possibilities. Yet, as of now, we have not been able to see anything that directly addresses this question. We know Ida was hell-bent on making sure Sam would not get the house. But why you?"

"Well, I guess that is the ten-thousand dollar question," I replied.

"Right, but then while Linda was going over the letter you brought, something caught my eye. The combination to the safe."

"What, you think there is a clue in there?" I asked.

"No, probably not. I am not concerned with the safe,

more the combination. Well, that combined with her cryptic words saying the numbers should mean something to you."

"I'm not really following. Why would any of this shit make sense to me?"

"Read me the combination!" he demanded.

I pulled the folder open and retrieved the letter.

"2, 27, 4," I said, still confused.

David followed by writing the combination on the whiteboard. Then underneath he rewrote it. '02/27/04'. Underneath he wrote February 27, 1904.

"That is the birthdate of Samuel Leopold... eh we'll just call him Sam Jr.," he said.

"Okay, isn't that how people make combinations, important dates?" I asked.

"Yes, of course! But people don't expect those dates to make sense to other people. Random people decades later. Not to mention it is the birth date of her child, the one child conceived by someone other than Sam. The one child conceived out of love. The one child she would wish to leave her estate to!"

"So, you are telling me I am her love child?" I asked.

"No. I mean you have a mom, a dad, a lineage of your own at least in the physical sense," he said. "Right now, this is just something to look into. I find it odd, to say the least."

I sat there shocked. I really didn't know what to say.

"Look, it is just something to look into," he repeated.

I noticed Kat wearing a troubled expression. I knew what she was thinking, and I knew it was about to shake up this whole conversation.

"So tell me, in all that you have seen, were you able to tell that I have no blood connection to the butler?" she asked.

Both David and Linda stared at her.

"What do you mean?" David asked. "You told me.... The letter, the penny..."

"Yes, he raised my great-grandmother and was a father to her, but my bloodline is through Samuel!" she yelled.

Silence hung in the air. I couldn't help but smile. Kat had taken the 'Fuck you' attitude and just dropped an atom bomb on the room.

"I have a letter," she said. "Apparently, Sam raped some poor maid at the estate. Edgar was asked by Ida to adopt the child and raise her as his own. Which he did."

David's' eyes were wild. Linda sat silently looking at us. After a few moments, Linda stood up slamming her hands on the table.

"Of course!" she yelled. "This explains everything!"

"What exactly does this explain?" I asked.

"This is why you have such a confusing presence in relation to the house. After holding the penny, I saw Edgar, who seemingly plays a minor role in all of this. Yet to you, both David and I felt an incredibly strong connection! You may be the key that unlocks this whole story! Tell me, do you have anything else personal from Edgar beyond the penny?"

"Uh... well, I have the letter he wrote explaining that we are of Samuel's blood," she said.

"I will need to see that. That will help me connect with Edgar but also hopefully fill in the missing pieces with Samuel."

After a bit more conversation, we decided to end the day's session and meet up again the next morning. Kat and I headed back to the hotel and clean up before going to dinner. Once we got there, she went to take a shower, and I laid on the bed. I grabbed my phone and started looking at the missed emails and calls from the day. There was one from the foundation contractor that caught my eye.

"Call me!" the text read.

I immediately dialed his number.

"Hey, this is Jim. What's going on?"

"For starters, one of my guys is in the hospital, barely clinging to life!"

"What happened?" I asked.

"Randy was attacked by a wolf on your property is what fucking happened. I heard the scream. By the time I got there, the wolf was gone. Randy was lying there in a pool of his own blood, babbling nonsense."

"I'm sorry. What can I do?"

"I dunno. Sorry, I'm just pretty shaken up by it. I don't mean to take it out on you. Randy will be alright according to the doctors. He might look a little worse, but he got lucky."

"I get it. If you are calling me to tell me you guys are done there, I completely understand given this all."

"Fuck no we aren't leaving. When my crew signs up for a job, we finish it."

"Well at the same time, if there is anything else I can do, just say the word."

"On that note, you mind giving me a heads up when you send other crews out to this place? When we rolled up this morning, there was another crew here working on the interior."

"That's impossible. The only other one I've even contracted is the roof and windows, but they are not coming out until you are done. Who was it?"

"I have no idea. Never seen them before. There were names on the trucks. I asked to speak to their foreman, and a guy named Fred came out. He said you hired him, and they needed to start working on the rooms."

"I have no idea who that could be. Certainly no one I hired."

"I told him to leave until I have word from you. He was pissed, but they cleared out."

"Shit man, I don't have any clue."

"Hopefully it was just some eager crew you started talking to that got the wrong idea."

"Listen, I'm in Tennessee. I'll be back on Monday. I know you guys aren't working tomorrow, but is there any chance you could keep an eye on the place for me? I'll make it worth your time."

We talked for a few more minutes. We agreed to an amount I would pay him for keeping an eye on things. I also agreed to cover any of Randy's medical expenses that the insurance didn't cover. I felt horrible about the accident and wanted to do anything I could to help.

I hung up the phone. There was a terrible feeling in my gut. I felt responsible for having someone hurt there, hurt by a wolf which matched every one of those damn stories. The rogue crew that showed up concerned me just as much. I knew damn well that I hadn't hired anyone else. I couldn't even imagine what crew would even want to go out there. Just then, Kat came out of the bathroom. She looked at me and immediately could tell something was bothering me.

"What's going on?" she asked. "You okay?"

"I don't know where to start. I just talked to the foreman of the crew at the house. One of his guys got torn up by a wolf while out there. On top of that, some other crew showed up today, saying I hired them to work on the interiors. Thing is, I haven't hired anyone else."

Her face went blank. She just stared at me for a second with a look of shock.

"A wolf, like those stories you were telling me about?"

"Yeah, same damn place on the property too. I mean, I guess it doesn't have to be supernatural. There's a lot of forest. It could be a real wolf protecting its home."

"Hold up. You had a crew there? I mean, I didn't know you hired anyone."

"That happened while... well you know," I stammered. "Anyway, yeah, I hired a couple crews. Right now, a crew is working on the foundation, which should be complete soon. Then, the roof and window people. But that's all I've hired so far. Certainly, no one for the interiors, because the foundation needed to be secured and finished first in case anything shifted."

She was pacing in the hotel room. "So, who was it? What were they doing there?"

"Hell, I don't know. It sounds like my foundation guys ran them out pretty quick. It's just weird. I never even thought about security at that place in the shape it is now. Beyond that, do I call animal control? There aren't exterminators for wolves that I know of."

I started realizing how odd it was that her focus was more on the work crew than the guy that almost got killed by a wolf. I was about to mention it when I looked at her pacing the room in her towel with her long, wet hair. I became completely distracted from the conversation. I walked up behind her and put my arms around her, kissing her wet shoulder. It was only a few moments before any thought of the house disappeared.

16

THE NEXT MORNING, we arrived at the office feeling much more relaxed. Everything between Kat and I seemed to have taken a light-hearted direction. David and Linda, on the other hand, did not seem to be sharing this light-heartedness. Linda, especially, looked as serious as ever. We took our seats. Instead of waiting for her to speak, I took the lead.

"Listen, I know we are supposed to go through what Linda saw yesterday. But before we do, I need to bring something up."

"What is it?" David asked.

"So, I did some research on my own before reaching out to you. Everything I came across talked about a wolf on the property. I got a call last night from my foreman telling me one of his guys at the house was attacked by a wolf. Before we go any further, is this all natural? Some wolf that has a den or whatever in the woods there, or is this related to all this crap?"

David silently looked at Linda. A few moments later, he nodded to her and turned his eyes to us.

"Based upon everything we know about the property

now, it would be foolish to assume this is a natural occurrence," David said. "Look, we have plenty to talk about in regards to this today, but I will cut to the chase for you here. Remember when I was out there and described the darkness of the property in contrast to the light of the house? We are certain that you have a couple entities at this place. There is Ida, protecting the house. But the outside... that seems to be occupied by a demon. I am certain that the demon is our friend Sam. And if you would do your research on demons, you would know they can take many forms, including one of a wolf."

"Wonderful!" I replied "This is just getting better and better."

"Wait a second," Kat interjected. "How are you referring to Sam as a demon? I thought demons were separate entities from people."

"Traditionally, you are correct. But do you know much about the concept of a Faustian Bargain? Essentially a deal with the devil. You know Robert Johnson, Ralph Machio, going to the crossroads and all that?"

"Yeah, but aren't those deals just getting what you want on earth before burning in hell?" Kat asked.

"Yes, again in the traditional lore anyway. However traditional lore only introduces the subject in broad strokes. Based upon what I understand of Samuel's role in the KGC, I wouldn't hesitate to believe he'd struck his own accord with the devil. I think it goes beyond that. I feel that he didn't simply strike a deal to get what he wanted in life. His bargain involved doing the devil's bidding in life and in return he would be stripped of his humanity and be able to take the role of a true demon."

"I feel like we are fighting over titles here," I said, trying to break up David's lesson in demonology. "Ghost, demon, hexes, curses, whatever... I am less concerned about what we call it than how we end it all."

"Jim, this is only the beginning. I fear the powers at your home are far stronger than we can comprehend at this point. Let's have Linda explain what she was able to see."

She began to explain her visions more in-depth. Yesterday, we heard about the basics. The who and what of everything. Today, it was clearly going deeper than that.

"There are many types of spells one can cast. I believe here we have a combination of protective spells and curses. Anyone who casts spells is equally schooled in both of these sides. One who casts curses must also cast protection spells to preserve themselves. We know curses were cast on both Ida and the property by Sam. Additionally, Ida cast spells of her own to protect herself and her home.

"So, can't all spells be reversed?" I asked.

"Well, yes and no. Many can be, but they require knowledge of the spell. Others, while they cannot be reversed, can theoretically be overpowered by a more powerful protection spell."

"But they are all dead," I pointed out. "Isn't there like a statute of limitations on this shit, or at least an open door to make casting a protection spell easier?"

Linda didn't respond. She and David just looked at each other. I could tell what came next was not going to be good news.

"James, these curses and spells, well they are just part of what is at play. If we walked into the estate in 1929, they would all work no differently than they do today. But now, in addition to these spells and curses, there is more."

"Okay, I'm listening," I said. "What else is going on?"

"This brings us back to our lesson in demonology,"

David said, "where Samuel's presence, which has taken the form of a demon, comes in."

"So, my house is cursed ten times over, and it is haunted?" I asked.

"Well, to put it bluntly, yes," David said.

The two then went on to explain how, they believe certain aspects of the house to be haunted. In short, it was going to be nothing short of a miracle to make the house peaceful. Honestly, they were beginning to make it sound like the estate sat at the center of Hell City, Hell.

"But we have an advantage here," Linda said.

"Really, what's that?" I asked. "Because it's sounding pretty damn bleak to me."

She looked over at Kat.

"Katherine is our advantage," she said.

"Hold up, I understand that you think I can help because of my bloodline, but what does that really mean?" Kat asked.

"My dear, you have a connection to Edgar and the blood of Samuel," Linda explained. "Both of those things give us the upper hand."

"Well, at least I got something going for me," Kat replied, "but that doesn't help me understand."

"It isn't just that. The connection with Edgar to this property is especially intimate. He was far more than a hired hand. He is directly involved in all of this. Yesterday I spoke of his connection with Ida. There is an incredible softness in Edgar when it comes to Ida. But there is also a definite connection when it comes to the demonic side of Samuel. With Samuel, his connection is dark. I feel he was more on the front line of fighting Samuel than anyone knows.

"With you having the connection to Sam, he may respond differently to you. Just like Ida's protection spells.

You both mentioned how it appeared that someone had tried unsuccessfully to enter Ida's parlor. For James though, the door opened freely. Ida responds to James. In that same way, it is possible that Sam will respond differently to you."

"I fear there is one more thing we need to talk about," David said cautiously.

"Okay," I replied nervously, not sure if I was able to tolerate more bad news.

"So you understand, a lot of what we know about the history here comes from extensive research Linda and I have put into the KGC," David declared. "So, while all of this happened in the past, the KGC is very much an ongoing living breathing entity,"

"What do you mean?" I asked.

"We don't have a clue where they are, who they are, or how powerful they may be, but we know they are here. Many knights passed down their knighthood from generation to generation. They have been able to maintain an underground existence. But go poking around, and you will find them."

"Most people assumed they disappeared or disbanded," Linda added. "Our experience has taught us otherwise. One thing we think is that it's an unorganized group. The Sovereign Lords fell apart, leaving the knights little objective."

"Fell apart?" I asked. "Wasn't keeping it together Sam's focus?"

"Well, you can't always get what you want." David laughed at his own statement.

"You're right up to a point," Linda explained. "The problem was that each of the Lords needed to have an heir willing to take the reins of an organization they had no involvement in. This proved to be far more difficult than simply having a child. Samuel himself did eventually get his son. Sadly, he was less than a suitable heir. He ended up spending the second half of his life committed to a sanitarium. The story of the other Lords wasn't much different."

"Today we know nothing of their leadership," David said. "We do know there are plenty of knights sworn to protect."

"Protect what?" I asked.

"We don't know. Some assume massive caches of gold. Others assume nothing more than the sheer secret of their existence. Point is, that they're out there."

"Okay, but how does that play into me?" I asked.

"We don't know if it does or if it ever will. This is more of a warning. History tells us that it's a group that lets nothing stand in the way of their objectives. This estate was owned and fought for by one of their final leaders. It only stands to reason that there is the potential of there being something there of interest to the Knights."

"Yeah well, they had, what, eighty years to go in there and take whatever they wanted. I'll take your warning, but forgive me if I don't seem too concerned."

"James, tell me, has anyone approached you about the estate?" Linda asked, refusing to acknowledge my sarcasm. "An odd phone call? A stranger lurking in the shadows?"

"Nah, not really," I said. I looked over at Kat whose eyes were wide. Then I remembered talking to my mother. "Wait! I haven't, but when I told my mom about the estate, she kinda freaked out. She told me about someone calling her after I was born. Whoever it was told her that this inheritance would be coming, and she needed to make sure I didn't accept it. But jeez, that was right after I was born."

"That was them! It doesn't confirm that they are looking

for you now, but there is something with that house worthy of their interest."

"Look the point is we don't know to what extent any of this matters," David warned. "Just be careful and be vigilant. I am especially concerned with my knowledge of how many of these protection spells work. See, Ida's parlor was protected for everyone but you. It is very plausible that you, being the heir, broke the spell. I don't know for sure, but I think it is best that we assume that Ida's parlor now sits unprotected."

We wrapped up the conversation and were saying our goodbyes when David asked if he could speak with me in his office for a minute. I followed him to the small dingy room.

"Listen, remember when I was at the house, and I asked you to go into that room alone?" he asked.

"Oh yeah, I totally forgot about that."

"Okay, do it soon. We know Ida is there, and I have a feeling she will show you something if you do. If my hunch is right on this, we could learn exactly what we need to do to reclaim your home."

"Alright, I will do it as soon as we get back. I have to go out there anyway to apologize personally to the work crew."

We said our goodbyes, and Kat and I got in the truck. As I started driving out, she had a confused look.

"This whole thing confuses me" she said. "I don't even know what to think."

I leaned in and kissed her on the cheek.

"That whole thing with Linda speaking about Edgar's connection was hard to follow," she admitted. She grabbed my hand and squeezed it in hers. "I thought she was talking about my connection to him, but then it sounded more like his involvement with Sam."

"Well, he did end up raising Sam's child, so maybe there was some confrontation that took place around that... So do you believe everything they said?"

"I'm not sure. I would have bought into everything she said one hundred percent if she was able to call out that little secret. But I'm the one that blurted out that my blood-line goes back to Sam. Still, she was able to see a lot. I kinda want to play this out and see what else we can learn. I want to know more about Edgar. I feel like there is something missing in all of this."

"Well if there's one thing I'm completely sure of, there is a whole shit ton of stuff that we're missing. All of this, combined with the research and everything else I learned, is clearly only the tip of the iceberg when it comes to what all happened there."

After a long drive, we finally arrived back home. I dropped Kat off at her mom's and took a nice long nap. When I awoke, I realized that I needed to tend to everything that happened while I was in Tennessee. I needed to get to the house, and I needed to meet with the foreman.

I felt driven to first go to the hospital and speak with the man who was attacked. It was odd. I didn't know the man. I'd probably never even seen him. Still, speaking with him was my first priority. With only his name and the hospital, I began to question this decision. Part of it felt wrong, like I was invading a personal space I had no business in. But that feeling didn't overcome the need I felt. I needed to look him in the eyes. I needed to hear his story in his words.

I arrived at the hospital and was directed to the proper section. There, a nurse greeted me and informed me that the man had been released from Intensive Care a day ago. She directed me to his room. Inside, a large man sat in bed changing the channels on the TV. He had bandages on every part of his body. I took a deep breath and knocked on the open door as I stepped in.

"Hi, look you don't know me personally, but I wanted to come here and apologize in person for what happened. I'm Jim. It was my property you were working on."

The man set down the remote control and stared at me intently.

"You're James," he stated curtly.

"Yeah, call me Jim...again I cannot tell you how sorry I am that this happened."

"Look, if you are here expecting some sort of thank you for the medical bills, you can leave now. I am not taking a dime from you. I want to be as far away from you and that property as possible!" His eyes narrowed as he stared me down.

I was completely taken back. "Please, I mean no harm. I see it as only right, considering that wolf was on my property."

"Wolf?" he snarled. "You think this was a wolf? What I saw only looked like a wolf. I have just one thing to say to you and then I beg you to stay the fuck away from me."

"What is it?"

"I was given a message for you, a message from the so-called wolf. Bring me what I need or this is only the beginning!" The man's face was so still it looked like it was etched in stone.

"I'm sorry," I replied bewildered. "I don't know what you are talking about."

"That's the message I was given. Now I've passed it on. Please leave." He picked up the remote tethered to the bed and pressed a button, his eyes never breaking their stare on me.

I was frozen. I knew I had to leave, but I felt I needed to

say something else. As I struggled to find my words, the man reached to the IV tube in his arm and ripped it out in one swift motion. Blood oozed to the surface of his arm and started to spurt out. In a matter of moments, blood was running down his arm. Just then, a nurse walked in. She saw the blood and immediately pushed me out of the room.

I staggered out of the hospital in a daze. I'd never seen anything like that and couldn't even comprehend it all. I decided to head to the house, hoping to have better luck talking to the foreman.

I didn't have to look hard to find him. As my truck pulled to the top of the driveway, he immediately stepped out of the tent set up outside the house and approached my truck.

After a hearty handshake and an exchange of greetings, he looked at me with a worried expression on his face.

"Jim, take a walk with me please." He paused looking over his shoulders at his busy crew. "I need to talk to you privately."

He led me down south of the house towards the pond. He didn't say a word. As we approached the pond, he turned and headed towards the forest that encroached on the west side of the pond.

"What's going on?" I asked.

He stopped dead in his tracks.

"Look, you gave me a hell of a job here with this house. I mean, it's enough work to keep my crew going for a month of solid work, and you have been very generous. You asked me to look after the place a bit and... well... I may have taken that a little far."

"And as I mentioned, I will pay you whatever you feel fair for that. I appreciate that more than you know."

He held up his hand telling me to stop talking. "Randy wasn't just a guy I hired. He was a friend. I've worked with him side by side for twenty years now. So, after what happened, I figured I knew one thing to lift his spirits and hopefully break him out of the shock of it all. I have hunted with Randy every year. So, I figured now I needed to hunt down that wolf and give him its pelt. Look, I know it ain't exactly legal, but I had to do it."

I took a deep breath, relaxing a bit. "I get it. No worries. As long as you don't get yourself busted, I really don't care."

"It isn't that. I can handle my own shit. Hell, I didn't really intend to tell you about that, but things kinda changed a bit."

"What do you mean?"

"Animals are pretty easy to track when you know what to look for. They leave a path everywhere. From footprints to scat. I've searched every damn inch of that forest there and haven't found the slightest hint of a wolf. That is odd, but what concerns me more is not what I didn't find, but what I *did* find.

"Just tell me. You can give me the backstory afterward."

He looked at me as he scratched his scraggly beard. "Tell you what, I'll do you one better and just show you. Here, follow me."

He walked closer to the wall of the forest. Barely even visible to my eye was what looked like a path into the forest. We entered and were immediately enveloped by the canopy of the trees. I could see the small path winding deeper into the woods.

"It's just up here." He grabbed my shoulder, stopping me. "Look, before we head in there... this is... well... pretty fucked up. Take that as my warning."

17

THE TRAIL LED to a clearing a few feet deeper into the woods. It was a circle about fifteen feet in diameter with nothing; no grass, no weeds and no trees. It was barren earth. As my eyes scanned the clearing, I realized it wasn't just barren, it was scorched. In the center, the ground was blackened as if there had been a massive bonfire there recently. The trees that surrounded the circle were also charred.

"What the hell is this?" I asked.

He looked at me and pointed to the far side of the circle. A beaten, yellow-handled shovel lay there. "I could offer some theories, but you better see for yourself first. I couldn't figure it out. The burn is fresh, but a fire this size could never be contained with all these trees around it. The flames would have been high enough for someone to notice, even way out here. With no ideas of my own, I decided to dig up some of the soil. Here, I covered it up now, but take a look." He approached a small area where I could see freshly disturbed dirt.

I picked up the shovel and started to remove the dirt.

After the loose soil on the top was removed, I heard the tip of the shovel hit something solid. I knelt down next to the hole and brushed away the remaining loose soil with my hand.

I saw what looked like a blackened tree branch. I grabbed it pulling it out of the hole. I realized it wasn't a branch but a bone. Startled, I threw it back into the hole and jumped up.

"To answer your next question, that isn't from a deer."

"You sure?" I asked, trying to compose myself.

"Jim, it isn't just one bone. You're standing on a fucking graveyard. It's like something out of a movie. Look around. I must've dug about fifty damn holes here. Every one of them was the same. I'd guess there are at least twenty to thirty bodies buried here... all human, all charred."

I just stood with my mouth agape, looking at the blackened bone sitting in that hole.

"I know this isn't you," he said. "I mean these are old, and you just got this place. I get it. I'm not gonna tell anyone. Christ, the last thing I need is to be interviewed by some cop asking me questions about what I was doing out here in the first place."

"Fuck me!" I yelled. "I need a drink!"

"Now that, I can help with." He pulled out a shiny flask from his pocket and handed it to me. "Keep it. You need it more than I do."

I unscrewed the cap and took a long swallow. "What the hell am I supposed to do now? How does one even call the police station and say 'Oh, by the way I have like 30 bodies buried on my property.'"

"You want my advice?" He grabbed the flask from my hand and took a sip before handing it back to me. "You better be ready when you make that call."

"What do you mean? I'm pretty fucking sure I will never be ready."

"Look, first off you need to have a really good story about how this was found that doesn't include me hunting out here. Also, know what you are getting into. Your little restoration project here will likely be halted for at least a year while they investigate all this. It's gonna be one hell of a mess. And there is more."

"You just told me there are 30 human bodies here, and that you don't want me to report it, and there is more?"

"What you want to do with the cops is up to you. I don't want to be involved. But look, these are fucking old, so all I am saying is there is no urgency here."

He paused to grab the flask and take another sip.

"I'll be straight with you. There's something messed up here. Messed up in a way I don't even understand. Randy... look, he went a bit off the rails after the attack. I just assumed he was in shock or some shit. But now...well, I think he was telling the truth."

"Telling the truth about what? What's going on? You know, I visited him in the hospital today. He ripped his goddamn IV out of his arm for no other reason than to ensure that I had to leave. I assume you know why he was so freaked out?"

"Oh hell, I wish you hadn't gone there. Listen, Randy can be a bit dramatic for sure, but something here spooked him good. I don't think it was a wolf. When I first saw him after the attack, it was obvious that he had been injured by an animal. The wounds were very consistent with that. The first word he said was 'wolf' as he pointed towards this path." He stopped and took a deep breath as if he was unsure of continuing. "Look, I don't know you. I don't know if you believe in things that go beyond the norm." He looked around nervously.

"Just please continue," I pleaded. "If this house has taught me one thing, it's that there is a whole world beyond the normal."

"Well, as I sat with him, holding his wounds, waiting for help... he started talking about some strange shit. He said that the wolf was a man. That a man did this! He talked about him being the man's messenger. It was all fucked up. Like I said, I thought he was just in shock."

"And now you think it is more than that?" I asked.

"I'm a very logical man. Take this pile of bones out of the equation for a second. Wolves don't just attack like that. Not here. Sure, there is enough untouched land that it's possible, but I'm one hell of a tracker. I spent the better part of two days in this woods and haven't seen any indication that a wolf or anything else lives here."

By the time I left, I was in a state of shock of my own. Everything was taking its toll on me. This house which started out as a great windfall and direction in my life. It quickly spiraled into a curse. For every piece of the puzzle I seemed to fit together, another entire realm of unanswered questions opened up. Initially I wanted to simply call the police and let them handle it. As I thought back to my conversation with Randy, I realized I wasn't ready for this. There was so much going on with David and clearly the demon of Sam was tied in. Right now I was not ready to make that call. I was tired of thinking about it. I needed to step back.

I decided to do just that... run away. For a few weeks, I avoided the house and any conversation about it. David kept calling me. Telling me I had to return to the house, to Ida's room. But I just ignored his pleas. I never got too far away.

As hard as I tried, the house seemed to keep trying to draw me in. The more I resisted, the worse it became. My mind would show me scenes of the house. Scenes that included everything from Ida to the graveyard in the woods. Then my next dream came.

When I opened my eyes, I was alone in the gardens of the estate. The air was cold. I walked directly to the pond. Everything was silent and still. I walked at a very fast pace. When I turned the corner between the shrubs and the pond, I saw the wolf. It was standing behind the granite bench on the far side of the pond. It stood motionless, staring at me with its cold calculating eyes.

I stood there silently, unable to divert my eyes from it. My breath created a fog as it hit the cold air. As the fog quickly dissipated, the wolf was gone and in its place was a man. The light was dim, but there was no mistaking it was Samuel. But what was he doing? I held myself back from approaching him. I wanted to observe as long as I could. As I watched him, the hair on my neck stood up. I was overcome with a chill. Everything around me started to swirl.

It was as if I had been drugged. I squeezed my eyes closed, hoping I could reset my vision. When I opened them again, I could see clearly. Samuel was standing there, and he was talking. Talking to others. The sight almost knocked me off my feet. There were four other men, wearing black cloaks, surrounding him, two on each side. Two red candles, on either side of the bench, flickered in the breeze.

Then, a voice echoed as if through loudspeakers.

"What are you waiting for? I am glad you could make it in time, James. I was beginning to think that you didn't receive my little message."

I shook my head. I didn't know what to say. I saw this as my chance to turn and walk away, but I couldn't. Something drew me in. I took a deep breath and looked at Samuel. He held out his hand as if inviting me to come to him. I stepped out into the open path and began walking towards him. I wanted to run away. I wanted to do anything but approach him, but I had no control. I felt like a fish on a hook. He reeled me closer. I stopped about ten feet away from him.

Now, I could see the men surrounding him. A cold shiver shot through my spine.

"James, I thought you understood that you could not win," he said. "I really didn't want to be forced to prove my point."

He stopped and looked at the other men.

"It is time," he declared to them.

One by one, they turned and walked off slowly in a single line.

"You completely misunderstand me," he said. "I am not the monster your mother makes me out to be. Really, I can be quite agreeable. Well, that is, when you do your part. I am not here for the house. I could care less about this useless place. I need that which was taken from me and locked away. So, if you would be so kind to return it, I shall leave you, never to return."

"And if I don't?" I asked.

"Master James, you are hardly in a position to negotiate," he replied.

"Who said anything about negotiation? What if I refuse?"

"You do have a strong will. Quite an excellent character trait. Although, battlefields are often littered with the bodies of the strong-willed, dying for their cause. I really had hoped you would be more understanding than this."

He retrieved a long knife from his cloak. It reflected the light into my eyes, blinding me for a moment.

"How far are you willing to go, Master James?" he asked.

"Are you going to kill me? Add my body to your little graveyard in the woods?"

"Please James, if it were only that easy. Those bones back there... well those people were very different from you or I. I'm afraid we are both difficult to truly kill. Besides, what use would you be to me then? Sadly, I do need you. I've been waiting many years for you. Only you can bring me what is needed."

"Well good luck with that!" I yelled as I gave him the middle finger and turned to walk away.

"As you wish, James," he said. "But you might want to stay for a minute. I would hate for you to miss the show."

I turned to look and saw the four men laying a body covered in a white sheet upon the bench in front of him. In a grand flourish, Samuel tore the sheet off of the limp body. I went numb. It was Kat, lying there, peacefully sleeping.

Without a thought, I sprinted at Samuel. Within an instant, I was tackled by the cloaked men. They held me down as I fought to get free.

"Fuck you!" I screamed at him.

"There, there Master James," he said. "This was your choice."

"What do you want?" I spat.

"You know what I want," he said. "Now let me begin. You see James, I can be very agreeable. However, when someone fails me, there is nothing left but to spill their blood. Katherine has failed me no differently than you plan to. I will not be stopped. I will not stop with her. I will kill everyone who stands in my way, everyone you care for in the slightest until you give me what I need. Now watch James. Watch what you have done!"

He raised the silver blade above his head with both hands clutching it.

"I hope I have not underestimated you, James, I would hate for you to derive a sick pleasure in the blood." He brought the blade down thrusting it into Kat's chest.

I jolted up out of bed, dripping with sweat. My hands were shaking. My head throbbed. It took a few moments to figure out where I was, even when it was. My hands still shaking, I picked up my phone and called Kat.

"Morning baby," she said as she answered the phone.

"Uh... morning. Are you alright? Uh... I mean, is everything okay?"

"Jim, what's going on?" she asked.

"Nothing, I was just worried about you."

"I'm fine, but what is there to worry about? What happened?"

"It was nothing, I just had another dream. It just freaked me out a bit. Everything is fine."

"Don't worry about me. Everything is great. I just gotta get ready for work. Want me to come over tonight, afterward?"

"Have I ever turned you down?" I replied.

"Mmmm, that's what I thought. But I gotta run. I love you, babe."

"I love you too!" I replied as I hung up the phone.

I sat on the edge of the bed trying to collect my thoughts. Dreams of the house had become somewhat frequent, but this one was different. This one didn't feel like a dream at all. The only reason I could believe that it was a dream was the fact that I woke up in my bed.

I had chosen to stop obsessing about the house in hopes I could approach it from a place of logic instead of emotion. This dream however, made me understand without a doubt that the house would not let me do this. The house and I were connected and now I realized that I couldn't hide away, I needed to get involved.

Kat and I were having a wonderful time together. Without being obsessed with the house, things between us just became natural. Without my intervention, the renovation at the house was moving forward smoother than ever. The foundation was complete. This meant no one currently at the house knew anything of the bones in the forest. The roof was about half done, and another crew had begun building the custom replacement windows. I had even contracted out to have the electricity and gas done. A week from now, a massive heating system was set to be installed. According to plan, while the house would be far from being done, it would be habitable before Chicago's chilly winter hit with full force.

The last thing I wanted was to derail the positive momentum because of a dream. But this dream cut through me in a different way. After an hour of replaying it in my head, I decided I needed to talk to someone about it. I picked up my phone and called David.

"Hey bro, where you been?" he answered.

"Hey, David! Listen, I gotta ask you something."

"Well, I hope you're gonna ask if we are available to come up there this weekend, 'cause the answer is yes!" he exclaimed.

"Nah... well, maybe. I just got something else for you. What do you know about dreams?"

"Depends what you're asking. I mean shit, that is a pretty wide topic. Wanna narrow it down for me a bit?"

"Can spirits overtake one's dreams?" I asked.

"Of course! There are mediums I've worked with that can only communicate with spirits in a dream. Actually, dreams, and taking the time to look into them, is where a lot of mediums first realize they have the ability to communicate. But this isn't a theoretical question, as much as I love those. Is it Jim?"

"Okay, but if spirits can contact a person via dreams, and at the same time dreams can also be a manifestation of something in your head or subconscious or some shit like that... well, how the hell do you tell the difference?"

"I don't dream. So, I don't have first-hand experience with this. But from what I've learned, most mediums will say that there is something starkly different about these dreams. The feeling, the clarity of it, the emotional pull of it. I know that isn't really tangible but that is the best I can do on that front. You wanna cut the crap and tell me what you are dreaming?"

"I had another dream with Sam in it," I confessed.

"See, now that is something else. I mean now, sure, there is a lot in your head with Sam and the history of everything. But, this isn't your first dream of Sam. You had a dream of him; you also had one of Ida. And if what you are telling me was real, both of those happened long before you knew the story, knew the people. You recognized Ida in a photo, having never seen a picture of her before. Kinda hard for that to be a manifestation of your subconscious. Am I right?"

I told him the dream. My mind was focused on the sheer fact that I saw Sam killing Kat. The horror of it. The pain of it. It was like there was brightly flashing warning signs everywhere. Yet, while I told David, he almost bypassed that. He was focused on the details. He zeroed in on the words. What Sam was saying to me. He made me recite them over and over.

"You know there is a lot here, but there is one thing that really sticks out in my head," he said.

"Yeah, like the fact that I got a warning from some dead asshole that he is going to carve up my girlfriend!" I huffed.

"How did Sam refer to Ida? He didn't say his wife, that bitch whore, or anything else. He said your mother!"

"Okay, what's your point?" I grumbled.

"There have been quite a few things that point to... well, refer to anyway, to the idea that you, are in fact, Ida's child."

"Well, too bad she was about eighty years too early for that to happen." I was annoyed.

"No! Listen to me dammit! I am beginning to believe that Ida left this estate to you because she believed you are her son. I mean, I get it. That was forever ago. You have a mom and everything else on this plane. But what if? Just what if, on the spiritual plane, she was right?"

"Are you fucking kidding me right now? Look, I appreciate all your help, but I'm not sure I can buy into this crap."

"Look, I am not going to say we understand everything, but hear me out. Just because the idea of reincarnation doesn't make any sense to you, doesn't mean it isn't true. It is a belief held by billions. Generations and generations of people steadfastly believe in it. And you know damn well the minute anyone tries to apply scientific proof to any belief system, they get nowhere. So, who are we to just instantly deny thoughts like that?"

"Seriously? You are too much." I waved my arm dismissively.

"Actually, if you apply the idea of reincarnation to this, it makes a lot of sense. Provided of course someone, in some way, would be able to predict reincarnation. I think we need to start digging into this concept. See if there is anything we can find out about reincarnation being of interest to Ida.

This could answer a lot of questions and help us with the house."

"How exactly will this help us?" I asked.

"Let's just pretend you are her son reincarnated. Then the spells, the charms, any magic she used, could have been done specifically for you. Meaning, you could be the key to solving all of this and ultimately putting all of this stuff to rest."

We continued talking for a while and I finally updated David on the crewman who was attacked and subsequently the bones in the forest. Kat had been surprisingly really easy to talk to about that. David, on the other hand, grew increasingly concerned. The conversation ended with an air of real danger. For the first time after talking to David, I felt that something bad was about to happen.

18

AFTER TALKING TO DAVID, I drove out to the house. After that dream I felt a drive to just face the house and everything head on. I didn't have any plan, aside from appeasing David's request to go into Ida's parlor. Outside of that I simply realized that the only way I could accomplish anything was to be present at the house.

I drove up about twenty feet from the front door. The crew was hard at work. I noticed that they were parking off to the left of the house. The front of the house was covered with ladders and scaffolding. I slowly made my way to the makeshift parking lot and parked in a spot deep in the trees. The foreman must have assumed I was there to inspect the work as he quickly came out and greeted me.

He walked me over to a tent he'd set up and started going over the plans and the progress. For the most part, I was uninterested. I just assumed they were doing their job, and really, my visit had nothing to do with their work. Then, something caught my eye. On the desk, were large sheets of the plans for the work being done. Also, there were copied sets of the original plans I'd gotten from the library. One of the originals was slightly peeking out of the pile. The area exposed was the front corner of the second floor of the house. It was the parlor. I pulled the copy out from under the pile and started looking it over.

The plans showed the shape of the parlor as a perfect square. Yet, I knew from being in the room, it was nothing close to a square. It was a long rectangle.

"How accurate are these old plans to what is actually here?" I asked.

"They are as precise as it gets. I've found nothing even an inch off from them. We typically don't use old plans as much of a guide, but these were so accurate that we used them as a base model for our own plans. Of course, with ours, we took precise measurements to adjust them. But there was really little adjustments to be made."

"Hey, this might sound kinda odd, but have you guys seen anything weird going on here at all?" I asked.

"Aw hell, is this where you tell me there are stories about the place being haunted? I mean I get it. It's an old house. I've heard it all before." He rolled his eyes.

I suddenly felt stupid for asking. Part of me couldn't help but think this was all made up in my own head.

"Nah, not like that. I uh... well, when they were working on the foundation they had a crew show up supposedly to do the interior. The thing was, I hadn't hired anyone at that point. They left and all, but still, I don't know if somebody might be trying to get in," I covered my embarrassment.

"Ah. No, nothing like that. It's been as quiet as a work site can be, but I'll keep my eye out. I'd be surprised though; my boys don't exactly play well with other crews. So, if someone did show up we'd know it."

I finished up the conversation, thankful that I hadn't raised too much concern with the foreman. But now, I had a new mission. I was still going to the parlor, but instead of just going in there to see if I felt anything, I had to figure out this anomaly that I saw in the plans. As I walked into the house, I was thankful that the crews were working on the opposite side of the house. The sound of them working quickly faded away as I walked closer to the parlor.

I approached the door and looked at it. I hadn't stepped foot inside since I was there with David. A chill went up my spine thinking about the blood red wall I saw that day. I ran my hand across the door frame, discovering new marks. There were even new spots of red paint rubbed off from a pry bar. I took a deep breath and unlocked the door.

The door swung open easily. Much like the first time I walked into the parlor, it was calm and quiet inside. Every-thing looked like it had that first day. I shut the door and walked over to the chaise lounge and sat down. I closed my eyes and my mind instantly brought me back to that day in the room with Kat. I took a deep breath and could smell the scent of flowers. I was immediately at peace.

I began to think about that day with David. I couldn't help but question if that was real or just in my head. The room felt so peaceful right then, I couldn't believe that it had also been so dark and twisted. I stood up and started to walk through the room. Remembering why I was there, I started to pay attention to the size of the room. It was indeed how I remembered it, long and much narrower than the squared size portrayed in the plans.

The window, the door, and the fireplace were all in exactly the right positions, but yet everything was off. Then, I realized the wall along the west side of the room was wrong. It was as if the wall cut the size of the room. That was when it hit me. The room was not inaccurate to the plans. It was just divided. I started to analyze the wall. It was beautifully done. The top half was a light green color with a gorgeous dark wood covering the bottom half. The two sides were separated by an ornate piece of wood trim. I slowly walked along the wall running my hand across that piece of trim.

About five feet from the door, my fingers felt a small gap in the wood. I stepped back to look at it. There was a slight but unusual gap right where the two piece of wood trim met. As I looked at it, I realized that it perfectly aligned to one of the vertical pieces of trim on the green portion of the wall. As my eye followed this vertical line, I noticed a similar gap in the crown molding where the wall met the ceiling. Below the trim, this imaginary line also lined up with the tiny gap in the wood paneling.

I gasped. "Fuck me sideways! It's a door!"

I was convinced that I'd found a hidden door. What I didn't know was how to open it. I spent countless minutes looking at it and working my fingers along the edge, trying to find a way to pry it open. I found nothing. I began to realize there had to be a lock of some sort, but I couldn't even imagine where. I moved things all over the room, half-expecting to unlock it by moving a book or object. I couldn't find anything that could be used to unlock the door.

I again sat down on the lounge and was about to give up. Sitting down caused me to look at the wall from a different angle. My eyes were drawn to the centerpiece of trim. The length of the room was adorned with brass flowers every couple of feet. They were not bright or polished but dark and dull with age. I noticed that one fell just about six inches to the right of the door. I walked up and looked at it. It looked like all the others. I pressed it, and it pushed in easily.

There was an audible click, and all of a sudden, the hidden door swung inward a few inches.

I gently pushed the door open. Surprisingly, it opened with ease. I looked over my shoulder, half-expecting to find someone watching me. Satisfied no one was there, I took a step into the dark room. For as warm and inviting as the parlor was, this room was the opposite. The temperature dropped what felt like twenty degrees. It took a moment for my eyes to adjust to the darkness, with just the parlor light coming in. I grabbed my flashlight to get a better look.

While the room was far from an unfinished storage area, it was still stark and cold. It was a small rectangular room. The floor was covered in alternating black and white marble tiles. There were two chairs on either side of a small desk. The walls were black except for a mirror that hung on the one side. The ceiling was black. Aside from the white tiles on the floor, there was just darkness and a feeling of emptiness. The black walls and ceiling gave the illusion of empty space, like there were no walls and ceiling...like the room just went on indefinitely. The desk and chairs looked like they were just floating there in space.

On the far wall, there was a door. As I walked towards it, I could hear my footsteps echo in the empty room. The door was unlike any other in the house. It was painted black and instead of the massive wooden doors everywhere else in the house, this one was metal. There were rows of rivets along the edges that made it look more like a door to a battleship than something you would find in a house. I turned the handle and found it to be locked.

As I examined the door with my flashlight, I realized there was something drawn on it. It was hard to see against the black background, but there was what appeared to be a circle with a diagonal line through it. It was crudely drawn and so faint. It looked as though it was painted hastily. There were drip lines at the bottom edges of it. I then realized how to open the door. Surely, it was the door which could be opened with the other key I'd been given.

I immediately pulled my phone out of my pocket. I wanted to tell David about it immediately. The bright screen of the phone briefly blinded me. A moment later, I tried to call David. The call would not go through. There was absolutely no service. I put the phone back in my pocket and sat down in one of the chairs in the room. On top of the desk, there was an array of black and red candles, all about half burned, leaving long ribbons of melted wax on their sides. I opened the drawer on the desk and saw an ancient looking book.

I grabbed the book to examine it. It was older than any book I'd ever seen. The cover was an aged tan leather, but so old and brittle, it gave the impression of an old plastic that would shatter if you put any pressure on it. I kept myself from opening it because I was afraid the whole thing would disintegrate in my hands. There was a crude black handwriting on the cover. It read "Münchner Handbuch der Nekromantie."

Afraid of opening it and equally afraid of removing it, I used my phone to take a photo of the cover. The flash of the camera blinded me for a minute, and I gently put the book back in the drawer. I walked back into the warmer parlor.

After only a few steps into the parlor I started to feel dizzy. My feet became increasingly heavy, the muscles in my legs tensed and strained at every step. I made it as far as the chaise where I sat down. My hands stretched to rub my legs and try to coax them back into feeling, but it was no use. I gave into the dizziness and the aches and laid down on the chaise.

As I lay there, the room appeared to darken. The light from my lantern faded. I shut my eyes tightly and shook my head, assuming that when I opened them again everything would be back to normal... It wasn't.

"Dearest James," a voice said.

The voice was calm and soothing, but it frightened me. I sat up immediately and looked around the room to place the voice. I was alone. The room was the same, but I knew this voice was not in my head. I was dizzy, but I knew in my core this was real.

"Um, hello," I said.

I expected an immediate response but there was nothing. Everything was still and silent. My legs still ached, but I forced myself to stand.

"Who's there?"

I was constantly moving in circles, trying to observe the entire room, when the lantern turned off. I found myself in complete darkness. The darkness only lasted a second though. A warm glow began the sweep through the room, starting from inside the hidden room.

"James, please sit," the voice said. "It's me, Ida. I need to speak with you,"

I stumbled back onto the chaise. Within an instant, the room was illuminated, not by my lantern or even the glow I saw from the door. It was daylight streaming in from the windows. Windows that were broken and boarded up. Yet, right then, the afternoon sun was streaming into the room. The boxes were gone. The room was pristine.

I turned my head and saw Ida. She was beautiful, wearing a purple dress and she was walking towards me. She looked exactly as she had in the photos I'd seen. Her features were soft and delicate. Yet, she carried herself with unbridled strength and resolve.

"We must speak," Ida said.

I was unable to respond. I could only stare at her, second-guessing the reality of everything I was experiencing. She moved closer and sat in a chair across from the chaise. After settling into the chair, she looked at me. No... she looked into me. Her eyes bore into me. She was looking into my soul.

"I cannot tell you how elated I am that you are here. I poured everything I had into the hope that this time would come. And here it is. You are here, and you will finish the task I failed to do."

"What task? You left me a house."

"Well, I suppose I owe you a bit of an explanation. Yes, I left you this villa. But that was only a way to bring you into the plan I'd set in motion. You see, this isn't about this Villa or my desire for you to inherit it. It is about finally putting an end to Samuel and his reign of terror."

My head was throbbing now more than ever. I knew this was my one chance to get answers, to finally understand everything that was going on.

"Please tell me what this is all about," I said.

"Samuel is an evil man. I never wanted to marry him in the first place. However, that choice was not mine. My parents left me no say in the matter. In the beginning, everything was fine. Not perfect by any means, but fine. Unfortunately, as time went on, his true self became visible. He really was a despicable man, willing to go to any length to achieve his goals. Not only did he commit atrocious acts but, he thrived on them. He derived a sick pleasure from torturing others.

"It was around this time where I tried to escape this life. Samuel was particularly interested in ensuring that I conceive and carry his son. With my heart elsewhere, I decided that not only would I not give him this son, but I would bear the child of the man I truly loved. In my mind, it was a perfect plan. As soon as he found out, he would leave me, and I would be free of him, free to live the life I wanted and raise my child conceived in love.

"It was short-sighted of me. Upon discovering the truth, Samuel had the child executed. I was now to exist as his slave in this prison. I refused to give up. I refused to let him continue. From that point on, I was his prisoner. A fate I would never conform to. I was able to gain some freedom thanks to the public image of us that we needed to maintain. I exploited this freedom to plan my escape. I used the staff of the Villa to spy on him, to listen in to whatever dealings he had. Piece by piece, I started to understand that his evil extended far beyond what I had ever imagined.

"I learned of his dealings with the Knights of the Golden Circle. I had always known of his membership with the order but had always assumed it to be nothing but a bunch of guys drinking together. The more I heard of his dealings with them the more I realized this was not just a group of cohorts. It was a subterfuge to conceal an army looking to take over the country. I learned of munitions being stored and prepared for war as well as money to finance this war being stored around the country. How real or not this was, I really never knew. However, to Samuel, this controlled his every move. My motivation began to change with every bit of this knowledge I learned.

"I sought my freedom personally. Beyond that, he needed to be stopped. He was a murderer of countless victims and everything showed me that he had only begun. So I used my freedom to form a plan.

"The public's view of me soured, showing me as depressed, even mentally unfit. I was able to retreat to

Germany under the guise of receiving treatment. It was there I delved into the black arts. I studied incessantly under the tutelage of the most revered witches. Upon my return, I put this knowledge to work and tried to overtake Samuel and break his spells. While my power was not strong enough to overcome him, I was still able to subdue him.

"I was able to ensure that he would never receive an heir fit of taking his place in the KGC. I was able to cast a spell of protection over this home and its contents, items of unexplainable value to him. In my final act, I conspired with my beloved Edgar to put him to rest."

Hearing this was too much. I couldn't comprehend it all.

"Put to rest?" I asked.

"Yes, my dear Edgar took Samuel's life much in the manner that Samuel once killed so many in the forest beyond the pond."

"Wait!" I pleaded. "If you protected the house, and Edgar killed him, then what is this all about? Why am I here? Why is this happening?"

"Dearest James, no doubt you have seen that he is still around. You see, Samuel also had taken an interest in the dark arts. He was able to ensure that death could not hold him. He is here waiting to restore his bloodline."

"That doesn't explain to me why I am here."

"You are here because I called you. When I constructed this plan and realized I could not overcome him, I devised a secondary plan, one to ensure that Samuel's reign of terror is definitely ended. My protections on this home, my spells binding him to this property, all came with limitations. Upon my death, the clock started ticking and soon all that I have created will be gone."

"I take it I am your backup plan?"

"You are not a backup plan; you are *the* plan. You and only you have the ability to lift this shroud of darkness. Only you can defeat Samuel once and for all. It is a burden I never wished to give, but I only gave it to you because I knew you would succeed."

"What should I do?" I asked.

"The first thing you must do is retrieve the necklace in the safe. My protection spell on that room is gone. Take it, keep it safe, and let no one know that you have ever even seen it!"

19

IN A FLASH, Ida was gone. The warm sunlight was replaced by the jarring white light of the lantern. The parlor was silent.

I sat there sweating and out of breath. My hands were shaking. I was unable to make sense of anything. I had talked to David about ghosts and such, but this was something on a whole new level. In my gut burned the simple question. "Was it real?'

I sat there for a long time pondering that question. I knew so much more about everything going on. I had an explanation for the bones in the forest. To some degree, I had finally gotten the answers I'd been searching for. Part of my wanted to deny the reality of this vision. Yet, deep inside me, I knew it was real. I could no longer think this was all make believe. This was real, ghosts were real, and Sam was very real.

I took a moment to think about it all... to believe every word Ida spoke to me and visualize how that all worked together. It certainly correlated with things that David brought up, but it still left me with some questions. What did Samuel really want? Could he really be a demon who is hell-bent on taking over the world? More so, if his organization really was that powerful, how could they not have found a way to put these plans in motion over the past seventy years?

That was when things started to click in my brain. I realized that, undoubtedly, I needed to follow her advice and go back into that secret room to retrieve the necklace she mentioned. I didn't know why, but I knew it was something Samuel needed. There were more troubling thoughts when it came to Kat.

I knew that something with Samuel's KGC connection hinged completely on his bloodline. Kat was indeed of his blood. I began to understand what David meant when he stated that she needed to choose sides. Could she be somehow turned to take the reins of Sam's evil plot? It was a horrific thought. In the past months, I had grown to love her deeply. The last thing I wanted to consider was her somehow being on his side.

Something deep inside me believed every ounce of what Ida said. In a way, yes, I felt this to be my true destiny. I felt that saving this home and vanquishing Sam was what I needed to do, but I also clung to the fairy tale belief that love would conquer all. That no matter who Kat was or how much she was connected to this, our feelings for each other would rise above anything in our path.

I took a few deep breaths and silently cursed myself for my digression into thoughts questioning Kat. I stood up and found that the dizziness had passed. The pain in my legs was gone. I felt alive. I was alive with a deep sense of knowing what I had to do. I looked around the room. I walked toward the fireplace where the vase of dead flowers still sat. I eyed them for a moment before scanning the room once again. I blew a kiss. In my head, this was my way of showing Ida that I accepted the burden she bestowed on me and that I would not retreat.

I immediately felt a warm embrace, as if a set of invisible arms wrapped around me and held me tight. This was right! This was exactly what I was meant to do!

———————

UNSURE OF WHAT my next steps should be, I decided to continue with my original intention of going to the pond. I felt I needed to be there and see exactly where my dream had taken place. I slowly walked from the parlor to the front foyer. I was beginning to see the entire house differently. No longer the derelict mansion it was currently, but the stately manor it originally had been. As I opened the front door, I was struck with the view of a radiant sunset.

I shook my head momentarily to try to make sense of it. When I'd entered the house, it had been early in the day. How long could I have been in there? The events inside, as I played them through my head, couldn't have taken more than a couple hours, but here it was evening. I glanced down at my watch. It was near six o'clock. I couldn't understand how that was possible.

It made no difference to me though. I was driven and headed out towards what remained of the pond. With fall quickly grabbing hold, the path was covered in a bed of fallen leaves. The brisk wind howled through the trees and made it feel significantly colder than it was.

I tried to follow the same path I had waked in my dream. The walkways, being completely overgrown, were difficult to follow. As I turned the final corner, to face the far side of the pond, everything changed. At that moment, I was not looking at the dilapidated remains of the pond but the pond completely restored... the pond I'd seen in my dreams. I stood there staring at it, stopping only to rub my eyes. I knew what I saw was impossible, but yet it was real. It was right there in front of me.

I walked along the side of the pond, closer and closer to the marble bench. It was the very bench I saw Sam slay Kat on. I found myself shaking my head a few times. Still in disbelief, I tried to shake off the vision before me. Soon, I was standing beside the bench. While everything around the pond was pristine, the bench was not.

As I leaned in to look at spots on the top of the bench, I realized they were red wax. Droplets of wax had once dripped onto the surface and left reddish smudges all over the bench. As I looked at them, all of a sudden the sunlight dimmed. A dark shadow had fallen over the bench. I jolted up and turned to look.

A few feet behind me stood a wolf. Its blue eyes stared me down as it bared its teeth. I could see nothing but Kat's eyes on this wolf.

"Go ahead," I yelled in a moment of courage. "I know you won't attack me. You need me!"

The wolf responded by stepping back, still staring at me.

"That's what I thought," I taunted.

I turned away from the wolf and began walking along the edge of the pond. I felt a cold wind shoot across the pond, chilling me. I turned my head to look. The wolf was no longer there. I continued to walk a few steps when I saw another shadow cross my path. This time, the shadow was in the shape of a man. From what I could see, there was no person, only a defined dark shadow.

"Master James, I knew you would come," a voice boomed from all directions. "Yet, I see you have not heeded my warning and have chosen to come alone. Do not test my patience. Your time is running out. Bring me what I need."

"Or what? You're trapped here!"

"You know more than I assumed, James. Yes, I am trapped here, but that does not mean I don't have my ways of getting what I seek. In fact, I have already shown you what will happen if you choose not to heed my warning."

I thought back to the dream. I saw the vision of him taking Kat's life on that bench. I refused to let that become reality. I needed to stop him. Yet, at that moment I was paralyzed. I wanted to speak. I wanted to run. There were so many things running through my head as he spoke to me. I stood frozen, unable to move.

The shadow turned toward me in a vicious whirl. It struck me! The massive force shoved me in the chest. I was thrown back onto the bench, my head slamming against the cold marble. I fought to stand, fought to move! All I could do was feel the cold marble beneath me and the warm blood trickling down my forehead.

I OPENED my eyes to darkness. My head was throbbing, and I was freezing. I sat up and only then came to the realization that I was at the pond. It was dark outside. I could only see by the light of the moon. As my eyes adjusted, and I looked around, I could see this was not the pond in my dream. This was the real pond in all its dilapidated glory. I looked down at the crumbling bench I sat on and noticed the dried pool of blood. That was when I started to remember everything.

My head ached in a way I'd never felt. As I rubbed my fingers on my forehead, I could feel the large bump along with my hair, stiff with dried blood. I wasn't ready to stand up yet. I reached to get my phone out of my pocket and found the battery was dead. I was out there alone with no way to get a hold of anyone. I decided I had to get to my truck. Even if I couldn't drive, it would be warmer inside it, and I could charge my phone and call Kat for help.

I slowly got to my feet. I could barely stand without wobbling like a drunk. I cupped my hands around my mouth and blew a few deep breaths into them, hoping the warmth would bring some feeling back to my fingertips. I slowly started to take a few steps. I was weak and disorientated, but it was working. One step at a time, I made my way to the far edge of the pond.

I was getting a little bit stronger with every step but I was still wobbly. I reached into my pocket and found that I still had my flashlight. I was thankful. I couldn't imagine trying to navigate these overgrown paths without it. The bright beam of light allowed me to see each step in front of me, ensuring I could find purchase and not fall. The typically five-minute walk was taking me forever.

Finally, I exited the overgrowth and got a view of the house. In the light of the moon, it looked foreboding. The half-completed work made it truly look abandoned. I made my way toward the front of the house. I silently cursed the fact that I parked with the crew on the opposite side making my walk even further.

As I got closer to the front of the house, I heard a mumbled voice that stopped me in my tracks. I dropped to the ground, turning off my flashlight. I sat listening. It sounded like Kat. As I sat listening though, I only heard silence. After a few seconds I had convinced myself that I was hearing things and decided to proceed.

I stood up and stalked over to the front corner of the house. My body ached, but I was acting on pure adrenaline.

I peeked around the corner, only to see a car drive off. The car's tires spun, kicking up gravel as she sped away. As soon as the taillights faded out of sight, I collapsed onto the ground.

I laid there for a few minutes. I didn't know if what I was seeing was real, yet something made me believe it was Kat. Slowly, a feeling of rage overtook me. I couldn't think of one possible reason Kat would've been there yet I believed completely that she was. That rage soon got me to my feet and to my truck. It was painful to step up into the truck, but I made it. I turned on the truck, and the heater started blasting out hot air. I plugged my phone in and reached over to the glove box. I pulled out a silver flask and opened it. The whiskey burned as it went down my throat. It helped.

A couple swallows later, I put the flask back and opened the mirror behind the visor. I looked horrible. There was a swollen gash on the top of my forehead. The right side of my face was covered with remnants of dried, cracked blood. I licked my fingertips and tried to rub some of the blood off, smearing it and making more of a mess.

The screen of my phone lit up as it finally got enough charge to power on. As I started looking at my phone, there was a list of missed calls and texts from Kat asking where I was. My finger hovered over the call button, but I resisted. I threw my phone into the passenger seat and closed my eyes.

For a moment, I could hear a voice yelling at me. It was a man. I couldn't make out anything he was saying, but it was loud. There were bright lights, and then it all faded to black again. Black peacefulness. I floated in the darkness. It was just an endless open space. There were the desk and the chairs. They were floating in front of me, and I swam over to them. I pulled a chair to me and sat down. It felt as though I was spinning, but I couldn't tell because I was just floating in darkness.

Then I felt a warmth. A kiss on my forehead.

"Dearest James," a woman's voice said.

"Who is this?" I asked into the darkness.

"I have you. You're safe now," she said.

"What's happening?" I asked.

"James, listen to me. We are running out of time before he takes over. He is getting stronger every day, and if you don't stop him, he will end us all."

I felt another kiss on my forehead and smelled perfume. I felt arms wrap around me and then everything drifted away.

PART III

REPRISE

20

April 22, 1905 - Cloudland Hotel

Samuel Freidrich Muller sat in a large leather chair in the empty private library of the Cloudland Hotel. The evening was cool there in the mountains. The room was silent aside from the constant ticking of the grandfather clock in the corner. Samuel gently raised his glass of whiskey and took a swallow. As he set the glass down on the small table in front of him, he retrieved his gold pocket watch and compared the time to the clock. It was 6:59 p.m.

A moment later, the silence was broken by a gentle knock at the door.

"Master Muller, your visitor has arrived," a young female voice called.

Samuel rose from his seat and put the watch back into his vest just as the Grandfather clock started to make the mechanical grinding it did just before it chimed.

"Please send him in at once."

The door creaked as it opened. A young woman dressed in a maid's uniform walked inside, accompanied by a short portly man. He was dressed in a fine suit and carried a leather satchel.

"Master Muller, shall I get you anything, sir?" she asked.

"No, please give us some privacy!" he shot back.

Upon those words the maid left, gently shutting the door behind her, leaving the two men in the room alone.

"Sir, I have your order," the man said.

"Please lay it out on the table for me to inspect."

The man opened his satchel, removed a piece of velvet, and laid it on the table. Then he retrieved a small ornate wooden box. He opened the box and gently withdrew a beautiful necklace. He laid the necklace on the fabric and stood at attention waiting for Samuel.

The necklace was truly a masterpiece of jewelry. A large green emerald pendant hung in the center surrounded by white gold. The chain was heavily laden with diamonds and accentuated on both sides by a pair of spectacular sapphires.

Samuel approached the table and looked at the necklace suspiciously.

"I trust the engravings are done precisely to my instruction?"

"But of course. Here, inspect them for yourself." The man handed him a loupe.

Samuel set the loupe on the table with the necklace. "You understand, of course, a piece such as this must be properly examined before you are to receive payment. Please exit to the study and wait for me to call."

"But of course sir." The man walked towards the door.

"On your way out, please send for the maid," Samuel said.

"As you wish."

A few moments later, the maid arrived in the library.

"Miss, please call upon John, William, George, and Robert," Samuel instructed. "Instruct them to meet me here as soon as possible."

As the maid left, Samuel retrieved a folded piece of paper from his jacket pocket. He unfolded it, setting it on the table with the necklace. On the paper was a map with several points marked. A small stream was drawn through the center of it. Samuel laid the necklace on top of the map and gently aligned the emerald and sapphires to some of the points on the map.

A few minutes later, the four men arrived at the library. Samuel stood to greet them.

"My brothers, please come see my work." He gestured toward the table. "Never again shall our efforts be thwarted by a paper map, which can easily be destroyed or fall into the wrong hands. Our vault is now secured, with this being the key."

He held up the necklace for them to see.

"To the layman, it is a piece of the finest jewelry the world has ever seen," he continued. "But to those in our circle, it is the key to our funds, now secure for generations until the Knights are called into action."

Samuel picked up his glass of whiskey as the men inspected the necklace. George used the loupe to check the engravings while the other men looked on.

"Samuel, is it not risky to leave the entirety of our fortunes in the hands of your wife?" John asked.

Samuel slammed his glass down on the table. "Are you accusing me of not being able to control my spouse?" He glared at the man.

"Of course not! I am simply asking is it not possible that this too could fall into the wrong hands?"

"John, listen to me, please. This necklace is a work of art.

I have invested a fortune in having it made. It will be renowned worldwide. A necklace such as that does not go missing. Long after I am gone, the necklace will be out there and its whereabouts known. I cannot say that it will never fall into the wrong hands, but I will say we will always be able to retrieve it. People are expendable and when the Knights are called, it will be retrieved. George, is every inscription correct and the necklace completely aligned?" Samuel held his breath waiting for George to respond.

"It is. The alignment is perfect!" George smiled, his eyes wide with amazement.

"Then brothers, join me in a toast to the future of our knights being secured," Samuel said.

As the others raised their glasses, Samuel took the map from the table. He crumpled the paper and tossed it into the large fireplace.

21

I OPENED my eyes and saw a stark white ceiling. It only took a second to realize I was in a hospital bed. I brought my hands up to my head and saw that there were a couple tubes in my arm with tape holding them in place. I reached for the gash on my head and could feel the roughness of a bandage.

"Jim, you're awake!" Kat blurted out while jumping out of a chair.

I looked over at her. She walked up to me and kissed me. She then sat on the side of the bed, holding my hand.

"I'm so glad you're okay. You had me worried sick? What did you get yourself into?"

"How did I get here?" I asked.

"The foreman at the house saw you sleeping in your truck. But the truck was running, so he went to wake you up. That is when he saw the blood. He called an ambulance and then grabbed your phone. Seeing all my missed calls, he contacted me. You have been unconscious for two days. What happened?"

Her blue eyes were swollen and wet. She looked as if she hadn't slept in days.

"Two days? But I saw you last night, at the house."

"Tell me what you remember," she said.

"It was Sam. He hit me, and I must've hit my head on the bench."

"Sam? Are you sure this isn't the painkillers you are on talking?"

"The fuck?" I snapped back. "I know exactly what I am talking about. And you! You were there! You were talking to someone at the house. What were you doing there?"

"Jim. Stop. I'm sorry. I get it. There is something with Sam going on, and I believe you. But hear me out for a second. There are nurses, doctors, and even the police are following up on you being found like this. If you start telling them a guy who died a hundred years ago did this, they are gonna lock your ass up."

I sat silent for a moment. Despite everything I felt, I knew she made a good point.

"But you?" I asked. "Were you there?"

"Of course I was there! You were supposed to meet me. You didn't show up, didn't text, didn't answer the phone. What else was I supposed to do but look for you? Jeez, Jim, I was worried about you. I went to your apartment. I went to the house. Hell, I called David. I couldn't find any trace of you anywhere. I even called the cops asking about any car accidents."

"I'm sorry, I... I don't even know," I said.

Just then, a crew of nurses barged into the room. Kat was ushered out, and I was subjected to questions I didn't know how to answer. The story I told them was that I headed out to the pond and must have slipped, hitting my head, eventually making it back to the truck.

After changing a bunch of bags of stuff, they left me alone to rest. A nurse even returned my cell phone. The first thing I realized looking at my phone was that it really was two days later. I started going through the texts from Kat. First playful, then annoyed, then pissed. Then they were straight up worried. I started replaying the night in my head.

I went to the photos on my phone and found the picture of the book. I quickly sent that off to David simply saying: "This mean anything to you?"

Then Kat came back to the room.

"You okay baby?" she asked.

"Yeah, I am just trying to piece everything together. I'm really not crazy."

"I know. I called David and told him about what you said. That guy is flipping out. He wants to be included in any conversation about it all, obviously."

"What about you?" I asked. "You gonna grill me about all of it now?"

"Jim, right now I am just glad you are here. We can sort all that out later. But right now I just want to be thankful you are here and getting better."

She slid the chair across the room next to the bed and sat down holding my hands.

"I was really worried about you. I love you, Jim! I was so scared I was losing you."

Her eyes were wet holding back a river of tears. But these tears were different than what I had seen in her before. Her eyes were filled with nothing but sincerity.

"I love you, Kat," I replied as I kissed her hand. "But Sam is a real sonuvabitch, and we are gonna have to do something about it."

Just then, my phone started vibrating incessantly. There were a series of quick texts from David.

"Where did you get that????"

"Was that in the house?"

"Do you know what that is?"

"My god, that isn't supposed to even exist!"

"Legendary level shit!"

"CALL ME!"

Just reading his texts made my head hurt again. I looked over at Kat and decided David and the house could wait. I powered off my phone and laid it on the table next to the bed.

Kat moved to lean her head down on my chest. In a matter of moments, my eyes closed, and I fell asleep.

It wasn't until about eleven am the next day that I turned my phone back on. I had convinced Kat that she could indeed get back to work and life. I had been through a bunch of tests with a lot of initials I didn't understand. I ate some horrible excuse for a meal. Then, I was there alone with nothing to do but sleep or watch day-time TV.

I decided I had let David suffer enough and called him up. He answered on the first ring.

"Jim, what is going on?" he asked in a frenzy.

"Well, your man Sam kicked the fuck out of me," I replied.

"He made contact? This is amazing! I need to know everything!"

"Easy David. One step at a time. After all, I'm not getting out of the hospital for a couple days. Tell me about the book."

"Oh my god, the book!" he blurted out.

"Yeah, I take it you know something about it," I replied.

"Of course! Who doesn't? Well, I mean not really, because at this point we all believed it was a myth, an urban legend."

"What do you mean a myth?" I questioned.

"Okay, you ever hear of the Forbidden Rights?" he asked.

"David... pretend for just a second I am a normal guy with no knowledge of the paranormal," I replied sarcastically.

"Got it. Okay. The Forbidden Rights is one of the foundational grimoires. Consider it the Kelley Blue Book of witchcraft."

"Grimoire?" I asked.

"Yes, spell book. Do your homework! Anyway, the Forbidden Rights has been around forever but was not an original work. It is an edited incomplete translation of the original Munich Manual. Or Münchner Handbuch der Nekromantie as it was cited. Thing is, no one has ever seen the original manual. For decades everyone claimed that it was archived in some national library in Hamburg, but aside from claiming they had it, no one has ever seen it. After an audit of the library in 2009, it couldn't be located. Most assumed that the Forbidden Rights now was an original work crediting the Munich Manual only to alleviate the scrutiny of the author. But here you have sent me a photo of it."

"Okay, so in the world of witchcraft, I essentially uncovered a Dunlap Broadside, right?" I replied.

"Wait! You know what a Dunlap Broadside is? Kudos to you for knowing your history, but no! A Dunlap Broadside is the first printing of The Declaration of Independence. While incredibly rare, it is a printing. You found the actual original Declaration of Independence!"

"Okay, fine, but to that point, it's just an old book."

"Fuck Jim, when will you listen! No! I'll continue with your little analogy there. Say the Dunlap Broadside is the closest thing to the original Declaration that anyone knows or has ever seen. And here you find the original the Dunlap was pressed from, but there is a reverse side, a side no one has ever seen? Like I said, Forbidden Rights never claimed to be the entire manual, only a small portion. Yet, it's still powerful enough to serve as a foundation for all the spells we know and use. This is the holy grail and could quite possibly contain spells and magic more powerful than any modern-day witch has ever even dreamed of."

"Well, it's tucked away in the house," I replied. "So, I guess that's good.... but does that change anything? I don't suppose there is some sort of spell to get rid of Sam in there."

"There certainly could be. At the very least we can use that to help identify what spells may be at play and thus how to clean this mess up. But Jim...I need to understand what happened. Tell me everything starting with the last time I talked to you."

I told everything as best as I could remember. David let me talk without interjecting every five seconds. When I finished I really only had one question for him.

"Is Kat in danger?" I held my breath, waiting for the answer.

"You are both in more danger than I think any of us realized. You don't want to mess with this kinda shit. Full physical contact with a demon is not exactly common, but it is a very real thing and can be very dangerous. In this case, you are being contacted in your dreams which extend beyond when you are physically at the house. Then there is the part Ida mentioned to you about time running out. Spells like this do often have limitations including time. If she was only able to bind Samuel for a certain amount of time then I fear this could be catastrophic."

"Uh huh." I nodded along pretending I understood what he was saying despite the fact that I knew he couldn't see me.

"What I am saying is that this curse is locked onto you. Once this time frame is exceeded, you could move to Australia and this thing will follow you!"

This declaration made my heart sink into my stomach. "What about Kat?"

"As I said in the very beginning, she needs to choose a side. The better question is, do you trust her?"

"Of course I trust her!" I replied.

"Well your word is all I have to go on. If you trust her then I trust her. More important than that though, what is it Sam wants?"

"I have no idea but I think it is in the safe, by the book. Should I go get it?"

"Absolutely not!" he shouted.

"Alright, relax."

"Seriously, don't you get it. Right now, whatever he wants is protected by her spells. If you go in and take it out, if you remove it, it isn't protected anymore and it's free game. We can go there together. We can look at it and figure out our plan. Only when we are ready can we remove it."

"I get it, but I would like to get this done sooner than later."

"Jim, I don't think we have much of a choice in that matter. I will be there as soon as I can."

After talking to David, I had time alone. Time to think. My head was awash with every emotion possible. The confrontation with Sam freaked me out. Hearing David say that there was a potential danger for both Kat and me was completely unsettling. However, at that moment there was one nagging thought that I couldn't let go of: the fact that I knew I saw Kat there, and that I knew I heard her talking to someone.

It was easy to just believe that my mind had made that

up. It was easy to believe that she was there looking for me. Yet, there was something about that memory that wouldn't let me give into those tempting thoughts. Seeing her at the house was the clearest memory I had. As I closed my eyes and thought back, I could feel it all. Something was off, I was sure of that much. But I had no clue what it was.

The scariest part of all of this was that as I sat in that hospital bed, I realized I didn't know who I could trust, if anyone. My mind started to play with me and raise all sorts of absurd questions. I began to twist things to see that everyone from David to Kat could be simply using me to get something. I even began to think that everything I saw of Sam that night wasn't real. Maybe it was an elaborate ruse set up by both David and Kat.

Having these doubts about Kat was among the most frustrating feelings I have experienced. It was a doubt which I knew had no real basis other than a feeling. Also, I could not prove or disprove anything. Even if I were to question Kat on it, just asking the question had the potential of sending our relationship spiraling out of control. Maybe Kat was right and this was all in my head. I just didn't know. I was questioning everything, and I hated it. I wanted so badly to just blindly believe everyone.

I tried to clear my head by turning on the TV. I caught the cliffhanger of a game show and the commercial break came on. The first ad was for home security system and was clearly targeted to the old paranoid person living alone . But, while watching it, a thought popped into my head. 'What if I take some precaution and just see what is really going on?'

I picked up my phone and found the number for one of my old co-workers Cedric. I dialed and waited for him to pick up.

"Jim, is that you?" he asked.

"Cedric! You move into my old cube yet?"

"Of course! You know I always wanted that cube... A desk with a computer screen not in a direct line of sight from the bosses office! So, what's up, Paul has been telling us you up and moved to the Bahamas or some shit like that."

"Not exactly, I am around, just tryin' to work on this old house I inherited. But hey, I need your help. Remember when you were telling me about the system you rigged up to make sure your kids weren't breaking into your stash of liquor?"

"Yeah, it works great too! I busted 'em, and they still have no clue how I did it!"

I explained what I was looking for, Cedric agreed to meet me that night and help me out with my little situation. After I hung up the phone, I realized this posed a bit of an issue. Kat would be done with work and with me. I had been in a hospital bed for two days and could hardly push seeing her off. My head started running a list of excuses to use that would allow me to meet Cedric and also run over to the house. I realized that in my attempt to remove any doubt from my head with Kat, I was becoming the one hiding and making up BS excuses.

The next thing I knew I was texting Kat a lie. I had met with the doctors and cleared to go home. I told her I was beat and that I would prefer her to come over around eight to give me some time to recoup. I felt horrible lying to her like that. In my head, I justified it with needing to put this doubt to rest.

Once I was released from the hospital, I headed straight over to my old office and texted Cedric. A few minutes later he appeared carrying a laptop bag. He brought the bag over to my truck, unzipped it, and started pulling things out.

"Here, these are the plain English instructions I wrote out for you." He handed me a folded sheet of paper. "This is your camera. Like I mentioned, it is motion activated and battery powered. It will not record unless you manually turn it on or it detects motion. Keep in mind, it reads a change in the scene as motion. So, if the room goes from dark to light, it will trigger the camera. Once it is triggered, it records for five minutes." He handed me a small black box.

"So how long does the battery last?" I asked.

"It should give you about four to five days without a recharge. When you need to recharge, just plug it in like a phone, and it will be set in about an hour. It is fully charged now." He pointed to the battery life indicator.

"Follow the directions. I made it as easy as possible. This little guy doesn't need Wi-Fi or anything. It is like a cell phone that only takes video. Everything you need to control it and view it is in the app. You can set all kinds of alerts from it sending you a text message anytime motion is activated to even an alert when the battery is running low."

I held up the box to the light, marveling at the size.

"Oh, the one thing you need to be careful with is making sure it is viewing exactly what you want to see. You can remotely control everything except where you put it. So, test it out and make sure it covers the whole area you want it to before you leave it."

I nodded my head. "Got it. Thank you."

"Hey Jim, listen. I know I am just doing you a favor here, but I gotta ask, are you okay? I mean you look like hell and something tells me this is a little more serious than watching over a stash of fine bourbon." He looked genuinely concerned.

"No, I'm fine.," I replied. "I just had a couple people on my property, and I need to see what's going on."

"Uh huh. 'Cause a standard visible camera on your door won't catch that? Like I said it is none of my business, but you know, people don't generally get a camera like this unless there is a pretty serious trust issue somewhere. Look, I appreciate the business. I mean this is a nice little payday for me and all. Just watch yourself brother, okay?"

"I hear ya, I just gotta take care of this and put everything to rest. I'll be fine." I handed him a wad of cash.

"Alright, bro. If you need me, you can find me. But I am not technical support. Means don't be calling me in the middle of the night because you can't charge your battery or some shit like that."

Cedric left and I sat there for a minute in my truck looking at this tiny camera. It was a stupid idea, but I was tired of letting everyone else have control. One way or another this was all going to end.

22

I woke up the next morning in a panic. My head throbbed and I was completely disorientated. As I looked around trying to get my bearings I realized I was home in bed, and Kat was sleeping peacefully next to me. I gently rubbed her shoulder and quickly relaxed. That was until I heard my phone buzzing. I leaned over the side of the bed and picked it up. There were text alerts from the camera I'd set up.

I looked over at Kat and bit my lip. I slowly got out of bed and walked to the bathroom to see what it was all about. I sat down and logged into the app. There was one video file. I downloaded it, and it began to play.

The screen was black for a few seconds, then I saw two people walk in with lanterns. The light was blinding the camera to the point you could only see detail right next to the lanterns and then it blurred into shadows revealing only the outlines of the figures.

The two people moved back and forth through the room. About two minutes into the video, one of the figures set down the lantern on the floor along with something else. I paused the screen, looking at it. My mouth was wide open, and I was overcome with confusion. I turned off the phone and walked quietly over to my nightstand where I frantically dug into the drawer with my wallet, watch, and everything else I carried with me daily. It had to be here. Finally, I felt the cold metal in my fingers. I wrapped my fingers around the key and ran back to the bathroom.

I pulled up the video again and paused it at the same point. I looked back and forth from the key in my hand to the screen. It was the exact same key. Somehow, whoever was at the house had this key or an identical copy of it. More disturbing was that they appeared to be looking for the same thing I was.

I wanted to know what was going on, but I didn't know even who had the answers. If Kat did, I was not ready to call her out on this. If she didn't, I didn't even have a clue what that meant. Despite everything David had told me, I was leaning more to the side of letting them take whatever they wanted. On some level, this whole thing was more than I bargained for, and I just wanted it over.

I turned off my phone and headed back to my bed to rejoin Kat and hopefully forget any of this for a little longer. I laid down next to her, once again seeing her peacefully lying there. I looked back at the key in my hand and quietly put it back in the drawer. As I lay down, my head spun. I felt in danger. Not just in danger of some supernatural force anymore, but the real danger, from real people. Somehow, this felt worse. In my mind, I tried to connect all the pieces.

It didn't add up to me. I was missing something. Why was I the target of Samuel? What could he possibly want from me? But that was the supernatural part. The real part was just as confusing. I mean the money, sure, but that was so tied up with legalities. Someone would have just as good of a chance of taking it before I had it, while it was in trust, as they did now. Somehow, I knew they were all connected. How or why was what I couldn't figure out.

I started replaying conversations in my head. Then, as if I was hitting fast-forward on an old cassette deck, I heard David talk about the KGC and about how they were still around today. It was a long shot at best, but I had nothing else to go on. So, I had to investigate the possibility that there was some connection there.

As my mind ran through all of this, something changed. I was mad and wanted revenge. I wanted to take a stand. For me, for the house, for Kat. No one was going to force me to do or give anything. David could help me with the supernatural, but the KGC? I realized that was my own battle to fight.

I gently got out of the bed, trying to not wake Kat and stepped out of the bedroom. I opened the closet in my hallway and turned on a light. On the floor, I started moving piles of old shoes, and God knows what else until I uncovered the small safe on the floor. I opened it and grabbed the stack of papers in it. I started flipping through the papers. My passport, title to my truck, and just about every moderately important piece of paper I had. Then, I found what I was looking for. A quick glance at the expiration date told me I wasn't too late. I took the card and put everything else back in the safe.

Walking back to the bedroom, I looked at the card. It was my Firearm Owners ID card I had gotten years ago. I never dreamed it would be of any use to me, but today it felt like it was everything I needed.

I hurriedly got dressed and looked over at Kat. I leaned over her on the bed and kissed her on the forehead. She let out a sigh and stretched as she moved.

"I'll be right back baby. I am gonna get you some breakfast."

"Uh-huh, goodnight," she slurred in response.

Later that day, Kat and I arrived at the hotel David was staying at. We walked into the lobby where we found David pacing back and forth. He looked more out of sorts than ever before. We agreed to talk in his room as that was the only place "safe" enough to have a conversation. We entered his room on the third floor, and it was like walking into a crypt. The curtains were drawn with the only light coming from a small bedside lamp. Kat and I sat on the still made bed while David rolled the room's office chair over near the bed.

"Okay, well, are you ready for this?" he asked.

"We're here, aren't we?" I replied.

David shot me a look of disgust. "Listen, this is serious shit man! I need to know you are really ready for this."

"Yes dammit! But what are we doing?" I asked.

"Okay, okay. Here is what I got. I won't replay what has been going on or what we talked about because we all know that." He waved his hands dismissively. "Jim, was there anything else in that room you remember other than the safe?"

I shrugged my shoulders. "I dunno, some candles and shit. It was kinda like a sitting room."

"There is more. Remember that photo you sent me of the Grimoire?"

"Yeah, what about it?"

David moved to take his laptop off the desk and opened it up. "See, you were taking a picture of the Grimoire, but what happens every time we take a picture?"

"For chrissake David, just tell us," I shot back.

"Fine, here is the picture you sent." He showed us the photo on the screen of the computer. "But when you take a picture, you are also taking a snapshot of other things in the room. Granted it is dark and not in focus, but there is more there. So I took that photo, and adjusted some of the contrast and zoomed in behind the book. Look at this."

On the screen was a grainy image of the room behind the table. There were a couple sharp angles appearing on the screen which kind of looked like the edge of a picture frame.

"You know what that is?" He continued without waiting for a response. "I know. I know. Mr. Cranky Pants is not in the mood for questions. So I will tell you exactly what it is. It is a mirror."

"Uh, great. Sure there is a mirror in there because I don't have a couple in my house. Hell, there is one right there in this room. What is your point?" I had no more patience for his cryptic dialog.

"Not just a mirror. Well, it is a mirror, but I believe it is more. Look at the shape of the corner here. And this looks like a symbol here." He pointed to the image. "Now, I did a little research. I knew I had seen that before. Here, look at this, really the bottom corner of it."

Now the screen showed a hand-drawn image of a shield with some writing on it, but it did appear to be a match.

"This is a Black Mirror of Lilith!" he declared.

"I take it, that is a good thing?" I shrugged my shoulders.

"This drawing, care to guess where it came from?" he asked.

"I'm gonna just assume it's from the book that was written based on the book I found in the room," I replied.

"See, I knew you were paying attention! Exactly! This mirror was described in that Grimoire. And since I know you have not read it, you will want to know what it is, right? Okay, have you ever seen Snow White? You know, the evil bitch trying to kill off her stepdaughter because she is way hotter? You know, mirror, mirror on the wall?"

"Of course, I know my princesses!" Kat replied.

"Good! Because this is that mirror!" David yelled.

David got this silly look on his face. It was out of place and just plain maddening.

"What, David?" I couldn't hide my annoyance.

"Well, it's just that...we discussed a theory I had before. This... this gives me reason to believe that my theory is absolutely correct."

"Just say it already," I grumbled.

"Okay, so there's only one thing that connects all the dots in my mind on this. Ida, from what we know of her, was tormented forever at the loss of her son. From what I can tell, everything from her motivation to become involved in spiritualism, to all of this, was drawn from that energy. The Mirror of Lilith, well it can show you anything! Past, present, and future. We have all tried to understand how this happened, how you were picked by Ida decades before you were born."

"What are you saying?" Kat asked.

David stood up and started pacing back and forth in the tiny room.

"Well, I believe you, Jim, are Ida's son, Samuel Leopold Muller."

The room sat silent, aside from the sound of the noisy AC unit.

"I need a drink." I stood up and looked out the window to gather my thoughts. "Let me just see if I got this right. Samuel was the bastard child, killed by his not real dad. Ida then decides this mirror will tell her who Samuel will be reincarnated as, and that just happens to be me."

"Wow, you got it quite well actually," David replied giddily.

"Jesus... Let's just forget for a second how insane this all is! Let's assume we live in a world where Disney is reality and mirrors talk, and we live in a place where reincarnation is a thing. Now, we can first thank my lucky stars that I didn't come back as a pigeon or something, but all of this still begs the question of how the hell do we get rid of Sam!"

"Well for that, we need to get in that room. I need to see the Grimoire, and we need to use the mirror. While we're there, we need to find out what Ida has been protecting from Sam in that safe."

"Okay, let's get out there and get the book already," I said. "The sooner we can end this, the better!"

"As much as I agree with you, there is one more thing I feel I need to share before head out there," David said sitting down again.

"You mean beyond me being some reincarnated kid?" I replied.

"Unfortunately, yes." He had a very serious look on his face. "See, there is more to the Mirror of Lilith than simply hanging up the mirror and talking to it. First, a ritual needs to be performed. In addition, the mirror is very specific about where it can be used. In the instructions, it needs to be in a sepulcher of a murdered person."

Looking at David, I could tell I didn't need to ask this question.

"A sepulcher is essentially a crypt or tomb," he finished.

"So, you're saying that this room we are talking about is a crypt?" Kat shouted.

"I really don't know. I mean, I'm pretty sure you would have noticed if there was a body in there Jim." He looked expectantly at me. When I didn't respond, he continued.

"Look, maybe there is a body for all I know, but I hope not. That being said, I think it is safe to assume two things. First, this is a very private place that Ida used to pay her respects to her beloved son Samuel Leopold. Secondly, I do believe there is some piece of Samuel there, be it a lock of hair or an urn of cremated remains."

"Okay pardon my French, but this is kinda fucked up!" I said. "But as messed up as all this is, I also realize we're not gonna to accomplish a damn thing unless we get in that room. So, let's go already."

I couldn't stay in that hotel room any longer. I was desperate to get that book and figure this all out.

"Hey, David," I asked on the way out to the truck, "do you really believe that whole reincarnation thing? Uh, I mean, do you really think I'm her son?"

"Kinda hard to say. In the end, we really don't know anything. I will say I have seen compelling evidence that supports the theory, like your situation. There isn't much else to explain it." He paused. "Let me ask you, was there ever a part of this house or property, maybe even a picture of Ida or whatever, where you all of a sudden felt like you had seen it before?"

"Well, yeah I guess so, but who is to say what that means. I mean your head can do a lot of crazy stuff. You can convince yourself of anything if you want to."

"That is precisely why this is all theory. Look at everything in the paranormal world. It all can have a justifiable explanation both within the paranormal world as well as to the contrary. It's even worse than religion. Scientists need proof to admit it exists. Religious people hold their ground based upon faith. This is no different. I cannot say for certain whether you are Sam Jr. or not. I cannot say Ida is here or not. Being one who lives with an open mind, willing to admit I can't explain everything, I see compelling evidence that suggests this is all very real."

"What about the KGC? You said that was still a thing."

"Oh, they are still a thing for sure! But they are the epitome of secrets. People talk about the Masons being secretive. They got nothing on these guys. Very little is really known except for historical info that came out. I will say this, you want to know if they are real. Go to the grave site of a known KGC member, carrying a shovel and see how long it takes for a blacked out pickup to stop by ready to take you out. Not that I know anything about that...of course."

"I don't get it though. What are they after?"

"I'm sure it's some hidden plan for taking over the world. I mean that is what it was founded for. They are also believed to have hidden a massive hoard of gold to fund their new empire.

"The truth is we don't know much beyond that. It is rumors and legends. We know that people are still protecting KGC secrets, but that is all we know. From my perspective, I really don't have a clue what their current purpose or motivation is, but you will not see me cross them. They operate with some crazy Secret Service style communication and protection."

"Okay boys, enough of this theoretical stuff," Kat said. "What are we doing there today?"

"We need that grimoire for starters," David answered. "Anything else we can learn while we're there can help too. The problem is, we only have theories about all this. We need to find what we can to support or dismiss those theories and the longer we take.... well."

"Well, what?" Kat replied.

"Look, clearly this is all getting worse. Samuel is getting stronger, and the longer we spend pontificating about it, the more power he seems to gain. Jim has been hospitalized already. What's next?"

"Wait, you're the medium," Kat pointed out. "Surely there has to be some way we can just banish the demon and buy ourselves more time to sort this all out, right?"

"It isn't like that. This isn't a movie where a priest walks in with some holy water and everything is over! Yes, things can be done, but it's all like putting a band-aid on instead of stitching the wound. Unless we know what's going on, it's all temporary. We need to end this once and for all."

"Okay okay," I said, "we go in there. We get the book and have a look around. Let's just let David do his thing here. I will be the first to admit nothing I've done has been any help at all."

I pulled my truck onto the property and up the long drive to the house. The sky was grey, and the sun was absent. We stepped out into the cold of the day. The wind whipped across Lake Michigan, carrying a chill that bit to the bone.

"You gonna have this place heated before winter hits?" David asked.

"That's the plan. The roof is almost done. Then, a crew can come in and start, but who knows at this point. We seem miles away from the house being livable."

We stepped into the quiet house and slowly worked our way upstairs to the parlor. We all stood silently, holding our breath, afraid of what would be on the other side of the door. As the door swung open, we were all relieved to see the room was quiet and exactly what it should be.

My phone started going off moments after opening the door. The camera was texting me. 'At least one thing is working,' I thought.

We made our way inside, and I started to explain how

I'd found the hidden door. David was enthralled with the entire premise of the door. I unlocked the door, and slowly opened it. It was cool and dark inside. As we stepped in with our lanterns, I quickly saw this room was different.

The first time I'd stepped into the room, it was as if a living thing was inviting me in. Today, however, it was just a room. Like an old attic or basement. It was dusty and undisturbed. Looking down revealed every action I took the last time I was there. My footprints and my fingerprints were all there, painting a trail in the dust.

David immediately found the book and cradled it like it was going to turn to dust with the slightest movement. He opened the front cover and attempted to read it. At that moment, I noticed Kat out of the corner of my eye. She was standing there silent and motionless... just staring. As I approached, I realized it was the mirror she was staring at.

"Kat?"

"Look at it, Jim! It's amazing and precisely like the drawing." She never broke her stare.

"Kat, are you okay?"

She didn't respond. I walked closer to her and grabbed her hand. It was ice cold. I looked up and glanced in the mirror. It was indeed exactly like the drawing, but something was wrong. I raised my lantern higher and looked again in the mirror. Kat was still fixated on it. Yet, I could see nothing reflecting in the mirror. I could see nothing, just black empty space.

"Katherine!" I yelled. "Come back to me!"

23

THE NEXT FEW moments felt like an eternity. I tried to pull Kat back with all my strength but, she would not move. I put myself in between her and the mirror, and as I stepped, she slowly collapsed. I dove to break her fall and somehow missed completely.

It took a moment to recover and turn. When I did, I saw Kat sitting on the floor, her knees pulled to her chest. Her eyes were wide and unblinking. Streams of tears ran down her cheeks. David put the book down and knelt by her side.

"What the hell happened?" I yelled at David.

He put his hand up to me like a traffic guard, telling me to stop.

"Kat, we are here. It's safe. Come back." He gently pulled up her hand, holding it.

David snapped his fingers in front of her face. Immediately, her eyes closed, and her head fell slack only to instantly jolt up like a person waking up. For the next second, she looked around the room, then at the mirror, then at me.

"We need to leave now!" She was frantic.

"It's okay now Kat," I said. "We're here."

"No! We are all in danger. We need to leave now!" She stood up and bolted out of the room.

Rather than question her, we followed. David grabbed the book on the way out, and we locked the door and headed out of the house. Kat was running. I was behind her while David struggled to keep up. We got outside the house in darkness. The moon had risen high above.

"What the hell?" I said as we got to the truck. "How is it dark? We were only in there for what, twenty minutes."

"Just get in and drive!" Kat yelled.

We got in the truck. I started it and headed towards the entrance.

"Stop!" Kat shouted.

I slammed on the brakes, nearly killing David who slammed into the back of my seat.

"Look!" Kat pointed out the windshield. "Nobody else should be driving down here, right? Kill the headlights so we are not seen."

I looked up to see a pair of headlights through the trees. I turned my lights off and slammed on the gas taking my truck off the path and out of sight from the driveway. David's panting was deafening in the quiet truck as we all just stared out the window. We watched the headlights slowly get closer.

Soon, the driveway lit up, illuminated by the headlights. A shiny black SUV pulled up and drove past us, never slowing until it reached the front of the house. I immediately shifted my truck into drive only to have Kat grab my hand and put it back into park.

"Not now. They'll be back. They cannot get in. The room is protected." Her voice was monotone as she stared out the window.

"Can we get the fuck out of here please!" David was wild in the backseat. "I told you! Black trucks! They mean business, and we need to stay out of it!"

I gave into his plea and started to slowly drive the truck off the property. Once we hit the road, I turned on my lights and slammed on the gas. Soon, we reached the neighborhood with the fancy houses. I came to a cross street and slowed down enough to make the turn without flipping the truck, but its massive tires screeched on the pavement. I drove up a block and turned the truck around. I pulled halfway up to the turnoff for the manor and pulled over turning off the lights.

"I want to get a look at them," I said. "This is the only road in and out of the house. They will have to pass by here on their way out. While we wait, you think you can tell us what the fuck is going on Kat?"

It came out far harsher than I intended, and I could see the words attack her like knives.

"I'm sorry, I'm just a little...well fuck, you know." I took a deep breath abandoning my harsh tone.

She slowly looked up at me. I could see her eyes were tearing up.

"I'm sorry Jim." She was shaking her head.

I grabbed her hands and held them tightly.

"It's okay. Everything is okay. What did you see?"

"I saw Edgar. He spoke to me."

"David, is this real, or did she fall into some trance?" I asked.

"Let her speak, Jim."

"He told us to go! He told me someone was coming, and we needed to be gone. He was right! Do you need more proof than that?" She glared at me.

"I'm sorry Kat. My head is just spinning here."

"Hey, remember me?" David said. "Now you guys can work through this, but I just want to jump in and say we shouldn't really be sticking around to meet our visitors here. I got a feeling we need to get the hell out of here."

"David is right, Jim. Please just drive. Let's go to my mom's house. We can talk there, and I can tell you everything I saw."

Against my better judgment, I listened to her. My truck was a massive bubble of tension as I drove off and headed to Kat's house. We were all in a state of shock and were silent.

"Those assholes broke my watch!" David yelled breaking the silence. "My watch, it is nearly eleven o'clock, and my watch says it is just after seven."

"Nobody touched your damn watch," I replied. "Your battery probably died. Either way I think we have bigger things to worry about."

"There isn't a battery to die, and my watch is still running. It is like it just stopped for the time we were in that room."

"Alright, fine. Add it to the list of shit going wrong with this place. Let's just get to Kat's and sort this all out."

We drove the rest of the way to Kat's house in silence. Despite being annoyed hearing about David's watch, I still couldn't imagine how it had gotten so late. I had made a mental note to take a look at the video files when I had a chance. Somehow, we were all in a time warp, and I welcomed anything I could use to help figure it out.

I was an emotional wreck. Yes, there was plenty of tension in the truck, but I was adding to it, and I didn't know why. I felt like I was on the blade of a knife, and the slightest nudge was going to send me over the edge of it. The drive gave me a little time to hit the internal reset button. Right now, I was consumed with the voice telling me not to speak without thinking. I needed to be calm.

We walked into the house, and Kat led us over to the family room. She asked us to sit down. She excused herself for a minute, and I was left sitting there with David.

"What's going on?" I asked.

"What isn't? We have kinda hit just about everything today. Right now, I am more curious to hear what she has to say."

I didn't respond. I just sat there absently staring off into the distance.

"Listen, I get it," he said. "This is some pretty heavy shit, but we gotta let Kat tell her story. Hold down whatever you are feeling to let that happen."

"I hope she has some beer," I said. "I need a drink for sure."

"Now that I can agree with completely!"

A few moments later, Kat appeared in the room after having changed clothes. As if she was listening in on us, she handed us both an ice-cold beer.

"I figured we all needed a drink after that." She sat down, a beer of her own in her hand.

"What did you see?" David asked.

"Like I said, it was my great-great-grandfather. But before I get into that, do any of you know about a necklace?"

"Not really sure what a necklace has to do with anything," David said.

"I'm pretty sure that is what is in that safe, and I'm also pretty sure that is exactly what those men want. See, when I saw Edgar, he talked to me like I was the only person in the room. He called me by name, explained he was Edgar and then even held up this to prove it." She held up her steel penny.

"This is incredible!" David was unable to contain himself anymore.

"He talked about Sam and how he'd tried to stop him. He said that he killed Samuel, but even in death he wouldn't be stopped. Samuel needed the necklace, but he also needed me. He wanted me as the last remaining person in his bloodline to take over where he left off. Then, he went on to say that we are all in danger. A group of men is coming to the house to get Ida's necklace."

She paused and her eyes drifted off as if she were trying to recall the images she'd seen.

"He said the necklace is the only thing they are after. Then, he stopped and looked around. He told me we had to leave, that it wasn't safe, and they were on their way... to get out immediately."

We all sat there in silence not knowing how to respond.

"The next thing I remember was lying on the ground," she said.

"Does this make any sense to you, David?" I asked.

"The contact, yes, absolutely. The story of him slaying Sam coincides perfectly with what Ida revealed to Jim. But the part about the necklace, I'm afraid not. Let me look into it and see what I can find." He pulled out his phone.

"What kind of necklace could be so valuable that a team is coming after it?" I asked. "And for chrissakes, the house was empty for fifty years. They could have blown the door off the safe with explosives, and no one would have known or cared."

"Not necessarily Jim. Remember, Ida said that the room was under a spell of protection, preventing anyone trying to get in. Except you of course."

"I guess. I mean logic tells me that is BS, but then again we are sitting here talking about a message from Kat's great-

great-grandfather that came through some magic mirror. So, I'll just go along with that for now." I took a drink of my beer.

"Oh my god!" David exclaimed. "This has to be it!"

"What? What has to be it?" I asked.

"The necklace. Listen to this." He began reading off of his phone. "In attendance was Ida Mansfeld, heiress to the Mansfeld newspaper fortune and socialite. All eyes were on her as she flaunted the newest addition to her ever-growing jewelry collection. This spectacular necklace was a gift from her husband Samuel Freidrich Muller and marks their place on the throne of Chicago's elite. The necklace was commissioned by Samuel and was reported to take over a year to create. White gold is off-set by hundreds of diamonds. Two large Sapphires add contrast and color while drawing attention to the massive one-hundred-and-ten karat emerald pendant. The necklace is reported to have cost a staggering five-hundred thousand dollars to create and can only be compared to the jewels of Marie Antoinette." David handed me the phone to read for myself.

There was a photo of Ida dressed in a fur coat, a fur hat, and of course the necklace. It was unlike anything I had ever seen. It immediately struck me as something I would expect to see in a glass case surrounded by lasers in a museum.

"Okay, that is impressive," I said. "But can I just throw this out there? Say it did cost five-hundred thousand dollars. The increased value of both the gems and the rarity of its craftsmanship could bring that up to a value of what, five million today? First off, that isn't exactly something you melt down and sell off at a pawn shop. Anyone who sees it is going to question where it came from. Right?"

"Yes," David agreed. "Its value is in the complete piece, not the parts. But how many times have we heard stories of some rich guy having an original Picasso in his second bedroom despite half the world looking for it? Stuff like that does happen."

"I suppose. It still seems like a stretch to me. I mean sure, someone could want it privately. Someone could pay a ransom to have it stolen. I've seen movies too. I just find it a bit of a reach to assume that these thieves for hire are staking out an old decrepit house, waiting for the moment they can grab it."

"What else do we have to work with, though?" David asked.

We sat there going through pictures of the necklace, throwing different theories out. I noticed Kat was becoming distant, staring off into space. Just as I made a mental note of it, she stood up.

"David, I need to talk to Jim privately for a minute. We'll go upstairs. If you need another beer, they're in the fridge."

Now, I had never been married but knew from TV and movies that her needing to talk to me in private was not going to be a good thing. I nodded and swallowed hard as I followed her out of the room. I felt as if I was being led to the gallows.

"Jim, sit down," she said. "I just need to say this and if I don't do it right now, I don't know when I will have the courage to again,"

I sat down on a chair in her room and looked at her. She paced back and forth as she spoke.

"I think I know who is after us," she said.

"What do you mean?" I asked.

"Just listen. Remember that day at the lawyer's office?"

"Yeah of course."

"That lawyer Lutz had been calling my mom constantly

in the weeks before. This was like his graduation day. Then, my mom got sick... really sick."

I could see tears forming in the corners of her eyes.

"That first night in the hospital, my mom was just lying there with machines beeping and the door opened. These two guys walked in. I stood up thinking they were in the wrong room or something. They approached me and told me to sit down. They knew my name and my mom's name. They basically sat there and told me that my mom was in the hospital because of them and if she wanted any hope of her recovering, I would do what they asked.

"Initially, I told them to fuck off and threatened to call the police. Then, one took out a syringe and was going to inject it in my mom's IV, telling me it would kill her instantly. So, I listened to them.

"They told me about the meeting with the lawyer. They told me that I needed to go into that meeting for my mom and try to find out what you were going to do. They wanted me to get close to you. I didn't know you. I just knew my mom was in danger. Then, once I was talking to you, they raised the stakes. They told me about the room and the safe. They wanted me to go in and get the necklace for them. I refused. This was when we went to meet David. There was another key to the Parlor Edgar had left. I gave them the key and told them you would be out of town and that was the most I could do. They need that necklace, and they will not stop without it, Jim. They will kill us all to get to it."

She was now sitting on the edge of the bed sobbing. I didn't know what to think. My head hadn't gotten past the first part about the lawyer's office. That was where the first knife dug into me. It felt like all the air was sucked out of the room. The only thing I could keep thinking in my head was that this was all a set up from the first meeting. She was never interested in me.

"Jim, I love you," she pleaded. "I tried to stop it all, I really did."

"Or are you just saying that because you were told to?" I shot back.

"Fuck Jim! I'm serious! I'm telling you this because you are more important to me than any of this."

"You want the necklace, fucking take it and good luck! You know, you could have just had it if you asked for it." I didn't know if that was true, but right then it felt as though it was.

"I'm sorry!" she cried. "I never wanted this!"

"And I did? 'Cause I'm pretty sure you created it, not me!" I pointed a finger at her. "Oh wait, you can't just take the necklace. David was right. You still fucking need me!"

I turned and looked out the window. I was unable to look at her any longer.

"And that was you that night. While I was fucking dying at the house, you were there, not looking for me, you were there helping them. You were making deals with my stuff while I was bleeding out on the lawn! You did a great job of trying to convince me I made it up, but I fucking heard you!" I was livid.

"I was there. You're right. But I was there for you. I was in the house looking for you because I was worried." She took a deep breath and covered her face with her hands. "They called me while I was there."

"Yeah, and I know they have been to the house every night. In that room, trying to get to the safe, and I know they got in with a key."

"How did you know that?" she asked.

"Sorry, I didn't know you were the only one allowed to

keep secrets here," I spat in response. "Oh wait a second. I get it now. This is perfect."

"Jim, what are you saying?" she asked.

"You tell me all this. You tell me about the bogeymen who are going to kill your mom. Conveniently, you bring this up just after you get a message from the mirror, which no one else can hear. Well played." I clapped my hands with maniacal satisfaction.

"No Jim! It isn't like that. I am telling you the truth!"

"You know what, I have had enough of your brand of truth. I am better off on my own." I walked towards the door. "Oh, by the way, I take back my offer. You want that necklace? The only way you are getting it is prying it out of my dead fingers. So, good luck with that!"

I hurried down the stairs to see David in the family room. He stood up, setting the book down.

"Jim, look I think I found something. You have to see this!" He looked at me and immediately could see in my face that it wasn't the time. "Ah well, of course, we can just talk about it later or something."

"Look, I'm leaving. If you're smart, you'll get out of this house too. I'll drive you to the hotel."

"Yeah, um, great idea," David replied awkwardly. "It is getting late anyway... um, I should be getting some sleep,"

"If I am driving you, do me a favor and for once just shut the fuck up!"

24

THE NEXT DAY could only be compared to a massive hang-
over. I spent the day in my apartment, an emotional wreck. I
was all over the place. One minute I was angry, then sad and
crying. There were even brief moments where that little
voice in my head tried to get me to look at it all logically. I
kinda understood it all. I probably would have done the
same thing Kat did. But that was the moment in thinking
where the thought of her just playing me took over and
brought on a rage unlike any I'd ever felt.

My phone had gone dead, and I was in no hurry to
charge it. There was a constant barrage of texts and calls
from both Kat and David. I had no desire to hear from either
of them. I just wanted solitude. I decided I needed at least
one friend with me through this. So, I found my old buddy
Jim Beam to hang out with. That was probably not my best
decision.

Half a bottle later, the emotional swings had reached a
completely new level. The sadness became abysmal. The
rage became overwhelming. Thankfully, it was at that time I
finally fell asleep.

I woke up early and took a shower. I actually felt a bit more normal. I wasn't about to go calling Kat up or anything, but I felt as though I could at least play the role of a normal everyday person. I plugged my phone in and kinda went on with a normal morning. Then, while emptying the pockets of my dirty jeans I found my FOID card, along with my receipt. I made the realization that my waiting period was over. Today, I could pick up my new gun.

As I drove to the shooting range, I chuckled about how the purpose of a waiting period for buying a gun was to keep them out of the hands of emotionally destroyed people like me. Fortunately for myself I bought this before I learned about Kat. Soon I was standing in a gun range, inserting the clip into my new Glock .22. No matter what was going through my head, standing in that range and firing off clip after clip of ammo was exhilarating.

The gun was much easier to handle than I'd anticipated. After a few clips, I was able to at least hit the target with not too much effort. I was far from a sharpshooter, but in a pinch, if I had to defend myself, I felt I could. That was really my original intent with this whole purchase anyway.

Once I got back to my apartment, I started looking at my phone again. I couldn't bring myself to look at the texts from Kat. I started weeding through the texts from David. Even that proved to be more than I was ready to handle. Typical BS friend stuff. "I know it isn't my place but..."

"You're right David, it isn't your place," I said to myself. "You should have listened last night when I told you to just shut up,"

Frustrated with the texts, I tossed my phone aside and took a nap on the couch. As I closed my eyes, I drifted off and saw her. I was at the house, standing on the bluff overlooking the lake. Ida was there next to me with her hand on top of mine.

"It is your time, James," she said.

"What do you mean?" I asked.

"Samuel... I couldn't stop him then, and now I can only do so much to keep you safe from him. You need to make your stand and put things right again."

"You mean the necklace?" I asked.

"That gaudy thing? I should think not. I never did like it, even when he gave it to me. I have no concern for it, but it is still there because it did give me one thing," She gestured toward the house.

"What was that?" I asked.

"Control, my dear son. There was something about that piece. Samuel needed it more than anything I could remember. As long as I had it, he let me have the space I needed. It was through that piece I was able to protect this home and protect you for as long as I had. It was my bargaining chip." She giggled. "I always found it funny that the one thing he needed above all was the one thing he actually gifted to me."

"So that is what he wants now, then?" I asked.

"I should think not! He certainly needs the necklace, but he is still here for one purpose only and will not stop until he gets it. He is here to ensure that he finishes what he started years ago."

"What is it then?" I asked.

"James, a mother should never have to say such things. You stand between him and the restoration of his bloodline. He knows you are the only one capable of stopping him, and he will not rest until you are gone."

I looked her in the eyes for the first time. Despite the

tears now forming, they were bright and full of love. Looking at her, I felt at ease.

She let go of my hand and waved towards the lake. The water looked brilliant. The sun was setting behind us, and the sky turned a majestic orange. The orange glow blanketed everything.

"Look, James. Your time is coming. The sun will soon set. It is time for you to make your stand. I have faith in you."

I looked back over the waves crashing on the shore. Everything blurred out and turned black for a moment. When I opened my eyes, I was back on my couch in the apartment.

I felt at ease for the first time in days. I could see out the window that night was coming. I sat up and looked at my phone. There was a new text from David.

"Listen, bro, no matter what you feel about her right now, we need to finish this. We are all in danger."

My fingers tightened on the phone to the point I almost crushed it. I didn't care what David was saying. All I could think about was Kat's betrayal. At that moment, the rage boiling inside me took over. The voice in the back of my head was gone. Peace was gone. My ability to just push aside those feelings had slipped away.

I grabbed my gun and inserted the holster into my waistband. I put the second clip in my pocket and headed towards the door.

"You're right Ida. It's time to make my stand." I walked out the door.

My truck roared as I pressed the accelerator down. The stereo was turned up to the max. The windows were open, the cold wind chilling me to the bone. I was running on adrenaline. By the time I got to the driveway of the house, the sun had started to fall. Darkness was imminent. I drove up to the front of the house and slammed on the brakes.

I hopped out of the truck and started to make my way to the pond. The walk was quick. Soon, I was making my way through the overgrown shrubs and staring across the decrepit pond. I casually started walking to the far end where the bench was.

"You wanted me, Samuel? Here I fucking am!" I heard my voice echo.

As I continued walking, the pond began to transform. The cracks healed themselves. The shrubs became neatly trimmed. And then there was light. Two torches appeared with a massive flame illuminating the entire area with an eerie glow.

"I must say, I am surprised at your persistence. Much like your mother. She never did know when to stop."

Then I saw him. He was standing behind the bench, dressed in a full suit with a jacket over his shoulders.

"You are early for tonight's presentation I am afraid. You caught me off guard and sadly unprepared."

"No need for a presentation. We can end this now."

"Really? You say 'we' as if you have control over anything that happens."

I reached behind my back and my fingers rolled around the handle of my gun. I pulled it out and took quick aim at Samuel.

"A gun?" His laughter echoed. "Apparently, I overestimated your intelligence. I have been dead for a long time. Just what do you think a gunshot will do to me?"

Ashamed at the thought, I lowered the gun and put it back in its holster.

"See James, this is what happens when you take the finer qualities of a woman of your mother's stature and breed it with a dimwitted servant like Edgar. All the persistence in the world but not a lick of intelligence to back it up. Your father thought he could end this with a gun too. And well, I think you can see for yourself how well that worked out."

"Enough! You want me dead? Well, here I am!"

"Right you are James, but let's not jump into anything so quickly. My necklace is still not in the hands of those who need it and you have still come here alone."

"I won't get it for you. It is you and me, right now!"

"As I said, you are early, the sky is turning red and my return to power is drawing near. There is nothing you can do to stop me now, and if you choose to wait, you will still die, but in a more agonizing way. Do you know what is even better than feeling the last heartbeat of someone you want dead, James?"

"No, but I'm sure you'll enlighten me."

"Seeing them suffer. See, death is rewarding, but it is so quick. To look into a person's eyes, as you destroy everything they care about is the true reward. Killing their soul, then their body." He walked closer to me before continuing. "And you made it so simple James. I can feel it now. Soon, everything will be ready."

"Let's just finish this now. I know you want the necklace!"

"Such a shame. You know, I am afraid that little trinket has turned me into a bit of a mockery in the eyes of my brothers. It is time for that to be put back into the proper hands. Of course, after tonight, it doesn't much matter. With you dead, that little bit of magic your witch of a mother used will be gone, and the necklace will be back where it should be."

"What is it about the damn necklace anyway?"

As I spoke those words, I felt my phone vibrate. I knew

that alert. It was the camera. Someone was in the room. I was trying to get as much understanding as I could before I dealt with them though.

"Secrets are not meant to be shared outside the circle, James. Yet, you have nowhere to run, and there is something terribly enjoyable about seeing you make the connections." He chuckled. "The necklace is a map. A map my brothers need and will have again tonight. The biggest mistake of my life was entrusting it with your mother. She made a mess of everything. Things would have been so simple if she would have just done as she was told. Like I said though, at this point it doesn't much matter if you choose to get it or not. Your mother's power is all but gone. Understand this: by the end of this night, you will be dead and the necklace will be gone. There is simply nothing you can do. Actually, I forgot to mention, your little friend Kat is helping me out with the necklace right now."

I had controlled myself this long, but that last sentence put me over the edge. I came here believing I could end this myself. At hearing that Kat was in the room, I realized I had to first stop her. I had learned everything I needed to. It truly was my time. I took the gun from the holster and held it tightly in my hand and raised it. Samuel let out a laugh, and I turned to run. I took off in a sprint back to the house.

"Oh, James you are too much! Be careful dear boy. I wouldn't want you to do something too stupid and take away my opportunity to kill you myself." I could hear him laughing in the distance as I ran.

That was the last thing I heard as I reached the shrubs at the far end of the pond. As I jumped through and saw of the house, everything returned to normal. The house was under construction, the shrubs overgrown. I moved quietly with my gun drawn. As I made it around to the front of the house, I stopped and took a deep breath. I holstered my pistol and cursed under my breath.

Kat's car was sitting there. She was here to finish things for herself. Out of breath, I spat. I bit my lower lip, moving my rage from Samuel to her.

I entered the house and slowly made my way to the staircase. Quickly, my eyes adjusted to the darkness. I started climbing the stairs, hesitating with every step so the creak of the aged wood wouldn't give away my presence. Once at the top, I made my way down the hall. Soon, the parlor was in sight. The door stood open, and I could see light inside. I stopped to catch my breath. I couldn't hear a sound coming from the room.

With a swift movement, I darted inside. I was anticipating surprising Kat, but what I saw surprised me in a way I will never forget.

Walking into the room, I saw Kat on the couch. She was gagged and her hands and feet were tied. Even before the sight of this registered in my brain, I felt the cold metal of a gun barrel pressed against the back of my head and a hand removing my gun from its holster. The next thing I felt was a shove on my back, throwing my body onto the hard floor.

I opened my eyes and saw a man pointing a gun at me. My sight was blurred. As things came into focus, I recognized him. It was the lawyer.

"Welcome back Jim. Glad you could finally join us."

I slowly worked myself up to my knees.

"The fuck do you want?" I asked.

"Please. Enough with your stupidity. You have been running us in circles for months now. You know, most bottom feeders like you would have gone to the safe immediately. Although, I suppose what is a couple more months when we have waited so long?"

In my head, I was calculating the distance between us. 'How long would it take me to step up, close the gap and disarm him?' I thought to myself.

He was an old man. His reflexes certainly were not the best. Although, I realized I had to do about five things, and all he had to do was pull the trigger.

"Look around the room before you do something stupid," he said as if reading my mind.

I looked around and then I saw two men behind me with guns drawn. Only, the guns were not pointed at me. They were pointed at Kat. The only thing standing between Kat and a bullet in her head was the slightest order from Lutz.

I raised my hands in defeat.

"You know we wouldn't shoot you. We still need you. Finally, tonight you will prove to my brothers that patience and planning are always more powerful and effective than brute force."

He stepped over to the hidden door. It was already open. "Shall we, Jim? The sooner I get what I want, the sooner you can go back to your life. Once we have the necklace, you will never hear from us again. And really, it is a small price to pay, given this fortune you just literally walked into. So, let's just get it over with." He extended his hand to the hidden doorway.

I made my way over to the secret room and Lutz filed in behind me.

"Listen, kid. Do what you're told, or she will be gone in a heartbeat, and that will only be the start of it. This can all be over in a matter of moments."

As I walked in and headed towards the safe, I realized the mirror was gone. I also noticed some marks on the wall where it hung. I didn't want to show that it held any of my attention. So, I kept my eyes straight ahead. I walked all the way to the steel door of the safe. I retrieved the key from my pocket, inserted it, and turned it. In the silence the sound of the door unlocking echoed through the room.

The door creaked open. Behind the steel door, were a couple of empty shelves. Below the shelves was another safe. This one was black with a massive dull brass dial and handle.

"Go ahead. What are you waiting for?"

I had memorized the combination after seeing it at David's office on the whiteboard. It was a set of numbers that meant something to me, because it was her son's birthdate. I took a deep breath and began spinning the safe dial to the left. After a couple spins, I stopped the dial on the two. Then to the right over the twenty-seven and back. On the second turn, I spun too much and missed the number.

"Damn," I mumbled.

"Are you trying to stall, hoping someone will come save you?"

"No, I just fucked it up."

I again, spun the dial a few times to the left and then stopping on the two. Now to the right over twenty-seven and back to it stopping the dial. I took my hand off the dial for a moment and took a deep breath. Back on the dial, I took my time to slowly bring the dial to the four. I took my hand off the dial and moved it to the large brass handle. I held my breath as I started to turn it. It turned slowly until it engaged and unlocked the door.

The door popped open about a quarter of an inch. I pulled it open the rest of the way. Inside were two shelves. The top shelf was empty aside from a lock of brown hair tied together with a purple ribbon. On the shelf below, was a flat carved wooden box.

"Hand me the box," Lutz commanded from behind me.

I slowly reached inside for the box. If this was my time, I was blowing it. I racked my brain to think of something equally valiant and stupid to turn this around. Unlike the movies, there was no random piece of steel lying around I could take him out with. Every thought I had met with the same ending, Kat and me both. I retrieved the box and pulled it from the safe. I turned and saw Lutz watching my every move with a huge smile on his face.

I handed him the box, praying he would set his gun down to open it. He didn't, of course. He set the box on the small table and opened it, never taking the gun off of me. With the box open, he stared at its contents for a moment.

In a quick motion, he closed the box and turned his head to me.

"Where the fuck is it?" he roared.

"Where is what?" I spat in response.

"What have you done with it?"

"I haven't done a damn thing. I opened the safe for you. That is the first time I touched it."

"You think I am that stupid?" He walked up to me, stopping within a foot of me. "This is not over. I am sure Katherine will be able to remember what it is you have done with that necklace."

Just as my brain started to track what he was saying, I saw Lutz raise his hand with the gun. His hand came down with fierce velocity. The butt of the gun slammed into my forehead. Everything went black.

25

WHEN I GOT UP, it was completely dark. It wasn't until I felt the cold marble floor underneath me that the reality of it all came back to me. I jolted up, trying to get my bearings. My head throbbed. I stood up and stumbled like a drunk. Unable to see, I reached out with my hands, trying to feel the wall. Anything to guide me. I took a few steps forward, and my foot caught on the chair. I tumbled forward, knocking the chair down beneath me. The chair broke into pieces with my impact.

Now, getting up to my knees, I felt around my pockets until I found my flashlight. I pulled it out and turned it on. The room was the same and empty. I stood slowly. I closed my eyes for a moment, trying to push away the pain in my head. When I closed my eyes, the only vision I had was of Kat tied up on the couch.

With a burst of adrenaline, I ran into the parlor. My light shined on the empty couch. The startling sight of her being gone sent a shock through my body. I dropped the light and went to my knees. Tears streamed from my eyes. I sat there for a few moments. My breathing started to slow. I realized at that moment, that Kat was not to blame, she had told me the truth. She had no choice and now she was in even more danger. I felt responsible for this. I was changing. With every tear that dropped, my sorrow was replaced with rage. Finally, there was no sorrow left.

I grabbed the flashlight and went back to the hidden room, looking for anything that could help me. I went back over to the safe and grabbed the lock of hair and shoved it in my back pocket. My gun was on the ground in front of the safe. I grabbed it. I checked the clip and the chamber. It was loaded and ready to fire. I put it in its holster and turned to walk out of the room.

As I swung the light around and caught a glimpse of where the mirror hung. Remembering there was something there before, I moved the light along the wall until I could see the markings. Looking closer, I could make them out.

"TEXT," was written on the wall in what looked like a red pen.

My mind cycled through a thousand images from the past month, stopping on everyone when I saw David writing something. He always wrote with the same red pen. I realized that had to be from David.

I pulled my phone from my pocket. It was 3:02 in the morning. There was a new text from David sent hours earlier.

"Go to the pond. When the time is right, say these words 'I conjure you, Lylet, and your companions and command you to banish this demon, Samuel Freidrich Muller, from the land of the living and return him to the hell he was delivered from.' When he is gone, destroy the mirror."

I re-read the text over and over. I had no idea what it would do or if it would work. At that point, it was my only hope. I continued to read it until I had committed it to memory. I put the phone back into my pocket. After looking at the bright phone screen, it took my eyes a bit to adjust to the darkness. When they finally had, I walked through the parlor and out into the hall.

The door locked with a thud that echoed through the hall. I realized that if anyone was waiting for me, they would certainly have heard that. I stood frozen in the hall for a moment. I turned off the light and waited for my eyes to fully adjust to the darkness. I could make out the edges of the hallway. I retrieved the gun from its holster. I held the gun with both hands and let it lead my way silently through the hallway, all the way to the staircase.

My heart raced. Yet, I took every step with caution. At every doorway, I expected one of Lutz's men to jump out, but no one did. Still exercising caution, I reached the bottom floor and stopped. I needed to take a deep breath and compose myself, to calm myself. I recited the phrase David texted to me.

I began to move toward the front door of the house. I recited the phrase over and over. With every step closer, I moved with more haste. The front door was in my sight. I had no more fear of someone jumping me. I had to keep moving. I reached the front door and slowly started to open it. As It opened, the cold wind of the night caught me off guard and took my breath away.

I stepped out into the light of the moon. It was a full moon and lit up the grounds like daylight. There was my truck, exactly where I'd left it hours earlier. Kat's car was there as well. My mind raced, trying to think where she could be. I thought about the possibility of Lutz having her killed. I thought of her being hidden in the woods. In the end, I shut the thoughts down because I knew exactly where she was. She was at the pond. I had no reason to know this, but I felt it.

This feeling gave me a new burst of energy. I holstered my pistol and headed towards the pond.

It was dark outside. I could see the murky water reflect the light of the moon beyond the shrubs. Everything looked quiet. There was a pang in my heart as I doubted my feeling. I pushed forward until I made my way through the brush.

Finally, I was able to see the entire pond. There was Kat lying on the far bench, still tied up. The sight sent me in a dead sprint towards her, forgetting any concern for my safety.

"First you arrive early and now late," Samuel's voice boomed.

Hearing this, I stopped dead in my tracks. The transformation took place again and Samuel was there standing before a completely restored pond. He was wearing his hooded cloak, standing behind Kat who laid unmoving on the bench. Now, in the blinding light of the torches, I could make out more of the scene.

"I had expected her eventually, but you all made this far too easy. I thought surely she would come here chasing you."

I began to slowly step closer to his makeshift altar. My eyes were focused on Kat. I could see her chest rise slowly with breath, relieving me.

"So this is it?" I yelled. "You tie me up and kill me?"

"Oh James, I have waited decades for this moment. Let's not rush into anything here. Besides, I see no reason to tie you up. Sure, you are stupid and heroic, but even that cannot overtake your need to watch this."

"Why Kat?" I asked.

My question resulted in an echoing laugh from Sam.

"You really have not figured this all out yet. James, you disappoint me so. You are so much like your father. You think this is about you and your poor mom. Please sit down. Let's chat a moment."

He motioned towards another bench on the side, across from Kat. I followed, taking every opportunity to delay this. I sat down and looked at Samuel.

"Then, why are you here?" I asked. "The necklace wasn't in the safe."

"Again with the necklace. You really need to learn to listen dear boy. The necklace would always fall back into the right hands, but this is why I am here." He gestured to the altar before him.

"This is my day of reckoning. My final chance to right my wrongs and restore everything to its proper balance. I never dreamed it would come together this easily. I always knew I would have you when the time came. But her... you practically handed her to me."

"What does she have to do with this?" I asked.

"Because she is my blood, James. Who could have ever predicted the twist of fate this took. Two half-breeds brought together. First your mother and that halfwit butler father of yours. Then, my little indulgence produced this bloodline in her. I would have taken care of that little situation the same way I did you, but of course, Edgar stepped in. This story just oozes with irony at every turn. I would love to give Edgar some credit for thwarting me, but we both know that was nothing more than dumb luck. Besides, if it weren't for his actions, I wouldn't have this pristine body full of my blood here today."

While he spoke, my eyes scanned the area for David. I prayed he was here somewhere, or at least that his saying would work. My eyes darted back and forth, finding nothing to even hint that these prayers would be answered. Quickly, I realized there were only two ways this night would end. Either we'd all be dead, or, David was right, and Samuel would be gone. I trusted David to a point, but honestly, the idea of trusting my life to him was a bit more than I could easily do. Rather than leave it all to the chance of David being right, I decided I had to try something.

I stood up from the bench and walked towards Samuel, who just stared at me with a confused look. Without another thought, I lowered my body weight and charged at him. I intended to hit him with my shoulder. Instead of making contact, I hit nothing. Nothing stopped me. My feet, braced for the blow, were unable to keep up with my body's trajectory. I stumbled and slammed onto the ground.

When I turned my head to look at Samuel, he was standing there as if nothing happened.

"Again with the heroics? Why must you keep embarrassing yourself?" He laughed loudly.

I slumped my head in defeat.

"Now, you will sit there and watch this," he commanded.

I chose to listen and moved slowly into a sitting position. Then, out of nowhere, something grabbed my hands. They were forced behind my back. No matter how hard I tried, I couldn't move them. I could feel the rope on my wrists, tightly securing them behind my back. Samuel did not move. He just stood there looking at me with a smile.

"Now that there will no longer be any interruptions, we shall begin."

Samuel turned towards Kat and knelt down before the bench. In a moment, he circled his hands on the ground. The next thing I could see was his hand raising a silver chalice. With a grand flourish, he set the chalice on the bench next to Kat and pulled a long shiny knife from his robe. He held it over her for a moment and then lowered it. He turned to face me.

I knew I needed to act. I quickly ran through the spell David gave me in my head.

"I conjure you, Lylet and your companions," I shouted, "and command you to banish this demon, Samuel Freidrich Muller, from the land of the living and return him to hell!"

Samuel sharply turned to face me. He stared me down for a moment before bursting into laughter.

"You really are new to this, aren't you?" He walked towards me.

He knelt next to me and moved in until his face was only an inch from mine.

"You picked up a spell for your mom's mirror. Pity that will not help you here. You haven't brought the mirror with you. Do you really expect the mirror to hear you from here? You should understand one thing before we continue, James. Your mother, even your father, were not particularly skilled. They simply provided setbacks. For certain, everything would have been easier if they had not made their attempts, but there was nothing they could do to overpower me completely."

He stood up and stepped back towards Kat while watching me.

"This is too easy. You know what is the most satisfying way of waking a person who lies unconscious?"

Out of spite, I chose not to reply.

"Taking a knife and cutting them like a surgeon. It never takes long. Then, we not only have the sweet blood, but we have a victim who is awake. Oh, there is such satisfaction of watching a person's eyes as the life is taken from them.... or should I say given to them?"

He turned to Kat and lowered the knife, cutting off her

sleeve. He shuffled back and forth with delight before he slowly sunk the tip of his blade into the flesh of her arm. Within an instant, her body writhed in pain, and he removed the blade.

"There, there Katherine. It is time for you to sit up."

She moved and slowly sat up. I watched her open her eyes, first staring at Samuel, but then scanning her surroundings. Her eyes widened. They locked onto mine. Without being able to discern any body language aside from her eyes, I had no clue what her reaction was. It could have been surprise, love, anger, anything. I saw the response I couldn't deal with. She was looking at me with disappointment. She was waiting for me to rescue her, and it was at that moment she realized I had failed. It was clear to me now that I had sealed both of our fates.

Disappointment, rage, and fear consumed me as I sat there. Kat's eyes were locked on me, and I had failed. I shifted my weight slightly, and my hand brushed against the butt of my pistol. I could not help but show a twinge of a smile. It was not an answer or an escape. It was a chance, and it was a chance I had to take. I tried to signal to Kat what I was planning with my eyes. Although the message certainly did not come across as I intended.

As I continued to look at her, my fingertips ran themselves over the handle of my gun and down toward the holster. Soon, I could feel the edge of my pocket knife, which was clipped in the holster. With every ounce of energy I had, my fingertips were able to free it from the holster and move it into my hand where I could hold it properly.

The knife was a one-hand open. As long as I could press the lever hard enough, I could open the blade. With my fingertips resting on the lever, I shifted slightly where I sat.

This gave me the opportunity to press the lever and also cover any sound it made when opening. I pressed the lever. The blade opened. Now there was true hope.

I gently moved the tip of the blade along the inside of the knot that bound my hands. Thankfully, the blade had a serrated edge which I sunk into the rope. I just needed a few good tries to saw through the knot, and I would be free.

"Samuel, remove her gag," I said. "Let us both speak."

Samuel turned and glared at me. "You want her to speak? I suppose that could be quite entertaining."

He turned back to Kat and began to slowly untie her gag. This gave me the opportunity I was looking for. I pulled the knife, feeling the blade tear through the fibers of the rope. Quickly, I planted under the knot again and pulled again. The rope was thick. Kat's gag was almost removed. I knew I had one chance left. I flipped the blade in my hand and inserted it under the knot. Hoping I found the right spot, I pulled the knife up. I could feel the rope straining under the pressure of the blade until it stopped. The blade was free in my hand, and the ropes loosened around my wrists. I had done it.

My hands were free, and I had to make a move. The question was, what move? I knew I didn't have the ability to overpower him. I started thinking through everything and realized that I'd only ever been able to see him by the pond. Not only that, I had to be close enough to this side of the pond. I had to get to that side with Kat. The only problem was, as I estimated, that would take about ten seconds if nothing went wrong. Ten seconds with him not reacting. I needed a distraction as much as I needed to buy some time for me to come up with one.

"What's the cup for?" I asked. "I thought you just had to kill us."

"I will not be killing Katherine. She will no longer live, but her death will be at the hands of your father."

"How exactly is that?" Kat asked.

"The only death taking place between you and I happened years ago at the hand of Edgar. This ceremony will simply replace your years with mine so that I may live on and fix this."

"What about my mother. She has your blood too!"

"Your Mother? Yes, you are right my dear. Unfortunately, I simply do not care. The blood is required for the ceremony. It is your remaining life I am taking. You have far more left than your mother has."

While they spoke, I had a realization: if the chalice were to drop, would he stop to retrieve it. While it seemed like my only available diversion, being that he conjured up the damn thing to begin with, who knew if it would work.

I knew I was proving him right with his statements about heroics versus intelligence. That frustrated me to some degree, but there was absolutely one thing I knew for certain: I was not going to see Kat die tonight. I would save her or die trying.

I looked at Kat. Our eyes locked on to one another's. Through looking over towards the edge of the pond, I tried again to signal to her what was going to happen. I slowly stood up. I kept holding the rope in my fingers and my hands behind my back to give the impression I was still restrained.

He turned to look at me and took out his knife.

"I see you would like a better look, James. Do not be so bashful. Please, come closer."

I had one chance. I was going to walk up and kick the chalice. As Samuel dove to retrieve it, I was going to grab Kat and carry her out of the garden as fast as I could.

I obeyed Sam and slowly stepped closer. Now I had only two steps to go before I was within reach.

I took another. One step to go.

"You know James, there is only one thing I hate more than whores like your mother."

"What's that?" I asked.

"Imbeciles who do not learn from their mistakes!" he shouted at me with anger.

All of a sudden, it felt as though arms were restraining me. I writhed, trying to break free.

"Now, we will get to see how much Katherine enjoys watching you suffer!" he spat.

He turned to me with his knife gleaming in the light of the moon. I focused every ounce of energy I had left on moving to dodge his blow. It wasn't enough. While I shifted to my left, the blade of his knife plunged into my side. Instantly, the restraint was removed, and I fell to the ground. Lying there, I felt the warmth of my blood as it soaked my shirt. I looked up at Kat who watched in horror. I had no idea if she was screaming or not. I looked at her. Her eyes were locked on mine.

"I'm sorry," I said and then closed my eyes.

26

I LAID THERE for a few moments with my eyes closed, ready to give up. Then a searing pain ripped through my body as Samuel removed the blade. In shock and pain, my eyes opened.

"Get up!" Samuel shouted. "We will end this now, and I will not have your heroics thwart my desire to have you watch me take Katherine's blood!"

I shifted and rose to my knees. I couldn't even feel my arm. I looked back at Kat, and tears began to run down my cheeks.

Satisfied with my view, Samuel turned back to Kat and grabbed the chalice. All of my energy was spent staying up. I wanted to fight but could hardly move. I just sat there in shock. As Samuel raised the chalice to the sky again, I heard something. It was faint and distant. But it was there, and I knew that sound. It was my truck!

The massive engine roared and appeared to be heading closer to us. Samuel noticed too. He turned to glare at me. Soon, the lights of the truck were visible beyond the shrubs. Sam's glare was still focused on me.

"Something about heroics and stupidity," I said with the best cocky smile I could muster.

Moments later I saw the glare of the headlights fly over the shrubs. The truck was headed straight for us. The tires screeched as the truck came to a stop, nearly careening into the edge of the pond. Samuel stood there looking at it. The door opened and David stepped out, nearly falling as his feet hit the ground.

"How's that for an entrance?" David said. "You know, it really hurts that after all this, you didn't even invite me to your little party,"

Everyone was quiet, even Samuel. David turned and opened the back door of the truck.

"Don't worry guys. I don't hold a grudge or anything. This isn't the first time the mailman forgot my invite. No hard feelings. See, I even brought a present."

He shut the door of the truck and stepped forward revealing the mirror in his hands. Upon seeing it, Samuel laughed.

"This is your valiant attempt to stop me? Your mother's cursed mirror?" He laughed harder. "You know the mirror only works within that little seance room your mother built. Out here, it is just about as useful as that gun of yours."

"Actually, that is where you are wrong, Samuel," David replied.

He walked closer, carrying the mirror. He set it down at the edge of the bench so it was facing Samuel and Kat.

"You are right. It only worked in that room, but that had nothing to do with the room itself. The truth is, this little mirror will work anywhere. That is, of course, provided the place it rests is set up properly."

"How so?" Samuel asked.

"Why should I tell you?" David asked.

While they were talking, I started to try and focus my head on the words of that spell. I wasn't sure if we really had any chance left, but I knew this was all I had. Just then, David's body went stiff, and he started sliding closer to us. His arms were rigid behind his back.

"You will answer me!" Samuel commanded.

"Um the...the mirror needs to be placed in a sepulcher of a murdered person," David said.

Samuel let out a laugh.

"Well, the only person about to be murdered here is the only person here who can use the mirror. I applaud your valiant effort, but as with all other attempts, you lose. You all lose." He gestured towards us.

The effort I spent keeping on my feet was becoming more than I could handle. I looked down and saw blood everywhere. I didn't know how much blood one could lose, but I knew it couldn't be much more than I had already lost. Everything I viewed had a cloudy edge to it, and I was feeling very light headed and wobbly. I tried to focus on David hoping he would give me a signal. However, I saw nothing but fear in his eyes.

"Wrong!" I yelled. "You were murdered in this very place!"

Without waiting for any reaction, I immediately started reciting the phrase David sent me.

"I conjure you, Lylet, and your companions and command you to banish this demon, Samuel Freidrich Muller, from the land of the living and return him to hell!"

I finished speaking and instinctively closed my eyes, unsure of what would happen next. A couple seconds went by with nothing. Not even a sound. I opened my eyes and saw Samuel smiling at me.

"Again!" David yelled.

I recited the phrase again. This time as loud as I could with every ounce of energy I had.

"I conjure you, Lylet, and your companions and command you to banish this demon, Samuel Freidrich Muller, from the land of the living and return him to hell!".

Again nothing happened. Samuel was grinning more now, and I saw him raising his knife. As he did, I saw something in the mirror. It was slight, like a momentary reflection of a flame. The knife was directly above my head now, and I closed my eyes bracing for the impact. In that split second, I realized I could not die with my eyes closed. I needed to look at Kat one last time.

When I opened my eyes, everything was still. Samuel was no longer standing in front of me. I looked at Kat. Her eyes were wide with shock. I turned slightly to look at David who was also staring wide-eyed. I followed his gaze. They were focused on the mirror.

The black mirror now glowed orange. In the glow, I could see the outline of a figure. It was Samuel.

"This is only going to hold him for a few moments!" David yelled. "The mirror needs to be destroyed!"

David ran over to the mirror. He picked it up over his head and smashed it down on the marble bench. There was no shattering sound. The mirror landed with a thud face down. David bent down to pick up the mirror again. As he started to pull it up from the ground, a brilliant orange light poured out of the face of the mirror. David dropped the mirror, immediately falling backward.

"It's hot!" He screamed looking at his hands.

The mirror fell but landed leaning against the bench with its face towards me. The orange light was blinding, and I could feel a wave of heat wash over me. The light was more brilliant than anything I had ever seen.

"We need to leave," David yelled. "The mirror will not hold him!"

I could see him moving towards Kat. He was clearly trying to run and get to safety. I didn't move. I couldn't move. I was frozen in the brilliance of the mirror, but it was more than that. It all needed to end. I looked at Kat who was making her way to her feet.

I reached my hand around my waist until my fingers felt the handle of my gun. I removed it and swung it around in front of me. Taking aim at the center of the mirror, I pulled the trigger. Despite everything happening instantly, time slowed down, and I could feel and visualize everything. Barely able to stand, blow-back from the gun sent my body backward and into a fall. As the bullet crashed into the mirror, there was an explosion of light, blinding my vision.

I couldn't hear. I couldn't see. I couldn't move. The bright light faded into darkness, and I could hear shuffling. I tried to force myself to my knees. It was dark and still. The pond was only lit by the moonlight. I could make out blurred shapes of both David and Kat.

"Jim, Kat, are you okay?" I heard David yell.

"I'm here, I think," Kat said.

"Jim, my God Jim, are you all right?" Kat yelled.

"Still alive," I choked out. "Is it over?"

My vision was coming back to me. I could see David untying the ropes around Kat's ankles. I tried to make it to my feet. The pain was unbearable. As quickly as I stood up, my legs gave out, and I crashed to the ground.

"Jim! No!" Kat yelled.

I blinked and when I opened them again she was holding me. David was pressing on the wound in my side. I expected it to hurt but felt nothing. The only thing I could feel was Kat's arms around me.

"Don't leave me now, dammit!" Kat cried. "Jim, stay with me. We are getting help. You need to fucking stay with me!"

There was horror and fear in her brilliant eyes. I was struggling to be aware of her fear, but all I was able to see was her beauty.

"We need to get him to the car. David take his legs."

Now, I was fading in and out of consciousness. One moment, I was lying there in Kat's arms, the next I was being dragged. I was unable to do anything but let it all happen. The next time I opened my eyes, I was lying in the backseat of my truck. My head was on Kat's lap. Her one arm pulled my head tightly into her, while her opposite hand stayed pressed onto my side. We were moving now.

I could see Kat's face light up in short bursts as street lamps blurred past.

"We're almost there. Stay with me." She looked at me. Her eyes were full of concern as she spoke. I couldn't even hear what she said, but I could see her lips moving. I was drifting away. I tried to focus on her eyes, but they became blurrier and blurrier until everything went dark and silent.

I opened my eyes, and everything was bright and clear. It was warm, and the sun was bright. I was running through a garden. I could see the tea house behind the pond. I started to run towards it. When I finally reached it, there was Ida and Edgar. Ida looked at me and grabbed my hand. She pulled me close to her as she wrapped her arms around me.

Then, she looked at me.

"My dearest son. I love you! Never forget that we are here protecting you. You may not always see us, but we are always here. Nothing that ever happens can break this bond."

She pulled me close in her arms and held me tight. After a moment, I pulled away and looked at her. Her eyes showed the love I felt in her arms.

"Thank you, mom," I said.

As the words flowed out of my mouth, my vision started to fade. The warmth of the sun was replaced with cold. It felt like everything in the world was being sucked away from me until there was nothing. Black, empty, nothingness.

Everything stayed dark. I felt nothing. It was as if every one of my senses was cut off.

I heard it in the distance. A beep and then another. The beeps were consistent and grew louder with each one. All of a sudden I saw everything. I was in a dark room. I felt Kat's hand in mine. I briefly closed my eyes as I gently squeezed her hand. I wasn't sure what happened or where I was, but I knew that was where I needed to be. As I drew a long breath, the familiar scent of her made me feel at peace. I moved my head slightly until my cheek brushed up against hers. I leaned into her just enough for my lips to touch her cheek. When I did, her body moved slightly and I felt her fingers tighten around mine. We rested there together.

Seconds later, she squeezed my hand again even tighter and jumped off of me.

"Jim!" she yelled.

She dove on top of me, wrapping her arms around me. At that instant, a jolt of pain shot through my body. With that jolt, I became completely aware of my surroundings. The hospital bed, the tubes running into my arms, the beeping machines, and the line of stitches in my throbbing side.

"Oh my God. I am so sorry." She leaned in to kiss me. "I just... I'm sorry. I just got excited. How bad does it hurt?"

"Well, I guess I'm still alive," I said.

"Yeah, I kinda lost it when you passed out on me in the car, but David got us here and carried you into the E.R."

"David? Oh fuck, the pond. That wasn't a dream?"

"It's over now. Don't worry about it ever again. You did it!" Her voice was full of pride.

We sat in the hospital bed for at least an hour before any nurse even knew I was awake. Kat told me her story. What she saw. How Samuel disappeared into the mirror. And of course how I ended up here.

Then came the parade of doctors and nurses to examine me. Finally, Kat and I were alone in my room again, holding one another. The door to the room opened, and David walked in.

"Morning everyone!" he yelled.

"David, it's 12:30 in the afternoon," I said. "Morning is gone."

"Nope, McDonald's serves breakfast all day now," he replied.

He threw a newspaper on my bed and he then walked around and made himself comfortable in the chair. "Go ahead. Take a look at my gift."

"David, no offense, but your last gift was enough for a long time," I replied. "And seriously, you have to work on your timing. You think you could have swung by thirty seconds earlier so I didn't need all these stitches, asshole?"

"I suppose I could have, but I figured I needed to make one hell of an entrance. I mean, it's not like I get to do this every day."

"Yeah. Your entrance that almost destroyed my inde-structible truck?"

"It's already at the shop. By the time you can drive again, it will be good as new. Seriously, look at my gift."

I picked up the paper and saw the label affixed to it from his hotel.

"Great a newspaper you lifted from the hotel. I didn't

know people still read these. How old do you think I am, eighty?"

"Maybe if more people read and did their own research..." he said.

"You'd be out of a job," I interrupted.

"It's not just a paper. Read the damn headline!"

I unfolded the paper and started scanning through the headlines. The third one on the page stopped me.

"Chicago Lawyer Found Shot in Wacker Drive Office," I read. "Oh my God. Is this Lutz?"

"See, I knew you'd like my gift!" He smiled proudly.

"Apparently, someone took him out good. It seems someone wasn't very happy that he came back empty handed."

"Good riddance," Kat said. "One less thing for us to worry about."

Something about how she said that brought a smile to my face. I suppose it was nothing, but the way she said 'us' made me realize at that moment that despite everything that had happened, we were truly still an 'us'.

EPILOGUE

9 MONTHS Later - Villa Ortenberg

David glanced at his weathered old watch as his truck entered the long driveway to the Villa. It was just before eleven in the morning. David was nervous, more nervous than he had been through any of the supernatural encounters he'd had there. He parked in the newly completed parking lot in front of the house and got out. His car was the only one there. He took a deep breath, trying to compose himself. He set out towards the lily pond.

The walk was nostalgic for him. As he slowly made his way through the gardens and to the pond, he was amazed at the transformation that had taken place in the last year. This was a completely different place than it was a year ago. He knew the very spot where the charred remnants of the mirror had once lain. But on that day, those were only memories in his head. The visual reminders were now replaced with the opulent beauty of the fully restored garden and pond.

Just ahead of him, David saw the silhouettes of Jim and

Kat sitting in the open-air Tea House. David clenched his hands and walked up to greet them.

"I will never understand why you make me meet you out here," he yelled, getting their attention.

Jim stood up and turned to greet David with a handshake and then a hug.

"Stop, those days are all gone thanks to you," Jim said. "This garden is exactly the way it was intended to be, and I'm going to make sure we enjoy it. Come on in and sit down."

David approached the table where Kat was sitting behind a spread of pastries.

"You got lucky on your timing, we just happen to be sampling these from the caterer." Kat gestured to the arrangement.

David took a seat at the table and nervously looked back and forth between Kat and Jim.

"Uh... No thank you," he finally said softly.

"Oh, c'mon David," Jim said. "We can't sample all of these ourselves."

Jim's demeanor changed when he looked at him. Apparently he could sense that this was not simply a jovial meeting.

"What's wrong? Why did you want to meet with us today?"

"I'll just say it!" David replied. "Look, you know I appreciate everything you've done for me, keeping me employed this past year even though there is clearly no more paranormal activity here."

"David you know that's the least we could have done, and the fact is we needed you. People don't exactly want to plan a wedding on a graveyard. I know dealing with the press and such is not your typical role, but you handled all of those inquires. You were able to convince the public that the hauntings were gone. How many people can convince the public that a place is beautiful and welcoming despite the 13 bodies the police found. That allowed us to turn this place into a home and a venue free from the stigma of the past."

"Let me finish. Anyway, while I was handling all the people wanting to know about the haunt or the bones, and assuring them activity here was vanquished completely, I... well... I got a job!" He was proud of his accomplishment.

"That's great David, where is this job taking you?" Kat asked.

"That is just it, everywhere! I got approached by some reality TV producers. They want me to be on a show investigating haunts all over the country. Not just be on a show, they want it to be *my* show! It's my dream job! Going place to place to the most renowned haunted areas and making good money doing it. It's just... well... I have to stop working for you."

"You're quitting?" Jim interjected. "That's what you're acting all weird about?"

"Yes. But it isn't like that. I even worked a clause into my contract to ensure that, if something comes up here, I will still be able to help you two out."

"David, stop. It's fine. Your work here is done. Hell, next weekend we have our first event here. A fundraiser for the Historical Society. I'm more than happy to keep you employed as our paranormal expert, but it isn't needed. You are my friend, and if you have the opportunity to do what you want to do, I'm behind that one hundred percent."

"David, you are still coming to our wedding, right?" Kat asked.

"Of course I'm coming to the wedding! I don't start the

show for a while. Apparently, they are setting me up with some personal trainer so I can look better on camera first."

"Good, 'cause if you bailed on that, the way I would come after you would make Sam look like a puppy dog," Kat said with a mischievous smirk.

"Well, if that's settled, we also have a surprise for you." Jim stepped to the corner of the tea house and picked up a plain cardboard box. He handed it to David. "Look, we never had a chance to formally show you how much we appreciate everything you did. So, we wanted to give you this to say thanks."

David looked at the box in his hand for a moment before a smile appeared on his face. He tore it open with reckless abandon. He pulled out a large black box. Opening the black box revealed a black fabric case with 'Omega Speed-master' embroidered on it. David opened the buckles on the case, and the new watch sparkled in the sunlight.

"We noticed how much you use your watch and wanted to get you one that was as reliable as you have been to us," Kat said.

"Shit, I've never even seen one of these in person!"

"That's not all," Jim said. "There's something else in that box."

David set the watch case down and returned to the cardboard box. He reached inside and pulled out a book. The Münchner Handbuch der Nekromantie. David held it in his hands and silently looked at it.

"We have no use for it. You understand what this book is. So, if anyone should be trusted with keeping it, it's you. It's yours to do what you want with. Donate it to a museum, sell it, keep it. Just don't bring it back here." Jim smiled at David.

As David was walking back to his car, Jim ran up behind grabbing him on the shoulder.

"Hey, are you really going home for the first time since all this started?" Jim asked.

"Yeah I figure it's about time I actually see my house."

"Look, I mailed you something back while Sam was still hanging around. Once you get home, let me know if it's there, okay?"

"Uh sure thing."

"Don't worry about it. You'll understand when you open it."

Two days later, David was back at his office. He wanted to make sure that he put the Grimoire into his safe. Locked within that office, he knew it wasn't going to fall into the wrong hands or get ruined by him accidentally spilling something on it.

It was the first time David had been in his office in a long time. He'd been so busy working with Jim and Kat all while securing his new television deal. He hadn't had another case in over a year. He walked into the conference room and looked at the whiteboard. It was still cluttered with notes and photos about the KGC and the Cloudland Hotel. He grabbed an empty file box and began taking all the photos and papers down and set them in the box.

The sleigh bell above the office door jingled, and David set everything down. He saw Linda walking into the office.

"David, my dear! I was wondering when you were finally going to come back here."

Linda hurried into the conference room and greeted David with a hug. When she stepped back, she realized what David was doing. Frustration appeared on her face.

"So, this is it? You think you're finished here?"

"Linda, this case has been over for a long time, and with the TV show, I'm not gonna to be able to take any more cases."

Linda walked past him up to the whiteboard. Her eyes settled on the word Cloudland. It had lines drawn to a photo of each of the Sovereign Lords.

"Your work is not done. The story of Sam may be closed, but there is much more work ahead with the rest of these Lords."

"Linda, please. I cannot take any more cases until I'm done with this show and then... who knows."

"Run if you want but remember what I told you when we started. You don't choose cases to work on. They choose you. Your work is not complete."

He brushed her off for the moment and retreated to his office. He sat in the creaky chair and turned to the pile of mail sitting on his desk. Amongst the typical mail there was a FedEx envelope that caught his attention. There was no return address listed. The label indicated that it had been sent months ago. He tore it open and poured the contents of it onto the desk. With a heavy thud a necklace dropped out. He picked it up and marveled at it gleaming in the light. He pulled a slip of paper from the envelope and read it.

David,

If you are reading this, I can only assume everything is finished. This was Ida's necklace from the safe. I took this out realizing it was what Sam wanted. That night, when Sam knocked me out and put me in the hospital, I realized I needed to keep this safe. After all, if there is no necklace, then no one will be after us for it. Please keep this safe and hidden. If it can be used for good, I know you will be the one who can make that decision.

Thanks,

Jim

David sat there with the letter in one hand and the necklace in the other. He looked at the necklace again with a smile on his face.

"I guess my work really isn't finished," he said.